SAVAGE JUSTICE

BRATVA SAVAGES BOOK ONE

PENELOPE WYLDE

READ THIS...

Hey, Penelope here! Thank you for picking up Savage Justice. As a reminder for new and returning readers to my books, I write dark romantic suspense with mafia ties and high heat. With that in mind, the Savage men have to fight to find their happily-eve-afters. As you will see in this series, some stories must start in darkness before the light can shine through. Ares and Nova's story is no different. Their story will take you through a dark mafia, MC romance experience before you reach their HEA.

There are several trigger warnings such as graphic depictions of violence to create a more vivid reading experience, mentions of self harm, human trafficking, drug use, and intense angst. While dark in theme, Savage Justice ends with a breathtaking happily ever after for this couple. There is no cliffhanger for the main couple.

Continue reading with this in mind.

He bought me. Now my enemy owns me.

Nova

They call him the god of war.

Damaged. Lethal. Ruthless to the point of savagery.

He is also my enemy and I am his captive bride.

He's bought me for the sole purpose of revenge.

And now he demands my help.

My heart says run, but my body says to trust his dark whispers.

They call him a killer. They are not wrong. But to me he's beautifully broken.

Ares

Savage justice is all I want.

It thrives in my veins and is my one true purpose.

Until her…

She sates my thirst for blood.

Beautiful, brave and a soul made for love.

But I can't have her and my justice at the same time.

Do I let her go, free her from me and the pain my darkness brings?

Or do I hold her to me and pray my jagged heart doesn't kill us both?

Savage Justice comes is a full-length 90,000 word novel and it comes with a TW warning. Ares and Nova's story is a twisted Bratva mafia, captive bride romance that I promise ends with a breathtaking happily ever after for this couple.

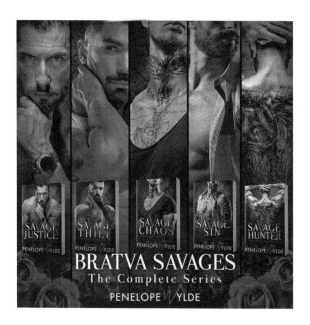

Series now complete!

Savage Justice - Ares & Nova
Savage Thief - Dragon & Asena
Savage Chaos - Riot & Lilith
Savage Sin - Rage & Persephone
Savage Hunter - Wolfe & Avery

Welcome to the dark, twisted world of the BRATVA SAVAGES where both blood and demons run freely. The cost of becoming a savage brotherhood—your undying loyalty. But once in, you'll have a found family for life.

Join the BRATVA SAVAGES in this raw, gritty series where its hard, damaged members ride the line between darkness and light. Life and death. All seeking redemption from a life of sin through the strength of the strong women they come to love.

Do you love dark anti-heroes with a heart of gold for their women? Check out the highly-loved series Bratva Savages and the connected Savage universe:

BRATVA SAVAGES:
Savage Justice - Ares & Nova
Savage Thief - Dragon & Asena
Savage Chaos - Riot & Lilith
Savage Sin - Rage & Persephone
Savage Hunter - Wolfe & Avery

SAVAGE UNIVERSE:

KISS OF DARKNESS
(Harlon, Cassius, Santi and Polaris)
Tarnished Kisses
Shattered Kisses

DARK MAFIA CROWNS
-THE MORETTI KINGS-
(Moses, Rhys, Zander and Aleta)
Stolen Pleasures
Unraveled Pleasures

DARK MAFIA VILLAINS TRILOGY
Her Dark Mafia Kings - Nyx & her men
Her Dark Mafia Beasts - Bailey & her men
Her Dark Mafia Sinners - Briar & her men

CLUB SIN:
Room One - Kandy and her men
Room Eight - Sapphire Constantine & her men

Room Two - Belle Constantine & her men
Room Seventeen - Laila & her men
Room Seven - Aster Constantine & her men
Room Six - Magnolia & her men
Room One Hundred and Six - TBA
Room One Hundred and Five - TBA

SAVAGE LOVE:
Mercy for Three - Mercy & her men
Honor for Three - Honor & her men
Justice for Three - Justice & her men

SAVAGE MAFIA
Stolen by the Mafia
Bred by the Bratva
Bred by the Villain

MAFIA DADDIES
Owning Amethyst
Ruining Lili
Possessing Bella
Stealing Grace

∾

Vitam meam. Mors Mea. Mea Via.

My Life. My death. My way.
- Nova Masters

∾

One

Ares

People go missing all the time.

Daughters, cousins, nieces, nephews. And worse. You know where I'm going with this. Don't make me spell this shit out for you any more than I have to. Acid rolls in the pit of my stomach just thinking about it and I don't need to be tempted into setting a few fuses and watching this place blow. Only the innocent trapped inside are keeping my raging demons at bay.

For now.

I straighten my cuffs before tapping my glass, signaling the barkeep to pour another when he looks my way. "Leave the bottle." I toss a crisp Benjamin on the polished black marble and find a nearby table to wait and let the bottom feeders of the top one percent of high society get a good look at their newest member.

From my earliest memory, I've played a role and tonight's no different. After nearly thirty-seven years of this shit you either get tired and fold or dig in deeper. Despite my father's wrath, I've never been one to turn my back on an opportunity.

I feel the burn of eyes drilling into the back of my head so I down a few fingers' worth of vodka and snag a passing captive by the arm.

"*Drugaya.*" I drag her to the edge of my table and she yelps. "Pour another," I translate gruffly. To be fair, if I treated the enslaved server any other way, we'd both draw unwanted attention.

"Yes, sir." Her tone is lifeless. Broken. Death, or the desire for it, flares in the depths of those flat brown eyes.

Fucking Volkov brothers. Another reason to want them buried and gone. We're the top two Russian families vying for the highest position in this city. But not for long. They're working to keep their enemy close while showing their growing strength. For now, I play along and let them have their fun. Letting them think they have the upper hand now will make their fall a helluva lot sweeter.

I've allowed them to operate under the radar, to eke out a living in their nightclubs and drug running. But I've heard rumblings from the shadows that they're moving into darker waters and I'm here to see for myself. The invitation in my pocket is their way of flaunting it in my face.

Around me, many of the members of The Society have brought their own purchased sex slaves to perform fellatio as we wait for the auction to kick off. Moans of pleasure ripple over the large room, the sounds making my fist tighten around my empty glass. And my dick has never felt so fucking dead in my life.

"Sir?"

The lifeless server signals for me to remove my hand. I wrap my knuckles on the gleaming table. "Hurry the fuck up and try not spilling it." Emeralds swing from her earlobes as she jumps at my tone, making me feel like a royal asshole. Her eyes are glued to the empty glass and her fingers tremble as she clutches the bottle. The flimsy black netting covering her tits and crotch are see-through with chains crisscrossing most of her body, leaving her exposed as a demonstration of wealth and level of quality.

The shit this poor girl must have been forced into makes me fucking sick.

"May I offer you anything further this evening, sir?" There is an inflection on *sir* that wasn't there before so I know she's moving into playing a role she's been trained for. She places the bottle on the table and lowers to the floor in front of me, her hands poised on the edges of her knees. Palms turned up. I watch her face as a pinch of fear works over her expression.

I wave her off. I'm every bit of the bastard everyone thinks I am. Mobster, murderer, crime lord, piece-of-shit biker trash with too much money.

They're not wrong. I'm all those things and more. But I've never taken someone by force. Or had someone feel they had to give me pleasure in order to draw their next breath.

"*Nyet.* Leave me. There's nothing you can offer me that I want." I regret my words immediately.

She remains unmoving. Panic creases the corners of her eyes and for the first time I see signs of life creep in behind those false lashes. This has me reconsidering my position.

"Please, allow me to pleasure you. If I don't, they will hurt me." She's trembling as she begs to suck me off. I can see the girl she used to be under the layers of caked-on makeup. She shuffles on her knees toward me and reaches for the buckle of my belt. I grab her hand, a delicate thing, and wrap my fingers around her.

"Please, sir." Eyes dart over my shoulder.

Her voice is low, timid, and laced with enough fear to cripple a grown man. Which steals away my attention from where I need it—memorizing every face inside these walls.

I take her chin between my thumb and forefinger. "Later, *dorogoy*." I speak up for anyone within earshot to hear. "You're a perfect specimen of what the Volkov brothers possess. Tell them I am pleased, but it's almost time for the auction to start. Come find me later and we'll see if that mouth of yours looks as beautiful wrapped around my cock as I suspect it will." I feel her desperation, but she's not who I'm looking for. I can't afford to get distracted.

Hope swiftly dies in the woman's eyes. She bows her head and sends me a silent thank you with her eyes.

She moves away slowly and I pin my gaze across the room. But in my periphery, I notice the older Volkov twin, Ivan, observing me interact with his property from a nearby table. The high-end traffickers and natural-born sadistic capitalists have been on my radar for a while now. Petty West Coast little shits who think they can muscle in and take what's mine because they've come into some money. Where they replenish the coffers is evident, but how they went from operating pop-up whore houses out west to this is another question. One I tend to find the answer to.

I had my men spread rumors about me being in the market for a bride and it was almost fucking child's play getting an invite Now that I have an in to one of their private showings, I resign myself to putting on a show of a lifetime. I can't give them any reason to doubt my motives. I've sacrificed a lot to be sitting at this table, and as the newest member of The Society everyone's eyes are on me. One wrong move that triggers their paranoia and all my work will be for nothing. I need to remember that.

One more look into the soulless pits for eyes of the woman and I know I'll murder someone for breaking such a fragile soul.

This brings me back to the shit I was saying before. We all know the world is a fucked-up place, but what goes on here is worse than the darkest pits of hell. And all for money. Why? Greed and power. Both put whoever controls the most at the top of the food chain. And I'm not such a saint to deny I love having both. From my throne at the top of the summit, the view is spectacular. Anyone challenges my authority and I'll spill their blood in my streets.

The Volkov brothers are stupid enough to think they'll take me out and step into my shoes. They haven't been in town long enough to learn my word is what governs the underbelly of New York City. My crew and I keep these streets clean, safe, and protected from trash like them. I rule with fear, strength and I'm not afraid to let rivers of blood coat my territory to maintain my reign. It's the only way to keep people like my father from emerging. I learned having full control is the only way at the knee of that brutal piece-of-shit. There is no end to the hatred thriving in my blood for him. He sparked a fire in my veins the day he killed my mother with his bare hands. And now he lives with the fear I'll come after him someday.

The bastard is not wrong.

Which naturally leads to another truth. The one universal law that makes humans seem like the scum of the universe —in all its filthy, faceted, fucked-up forms, sex sells. And those who have the money to throw around will pay any price to get it. Or, control over those who want it.

It makes criminals out of the nice guy next door, and broken souls out of those unfortunate enough to find themselves in places like this.

Auction windows. But don't let the name fool you. Nothing that goes on here happens in the light of day. The *windows* are underground pop-up locations so far off the grid not even the most crooked of cops are let in on this secret. Elaborate mansion basements the size of football fields, underground cave systems that have been converted into luxurious dens of sin, or a remote deluxe cabin in the woods. All on highly guarded, private property and away from curious eyes. Anywhere the Volkov brothers can host a gala that doubles as an auction. Princes, foreign politicians, men—and women—in power with too much money and a lack of morals all fill these walls wearing smiles and tuxedos more costly than your monthly car payment.

My crew is thorough in their intel gathering.

And by no stretch of the imagination are the women here by choice. Most of them walking from table to table have been here a while and are referred to as house samples. Women and men barely old enough to vote are forced into this life of degradation as samples of the Volkovs' product.

Anyone holding membership to The Society can demand anything of these poor souls and they either perform on command or be killed. Every last one of them is kidnapped off the streets, ripped from their lives, stripped of their dignity with daily beatings until they give their full submission. Some don't make it.

It's hard to believe, but these have it better than the ones drugged and held in cages just out of sight behind large curtains in the next room. Those are to be sold tonight to the highest bidder. And I have deep pockets. It's what pisses these Society fuckers off. I ride up here on my sled, look like I should be behind bars Upstate, and yet have more sitting in my bank account than all of them put together.

I let a wolfish grin slip.

And you thought I was a bastard. You're not wrong, because I plan on buying one of those women and making her my wife.

And the worst part is there's not a damn thing anyone will do about it. Yet.

But I'm getting ahead of myself.

"Sir." I look up to find a raven-haired woman in her mid-twenties bare of all clothing standing beside me, the one in emeralds nowhere to be seen. I gesture with a flick of my fingers for her to speak. "Your booth is ready."

Two

Ares

While the other server asked to touch me, this bare-breasted woman places a bold hand on my arm and leans in close. Her exposed nipples brush against my sleeve as she whispers in my ear. A blind man can see the Volkovs spent extra time training the woman in the art of seduction. Glitter dusts along her body and she has strategically placed jewels dangling over her nipples and folds that catch the light, drawing the eye to her many assets.

"Your broker for the evening is waiting for you by the door, Mr. Ares. If you'd like to follow me, I'll make the introduction. Once the auction draws to a close, the Volkov brothers would like to offer you an invitation to join them in their private rooms."

My little scene with her friend in emeralds paid off. I hold back a smirk and keep my face draped with indifference.

The lilt of her accent pins her origins somewhere south of Mexico. Colombia, possibly Ecuador. Doesn't fucking matter. She ticks a lot of boxes for anyone with a dick and a taste for the exotic. Beautiful, lithe, willing from the spark of fire in her eye and lingering touches, but again, not who I'm looking for. I guess some adapt to this lifestyle, becoming as twisted as their captors.

Perfect made-up eyes turn to mine. "If you so desire, *Señor.* I can also arrange for a private room for us this evening. The Volkov brothers wish for you to have a pleasurable time while under their roof. Never mind *la chica.* She doesn't know how to pleasure a man like you. Just ask for Salvaje after the auction. Maybe I can join you and your new bride if you find someone who meets your approval, that is."

I don't give a shit about some made-up name or her offer. Some people suck at reading body language and she's one of them. She mistakes my irritation for interest or maybe confusion and presses on. "The girl from before. Avery. She's new. But I've been here a while and know how to bring you to multiple orgasms in a night."

She pushes the lapels of my jackets aside and draws an invisible line down the center of my chest with a pretty pink-tipped nail and then wraps her fingers around my dick through my slacks.

I grind my teeth until my jaw aches. I wonder if she hears the enamel start to crack because she finally gets the hint and shuts her mouth.

I peel her hand from my cock and push it away. "I won't be needing your services tonight, Salvaje. And you can tell your bosses another time perhaps. I'm here for one reason only and it's not to get my dick wet in a pussy that has entertained a thousand men. As beautiful as you are," I add, offhandedly.

The woman blanches a split second before her face turns redder than her dyed hair. I take it that not a lot of people tell the Volkovs no, or her for that matter. Like I said before, my dick doesn't touch a woman who doesn't crave me as much as I do her. A sex slave isn't given a choice and that is a hard pass for me. I have plenty of pussy willing to take my cock back at the club if I want.

I cast a glance over my shoulder and give a stiff nod knowing the Volkovs are still watching. I stand, move past the woman and meet my handler. "My booth," I instruct him and he swiftly turns on a heel.

"This way, sir."

I follow through several clusters of guests all whispering and some trying to catch my eye. I keep walking.

Low-hung chandeliers cast soft lighting over a room full of ample-sized booths lining the edge of a large circular stage. There are a couple of plush chairs with a table in the middle holding a phone that links directly to the auctioneer, I presume. On either side of the chairs are large glass dividers offering the bidders a level of privacy.

My handler shows me to one at the end, draws the curtain back, and I step inside. I have a full view of the stage from here, but I'm unable to see inside the other booths opposite of me. They are not the smartest pair, but I have to hand it to the fuckers. The Volkov twins seem to have all their bases covered.

The light above the center stage flares to life and a disembodied voice carries over a sound system.

"Ladies and gentleman, welcome to The Society's eighth bridal auction of the season. Tonight we have twenty-three beautiful and exotic brides for you to choose from. As promised with this specific line of treasures, each piece has been left untrained so you may work and shape your purchase into your definition of perfection. Tonight's unique pieces are truly delightful. Let the evening begin."

With my curtain drawn, I don't have to feign interest. I tune out the male voice as one woman after another is paraded into the light dressed in nothing but a robe that is swiftly stripped away to reveal a drugged woman who can barely stand in the stilettos they were forced into.

I snap pictures, making sure the flash is off, and stuff my phone back into my jacket's interior pocket when a server refreshes my drink.

Jesus. The fucking acid in my stomach starts to churn. This is the part of the evening I dreaded. Seeing all these women being sold off like cattle. There's not enough vodka to dull this shit from my brain.

One ankle crossed over a knee, I down the swallow of vodka left in my glass. I push away from the table ready to leave when my eye catches a movement. A large swath of fabric dividing the holding cells from the viewing platform sways, but it's not the black curtain that holds me captive. It's the woman with blonde hair so light it's nearly the shade of an angel's feathers.

I sit back down.

Bids fly in fast. Half a million...eight hundred thousand. Now it's getting interesting. She throws her hands up and tries to cover herself, but it's like a battle of the lesser of two evils. Either the tits or the pussy. She can't decide which is more valuable. I smirk.

My eyes narrow on the feisty woman who is all tooth and claw. She abandons the idea of covering herself and swings at her handler, catching a swift backhand for her heroic efforts of fighting against the inevitable.

Two brutes wearing full-face masks and black suits step from behind the curtain. The smaller one grabs her by the shoulders earning him a nice elbow to the gut and the other receives a swift heel to the foot.

Ouch. Poor fucker. But not really. He deserves a bullet to the head in my opinion.

After a few more minutes of struggle, they place her in a collar with a chain linking to another around her ankles.

My chest tightens and I fist my tumbler so hard the glass cracks between my fingers. Knots form in my gut and I can't help but appreciate the way her bare body moves as she continues to struggle. The shape of her full lips, the flash of defiance and anger in her crystal-clear eyes. The sensual dip to her hips and the shapely size of her legs all work to create a beautiful masterpiece. Heavy breaths force her chest to quiver. My gaze drifts down to find her peaked nipples puckered against the cold of the room and I momentarily forget where I am at.

She is the one and why I'm here.

Unlike all the others who let fate happen to them, this one fights back and as fucked up as it sounds, that has my cock hard and my blood pumping.

I shake the mess of my broken tumbler away, uncaring of the few nicks along my fingers. Beside me is a small box and I hit the button signaling my interest before punching in my bid.

"I hear one million from booth eight. Do I hear one point five?"

Someone challenges my bid with an even two million when the foolish woman thrashes around the stage, raising a knee and slamming it into the fucker trying to hook a leash on the collar.

"Two million. I have two million for the wild lady who will be a delight to collar properly and tame. Who is in for a little bit of a challenge? Shall we make this a bit more interesting? Do I hear three million?"

I hit the bid button and up my ante to a number I've yet to hear anyone offer.

"Fifteen point five million dollars." The auctioneer sounds momentarily stunned. My gaze latches onto the woman and I don't let go. Every angle, strand of hair, and curve is burned into my memory.

"That's right," I mutter into my otherwise empty booth. "I can do this all night. You might as well give the fuck up now and let me have her." No one drops that kind of cash on pussy. Maybe for a harem of captives, but not for a solo prize.

The sound system grows quiet several seconds before the announcer comes back on. "Booth eight. Fifteen point five million dollars. Do I hear sixteen? Sixteen? Okay then, going once, twice... SOLD! The lovely lady with the spitfire attitude is sold to the bidder in booth eight. Congratulations on your new acquisition."

Blue flames for eyes blaze across the glass fronts of the booths and I know she's searching for the one who purchased her life. She can't see past the dark tint, but somehow, she picks mine to glower at through the masses of white hair hanging in her eyes. I don't know how but those knots in my stomach cinch tighter as I hold her gaze right back.

"Congratulations, Ares." My curtain moves aside and a stoic-looking Ivan Volkov walks in looking smug. Black hair hangs around his shoulders and unlike his brother, he prefers a clean shave. But he can invest in clothes and all the hair oils his deep pockets can supply, but he will still look like an ugly son-of-a-bitch. At least his brother tries to hide his fucked-up face behind a patchy beard. They say it was a fire that scared them in childhood. Bullshit. Truth is, a deal went sideways back west and shit literally blew up in their faces about a half a decade ago. Like I've said, I have good intel.

"We thought maybe our newest member would like to get the first bid on tomorrow evening's merchandise—see a few of our finer pieces before any other. Unless you're capped out and don't want to play."

I know bullshit. And it's coming out of his mouth at an alarming speed. They want to dick around and pretend we have some fucking long history of friendship together instead of them trying to move in on my city. And I hate dick measuring. It's a waste of fucking time when you have the ego to match the size of cock I have.

Ivan Volkov's Russian accent is not as thick as mine, but then again these bratva wannabes were born Stateside, never stepping foot in the motherland. Any Russian inflection they have rubbed off secondhand.

A parade of women is forced to kneel outside my booth. I stand, give them a glance and shrug. His little show of dominance is entertaining at best. After a couple of smooth years, the challenge shakes off the boredom. I cock a smile knowing the truth. I own him *and* his brother, only he's too fucking blind by money to see what's going on here.

It makes me want to spit venom to call them my brothers, but I move my lips anyway. *"Spasibo, moy brat.* Truly. Thank you for helping me find my bride. But I don't need more. I've already got a woman to run my bath and cook my meals. And now I'll have one to pleasure my cock. Now fuck off, Volkov. I can window shop for myself." I return to my scat knowing I'm playing hardball with an armed man with fewer brain cells than a weasel.

With my back to the entrance of my booth, I see a broad smile reflects back at me through the glass.

He steps into my booth. *"Da,* I knew you would make a great addition to our limited clientele. My brother thinks you should be put out of your misery and we should claim your territory once and for all. Enough of this live and let live bullshit."

His stance is wide and his watered-down accent makes him sound nervous. He should be. He's testing my boundaries.

The bold threat doesn't faze me as he likely intended. Intimidation never did. Words roll off me like water. Now point a gun in my face and you might get a reaction out of me—as unpleasant as it may be—but words are meaningless without action.

I take the cigar he offers from an inside pocket and snip the end off before lighting it. "And you? What do you think?" Smoke curls around my words as they hang between us for a few heartbeats.

He lights his own and sucks on the end for a few seconds for what I guess he thinks is a dramatic effect and in my boredom I let my attention drift to the phone in my pocket.

"I think lucky for you I am the older twin and that fucker does what I say. But I can only leash a bulldog for so long before he breaks loose."

A side of my lip curls up in a half-smile. "Is that a fact?" When you work years to gain the reputation of showing no fear, no weakness, and being willing to spill blood there are always fuckers stupid enough to test how far they can push the line.

I study the man across from me. Ivan and his brother have pushed my boundaries and this little game we are playing is nothing more than me toying with my prey before I swallow them whole.

"I think even you know you can't make money when you're dead."

Ivan lowers his weight into the chair opposite mine and I hold his gaze. "Maybe you owe me for being your protector."

I unhook the button to my tuxedo jacket, knowing the other man's eyes will drop to the pair of Glocks I have tucked into my double-sided shoulder holster.

I chuckle darkly, genuinely humored by his point of view.

"There's not a damn person I need protecting from. Especially your half-witted brother. Or you." I lay the challenge between us like a deadly viper trained to strike. If he wants to have a dance or two, I'm not hiding. But I am growing tired of the banter and games. "I made my purchase. When can I expect my product to be delivered?"

"Let's talk about a partnership."

The curtain behind me shifts and the woman in emeralds and chains from earlier steps in, a bottle in hand, and I recognize the coiled dragon head on the million-dollar bottle.

"A gift for you, sir."

Ivan snaps his fingers and she drops to her knees. "May I pour you a glass?"

I consider the bottle of Eye of the Dragon. It'd be easy to surrender to the darkness inside me, let the emptiness residing in me swallow my better judgment, empty a few rounds and execute this piece of shit. No one could touch me for it.

Or, I play along. Follow the chain and dig up the real money behind these clowns.

"You have the respect out on the street and I have the connections to make you more money than you ever thought possible. More than your clandestine arms deals."

"Is that why you presented me with an invitation?" I take the envelope out and toss it on the table between us.

"I wanted you to see the goods firsthand."

"Tell you what, Volkov. I'll give you an extra three million for her. And I'll take the vodka. Seeing as we both know the girl is used goods, I'm offering *three* times her worth which is zero." I give her a cursory glance. "Do this and I'll consider that partnership."

I'm betting on his greed to do the talking for him. It's not long before my bet pays off.

"Consider her a gift." Ivan snaps and the girl stands, her dead eyes blank windows that stare straight ahead.

"Since we are in the bartering mood, I require more material along the lines of your specialty. No questions. Just merchandise for cash. And as I said, you can keep the house sample."

I consider him for a moment, weighing my options. I need this man tied to me in every possible way. "Call The Genesis men. They'll get your particulars. Models, quantity, and then we'll be in touch." I take out a plain black business card with a single contact number. No names.

My broker moves around Avery and passes a tablet and I sign on the lines he indicates. I take out my phone and punch in Rage's contact. "Make the payment. Eighteen and a half million."

I move my new acquisition toward my handler; Volkov watches every move I make. I turn a hard stare on him. "I take nothing for free. Expect to pay full price for any materials we exchange. Let's see how this goes. Then we can talk about a partnership."

"*Da moy droog*, a pleasure doing business with you."

I live by keeping my enemies as close as friends. "*Moy droog*," I repeat and grip hands with him. "I'll be in touch."

"Your purchased wife will be shipped to you within the hour, sir."

"Make sure they both arrive unharmed. Any marks they have on their bodies I will personally come back and put on

19

you. No man touches my property."

I turn and find my way out.

You see, I'm not participating tonight to join The Society; I'm here to burn every single motherfucker into the ground. And I just purchased the element of their demise who will help me destroy my enemy.

THREE

NOVA

I am in hell.

Only minutes ago I woke to find myself in a dank-smelling hole and the back of my throat feels like I swallowed buckets of gasoline and lit a match.

The room is mostly dark with only hints of light filtering through the cracks of a door to my left. Muted voices seep through with the light but give me no clues as to where I am. It's not like I threw myself in here so someone has to know something.

Feeling unbalanced, I peel myself off the cement. Grim from the bare floor smears over my palms. I go to wipe the muck off only to find the slashed jeans and my favorite knee-high boots I'd left my apartment in gone. A sheer piece of cloth and my underwear is what I've been left in.

Confusion muddles my thoughts and I am having a really hard time piecing together the last few hours of my life. Or days. I honestly don't know.

After a few moments, I feel strong enough to rise to my knees and try to stand. I take a few careful steps and that's when I notice I have more than just a wardrobe change. Cold steel locks around both my ankles. A burst of anger forces a wave of hot tears to my eyes.

What the hell is going on? I yank one foot and then the other but the chains are short and barely allow me to move much in any direction. The metal tightens and tears into my skin every time I try to take a step. I shove the shards of fear down and push through the burn of what feels like fire and acid against the skin and give them another hard yank.

"ARGH!" I fight back the tears that want to break free at finding myself in chains again. "No, Nova. Don't go back there. Don't go back there." I crouch on the hard floor and I wrap my arms around my knees. I rock a little, trying to steady my breathing like I used to do.

"One, in. Two, out." I swallow back the lump of choking fear. No one will come looking for me. For years I've worked overtime making sure to keep layers between me and damn near anyone. Constantly moving from city to city. No boyfriends, no family besides my sister. Not until I arrived in New York City did I break and finally make friends with a couple of people.

Jacob won't even think to look for me when I don't show up in the back room of his bar. Not for a few days at least. And Ellie. Poor Ellie. Look what being my friend got her. Kidnapped.

I scrub at my face and pull my hair away from my eyes. Even if I did have someone in my life, they wouldn't know where to start. I cast my gaze around, tightening my arms. I don't even know where *here* is.

Goosebumps rise on my arms. This dark, cold room is a stiff reminder of how alone I am.

And why I can't fall prey to my past. Not again. I scrub at my face and grip the last strands of resolve I can find deep within.

First things first. My sister. I need to find her. She has to be scared to death. And my best friend. I try to think back to the moment before I woke, but a muddle of murky thoughts clog my mind. I'm not used to looking out for more than just my sister so having Ellie tacked on makes me feel like a worthless friend.

"Think, Nova."

The whiskey shots and beer from a girls' night out mixed with whatever is still burning the back of my throat make me lightheaded when I try to stand. My breathing is shallow and I can't seem to steady my racing heartbeat.

"What does all this mean? Come on. Think, girl." There is no way I've been here for more than a couple of hours, wherever *here* is. I can still taste Diablo's signature drink, Hell's Flame, on my tongue. It takes a solid five hours or so for the mix of liquors and tabasco sauce to fade. I use that little detail to mark the time. That means I haven't been out long and I am possibly still in New York City.

I close my eyes again and shove at the fog, but it's no use. Any memory of how I got here isn't coming easy.

"Polaris," I call out. Heartbreaking silence greets me. "Ellie!" I try again but only get the same response.

I test my restraints again and bite through the pain of metal on flesh. Nada. *Fuck.*

25

My gut is telling me I need to hurry. That I'm in more danger than I can possibly understand. I cast my gaze around in the dark with my hands trying for something to help pick or smash these damn things off me. Only rough cement meets my fingertips.

"Don't panic." I take a deep breath and let it out slowly, falling into old habits disturbingly easy.

"Polaris," I try again, but any hope of my sister being nearby dies every second I don't hear her voice.

My sister's name bounces off the enclosure. One door, small and cold. It has to be a basement of some kind. I think. Not that I can see the walls, but I feel their oppressive weight closing in all the same. Maybe not a basement. A dungeon? Oh, God. I listen for dripping water. The little squeak of mice.

"What are you? Back in medieval days? Get a grip." There are far worse places than basements and dungeons. I learned that truth the hard way.

I can feel old panic rise to settle in the pit of my stomach, gurgling and spewing venom into my veins.

Trembling fingers make for real shitty tools. I can't seem to get a grip on the metal cuff digging into my skin. I tear at it, scrape and slap but nothing frees me from the locked brackets.

"This can't be happening. Not again." I squeeze my eyes closed and try to calm the frantic lurch of a monster in my throat threatening to cut off my air. *Not again, not again.* "Breathe," I remind myself, but it's no use.

"Ellie. Polaris," I whisper into the shadowed darkness but there's no answer.

Fuck. It's cold in here, making my fingers stiff as I try to grab at the chains holding me in place. "Here goes nothing," I mutter to the darkness and lean my entire weight into pulling on the chains. This time I'm rewarded with the sound of old metal breaking.

"Thank you, sweet baby Jesus!" What sounds like chains feeding through a metal ring ricochets off the walls and I fall on my ass. Hard. My small victory is cut off when I land on something semi-soft.

I freeze. Oh, God. As in a body kind of semi-soft. I shudder and twirl around.

I try not to freak out when my fingers make contact with something other than cold stone. But my cool demeanor doesn't last long. I rush to my knees and move forward, scraping skin as I go. Cloth feeds through my fingers and I recognize the feel of sequins in my hands. My best friend had on a dress made of them tonight.

"Ellie. Ellie. Is that you? Oh, thank God! Why didn't you answer me?"

Shaking her, a sudden flood of relief fills me. "Have you seen Polaris?"

Nothing.

"Ellie? Ellie, answer me." When I don't hear the familiar softness of her voice, the panic I've held at bay up until now collides with the fear inside me.

"Ellie?" I try not to scream or let my fear control my voice but it's nearly impossible. My heart races so fast my fingers and limbs turn from ice to trembling fire. Not enough light filters through the door cracks for me to see her face and that is driving up my fear levels so severe I can't control the shaking.

I nudge her, but nothing. Not even a flinch or mumble. "Ellie, wake the fuck up already!"

I clamor in the shadows for the edge of the wall and shuffle my way to the door, but I'm drawn up short by the remaining shackle. I give it a hard tug but this one is not budging.

It's a good foot and a half too short, but I'm not letting that stop me. Panic sends my heart racing so hard dots dance in my vision. I have to do something. Helplessness is paralyzing. Stretching until I nearly lose feeling in my shackled foot, I manage to ball a fist and bang on the door. "Help," I scream.

The deep tones of men talking feed through the door when it suddenly bursts open sending me crashing to the floor and landing hard on my ass.

My eyes snap to the burst of light around two large beasts who prowl through with the smell of cigar smoke and pricey alcohol clinging to them. My gaze drops to Ellie's face and that's when I see she's more than not just answering me. She's a deathly shade of purple. My heart clenches. *No, no.* This can't be happening. I scramble to her but bear-like hands clamp around my biceps and I fight against them to clutch my best friend to me. "Something's wrong. Help me. Something's wrong with her. She's not breathing."

I'm shoved aside as the two asshats shoulder inside my… tiny cell? Where the fuck am I. The room can't be more than ten by ten. What the holy fuck! "Get the fuck off of me!" I kick out and my bare heel lands with a satisfying grunt from the beast trying to manhandle me.

"Do you want to die?" he bellows, holding his junk and trying to grab me with his other meaty hand. Unfortunately for him, I'm faster and have no problem playing dirty.

"What the hell kind of question is that? Do you really want an answer?" There's a fifty-fifty chance my mouth is going to get me into trouble but, hey, I'm more of a ride or die kind of chick. Balls to the wall. Nobody is going to get the best of me. Not without a fight first.

I scramble to my feet and move into a crouching position over my friend. "She needs help," I blurt, uncaring of my wellbeing when a gigantic hand swings out to catch me across the face from the one with the thick brown cancer stick clenched between the fingers of his other hand.

I catch a thick Russian accent in time with hard knuckles across the high part of my cheek. The force from the blow knocks me into the corner. No sooner do I hit the wall do I bounce right back out with my fists swinging. I know both men are bigger than me, but I've never let size or my lack of fighting skills determine my fate.

"Stupid. Don't damage the fucking merchandise. Fucking idiot." That's Beast One. He's larger than his friend and lumbers deeper into the room, thrusting a shoulder into the other beast.

Broad shoulders encased in black material block out the light but there's enough of it to where I can see the malice on their acne-scarred faces. I flatten my fingers, spread my thumb to create a V shape. Putting my weight behind it, I strike Beast Two with a punch to the throat, loving the sound of him instantly regretting getting in my face.

His cigar tumbles to the floor.

I lunge for it and drive the embers of burning tobacco into the closest piece of skin—his face. "How do you like that, asshole?" I dodge another swinging fist.

Beast One growls when his friend crumples beside him gasping for air. "That puckered burn mark must sting the ego a little, huh?" I blurt before thinking better of it.

Shit.

Primal instinct kicks in the second the other one realizes what I've done and reaches for me. My pulse hammers and there's only so far I get before Beast One catches me, slings me under his arm, and stalks toward the door with me in tow.

"Stop playing. Unlock her chains and let us go."

Beast Two, choking and looking like he wants to pass out, stumbles to his feet with murder in his eyes. He reaches over and releases my chains from locks with a set of keys.

"If they don't buy this one. I'll take her." His voice is strained but that only makes his threat sound more ominous. "Teach her manners and how to obey her master. Make her my ashtray."

"Yeah, fuck you. I'm no one's pet," I spit out but a hand muffles my next words.

I claw and thrash against the other one's side but his size keeps the vital parts of his body out of reach. Until he slips up and lets my unchained feet touch the ground. Two seconds is all it takes for me to turn the tables a little in my favor. I lunge up, knee raised, and drive home with the force of a sledgehammer. All my past horrors come rolling back and I'm right back where I was five years ago inside my head. Tied down, shackled, and willing to do anything to fight for my life and my sister's.

But apparently, this guy's balls are made of some kind of steel. Beast One barely flinches. He just growls down at me and I swear to God he looks at me like we just had a round of foreplay.

But his hand gripping the wall is a strong indicator I got to him and not in a good way.

"I like my woman to have some fight in her."

He takes a step toward me.

"I'm not your woman, asshole. You can go fuck yourself."

I seriously need to shut up.

I retreat and prepare for just about anything from these two. Beast One hisses, shoves into his friend's meaty hands, and glares at me so hard I'm contemplating if these are my last few minutes on this planet.

"Get her cleaned up," he growls and throws a hand out. Chunky fingers wrap around my throat and those dots from earlier come back to swirl in my vision. I claw at his hand but he only squeezes tighter. My lungs scream for air. I brace my hands around his, but he's not budging. My knees are ready to give and just as the vision starts to blacken, I can suddenly breathe again.

"You're getting sold at tonight's auction. If no one plucks money down for you, you'll make a good whore for the club. Volkov will love you. But first, we'll take a lot of pleasure breaking you in for your new job."

Visions of the life he paints make my stomach fill with acid.

Beast Two takes my hair between his fingers and twirls the ends with a look of detachment on his face. "Antonov hears the Volkovs are selling on their own; he'll slit all our throats."

"This is our city. Not theirs. Remember that," Beast One grunts.

"Won't it be some irony if that Savage asshole buys her?"

"Keep your mouth shut." There's a tense moment between them before the smaller asshole nods.

Whoa. What was that about?

"She needs her cuts properly tended to, and cover her bruises. Then get her lined up with the rest. We have to move the merchandise quickly. The bosses will want this one gone by the evening. Troublemakers don't make good long-term pets."

I didn't need his deeper meaning spelled out.

My gaze swings to the other man, unbelieving of the conversation passing between them. Like I'm not standing right there hearing their nefarious plans.

My view is blocked by these two thugs that I only catch a hint of someone in a leather jacket behind them. His hair is long and pulled into a knot on the back of his head. I watch in horror as he disappears inside my cell only to exit with my lifeless friend. Edges of his neck tattoo peeking out of his collar are the last thing I see before he's gone.

Noooo. My heart wails with grief.

"And that one?" Beast Two jerks his head in the direction the guy in leather took Ellie.

"You can explain to the bosses how you killed another one."

Another one?

Beast Two grunts like my best friend's life means nothing.

Did he kill my sister, too?

"And the other one? Where is she?" I ask, dreading the answer.

"Goes to Antonov. Virgins get more money on the black market. The underground market is where all the action is."

It clicks. "My sister. Where is she?" I wrench myself out of his tight grip and spring for the door. Not the best-laid plan, but I'm working on the fly. It's a miracle I get past them, but I manage to get a few feet outside the door before I'm cruelly stopped in my tracks and fall flat on my face.

I peer over my shoulder to find both beasts wearing disgusting grins, the end of the chain still connected to my ankle in the larger man's hand.

Beast One prowls over and takes a hard look at my ankle before clucking his tongue like some freakshow mother hen. "Look what you did to yourself. The brothers are not going to be happy. This will cost them on the sale." He says a string of something in Russian which makes the other man grimace.

Whatever he growled out to his partner probably didn't bode well for me in the end. If the rough tone didn't give me a clue the glaring murderous look Beast Two slices my way clues me in big time.

They drag me back and the other one takes my ankle in hand. I kick the guy who is kneeling in front of me away but he only shoots me an annoyed leer.

He grips a handful of my hair and I yelp in pain. My chest tightens and I start to tremble.

Don't go there, Nova. I slam my eyes closed and frantically shove the edges of a panic attack working its way through me.

I struggle but there's no getting free from his vise-like grip. "Get the hell away from me you freak show!" I grit through the stinging and keep my eyes glued to him waiting for the knife to the gut or throat. It's not that I've watched too many movies. Not a habit I ever formed. But more out of experience and past horrors.

On the outside, I might be all badass and uncaring. But that shit is only skin deep. Inside I'm a trembling poodle. But my sister is here. And I need to find her.

Another shake of my head and he finally lets me go. I scramble backward and pay no attention to the rough cement ripping at my palms.

Both swoop in and box me in. I'm over one man's shoulder one minute and thrown into a cold shower the next.

Someone forces liquid down my throat and I fight against the drugs making my head spin and fingers tingly.

My feet are shoved into shoes with heels as high as my forearm is long. I try to push away the old lady smearing something shiny over my skin and fixing my hair but my arms and legs don't seem to be on the same earthly plane as the rest of me. I stumble into anything within reach. Walls, chairs, and those freaking beasts with men's faces.

I fist the long waves of hair spilling over my shoulders trying to regain control over my body and snap out of this trance just as I am shoved into the middle of another dark room. I turn in a circle trying to get my bearings and all I can think about is why the fuck am I naked?

I try to cover myself but it's useless. Shadows move to either side of me and a hard hand lands on my shoulder. Instinct drives my elbow into his gut while his partner gets the pointy end of my shoe driven into his foot.

Both grunt and shake me violently but they fall back the second a light comes on.

Intense white light flares around me from above and small dome lights flicker to life in front of me. They are in a semicircle and a God-like voice booms overhead.

Two men wearing full-face masks step up beside me and I kick out with no real aim, but I land a heel where it counts anyway. Yay for me. I stumble forward but catch myself before tumbling to the floor.

My brain can't focus too hard but I catch five words that sober me the heck up pretty fast. The sound system grows quiet several seconds before the announcer rocks me to my core.

"Booth eight. Fifteen point five million dollars. Do I hear sixteen? Sixteen? Okay then, going once, twice... SOLD! The lovely lady with the spitfire attitude is sold to the bidder in booth eight. Congratulations on your new acquisition."

My eyes search the glass boxes I can only guess are numbered in order from right to left. Not that I can see anyone inside, but my gut tells me the man who just bought me for a crazy amount of money is in one of them.

And I'm going to drive a knife into his heart the second I see him.

FOUR

ARES

I chase the moon as she finally peeks from behind angry rain clouds. I twist the throttle and my bike grumbles over wet pavement resembling obsidian. I follow the shimmering white reflection as I ride the last handful of miles to the compound with the roar of the wind in my ears and the beast between my legs wide open. The deep purr helps my soul find a calm I can't find anywhere else. I lean into the curves and take them with ease from years of riding these back roads.

I shake the energy of the city off my shoulders and welcome the silence. The large clubhouse is more of a mansion sitting on ten acres not too far outside city limits. I have to be close enough to where I earn my money, but I like my privacy too.

The second I'm through the gates of the compound my mind shifts from enjoying the New York spring air to rumbling back to all the shit the Savages are handling. The Volkov brothers are just a fraction of where our energy goes. It's been slow going up until now given our limited crew. No surprise, but finding enough men willing to do fucked up shit all in the name of justice is harder than it sounds. Psychos need not apply. Rage, my righthand man, is crazy enough on his own.

When I kill the engine I can hear the thumps of loud music and rowdy whoops of my men cutting loose inside.

I notice a new car in the gravel driveway telling me my vice president, Rage, has gone on another shopping binge. It's that or a few lines of coke, so he calls it his lesser of two evils. The fucker doesn't understand living under the radar. A new Jag is slid in beside my Hummer and I smirk a little because I can appreciate the love of fine transportation. I pat the tank of my bike and give her a little rub. "Don't worry, baby. Nothing will take your place."

War cries and shouts ring in my ears when I swing the front door open. There are four levels. Basement, this floor and two above. This level is for anyone. The basement is for the patched members of the Sons of Savages. My brothers. The top level is off-limits. No excuses.

Beer and hard liquor flow and all the club candy is here with bonus friends. Everyone is in various stages of undress and the pool table is being used as a bed.

"Devil, get the fuck off the pool table, man. Nobody wants to see your ass in the air!"

Through an archway, I spot Riot ribbing our brother who only answers with a stiff middle finger before getting back to work taking his flavor of the night over the edge.

"Hey Ares, baby. How about a little fun time? You've been gone for almost a week, handsome. Everyone else is taken for the night but me." I stayed in the city knowing the Volkov brothers were keeping tabs on me running up to auction time. The peace and quiet were a nice change.

Kendra struts her tall frame from the main gathering room and winds her arms around me. I don't remember too much about her past but enough to know why she has a whiskey in her hand most nights she's not working the casino. I smell sex and booze on her in layers and I'm not about to touch that.

I peel her off and pass her to Riot, the club treasurer. Big eyes hit mine for a second before popping over to Rage as if either will move against my wishes. She pouts but gets the message.

"Where's Fergie?" Savage's only ol' lady of the club runs a tight ship maintaining the girls and keeps everyone in order.

Rage steps away from a couple of nearly stripped candies and comes up beside me, a fresh beer in hand. He shakes his head. He's clad in a black T-shirt beneath a worn, leather cut bearing the name of our motorcycle club and ass-kicking steel-tipped boots. He personified bad boy down to the sleeves of tattoos and a few piercings. Ones you could see and according to the club candy, some you couldn't. Crazy shit.

He puffs a couple of times on a cigar and blows out rings. "Don't know. But when I do, want me to send her your way?"

We spent a lot of years acclimating to our new country for the sake of blending in. Hard when you look like a fucking Russian polar bear like myself. Shaking our roots and adopting American slang and mannerisms wasn't easy except for Rage. The man could shift with the wind. One second he was an Irishman and the next he could make you believe he was a priest.

Devil, the youngest of our tight brotherhood strolls up, fixing his zipper. A prospect we patched in a couple of years back after spending three more proving himself to the brothers.

"Find Fergie. Tell her to get the top floor ready. The works. We're about to have a guest who isn't going to be happy about staying with us. And get another room ready on the second floor."

He nods, asks no question, and pivots toward the back of the house where Fergie can usually be found toiling around in the kitchen or home library. For an old broad who grew up in the crowded MC life and then married into it, she sure as hell takes her alone time seriously.

"You get a little greedy at the auction?" Rage's sandy blond hair slides around his face as he comes in close.

I don't consciously thrust my hand out and clasp Rage's. It's automatic. We bump shoulders and give each other a thump on the back. Solid as steel and just as trustworthy. A lifetime of running together forged a connection we both lean on from time to time. Like now. When we chase heat and light fires to smoke out the scum we don't want invading our territory.

"Moy droog."

"Brother."

"It was hard not to burn the shit hole down with the people in it and call it a night."

42

Rage pulls away and purses his lips in an *"I know what you mean"* manner and nods. "Copy that. Lucky for them you were in a good mood."

I clamp a hand over his substantial shoulder. "Call a meeting downstairs." The *now* is implied.

A crease mars the space between his brows but he nods and pushes away the club candy leeching to his side.

Rage swats her ass. "Get going, Pip. I'll catch you later, babe. Duty calls."

I shake my head when I see her bottom lip jut out. "Here we go," I mutter. I have no damn clue how any of them put up with all the pouty shit these candies dish out, but I chalk it up to all of them having soft centers under all their tough exteriors. But I keep my mouth shut and turn on my heel.

"Aww, but, Rage we—"

He huffed out a heavy breath and I already know where this is headed. "Babe, I said get rollin'. You're not new to how this shit rolls. I gotta go."

I leave my club brother to fend for himself. His dick problems are his alone. I'm about to have my own woman problems. I've told all the patches club candy is not for getting serious about but it seems he's failed to inform the girl that. Piper is decent with a good head on her shoulders but when she's not on the clock at the Asylum, my upscale bar, she turns into a carefree and willing party girl who doesn't like taking no for an answer. Usually, that gets her a good lay from one of the patches or a prospect, but she knows better than to play that shit with me.

I hear her try to get her way again as I walk down the main hallway and toward the stairs leading to the basement. I've made extensive repairs to the place since buying it almost a decade prior. Reinforced steel walls for the main floor took the longest but well worth the time. And then bulletproof glass for each window and down here soundproof padding lines the entire basement. The best fucking bar money can buy makes this level the best thinking spot in the entire clubhouse.

I descend into the calm and as soon as my feet hit the bottom step it's like a switch is flicked. I no longer hear the ruckus of the party. Tension ripples over my shoulders and I shrug it off hoping it doesn't come back as a raging headache later on.

With Volkov's parting gift in hand, I grab a couple of shot glasses and head to the long table in the middle of the room. Automatic dome lights flicker on above as I move through the large open space.

Rage is the first to clamber down the stairs and grabs a chair to my right.

I pop the top and pour us both a shot. As vice president of the club he takes his place as my best friend and righthand man literally and seriously. There is only one other person in the world I trust more than him.

We lift our glasses. "*Na zdorovie!*" we both say in unison and hit back our shots.

"Damn that's good. Not like the usual shit you drink."

He slides his glass my way and I pour us another.

Rage shoots off a low whistle. "You clean up nice, boss man. Maybe I should get some promo pics for the casino while you're not wearing bike grease and have a clean jawline." He shoots me a wink and I flip him off.

"I can't remember the last time I saw you in cufflinks and shoes shinier than your ride either. Back home it was always shit kickers and jeans."

I give a nod recalling the shit I used to do. My father would parade high-level diplomats to run-of-the-mill street thugs through our home, doing various levels of deals.

"Anything to piss off my old man, right?"

He nods and kicks back on the hind legs of the chair and rests his hands on his thighs. Typical Rage style. All like he has no care in the world when I know what goes on in that man's head and it isn't pretty by a longshot.

"Back home?"

"Yeah," Rage grunts and easily slips into our native tongue. "*YA dumal ob etom bol"she.*"

Huh. That has me pausing with my glass halfway to my lips. "And?" Rage thinking about *Rossiya* isn't a good sign.

"I've been thinking about it more. How we left shit with your old man and mine."

He's got that same smelly ass cigar clenched between his teeth and I swear to God he looks like Eastwood in the early days with that half-eye squint going on. Or at the very least the son. Some scruff on his face lends to the Dirty Harry look. Rough around the edges with a bigger chip on his shoulder than me given his name sits at the top of my father's hit list just below mine. Something neither of us likes to talk about. Or the drug addiction he went through because of it. It's a long story he hates getting into so I'm surprised to see him nostalgic.

"What the hell is that smell?" Three different perfumes permeate the space around him. "Did you roll around in the back flower beds?"

He puts on a shit-eating grin. "Club candy. Sweet, aren't they? What can I say? Women love me and I love them right back."

I lean my substantial weight against the back of my chair and pin him with a hard look. "Is that what you've been up to while I was gone?"

"Maybe."

I chuckle. "Better be careful. One of them will expect to be your old lady before too long."

He grunts and tosses back another shot before saying anything. "At any rate, my friend, glad you're back after taking a trip into the devil's ass. How did it really go?"

I rub my jaw. "They are amassing money and forging connections that will make them stronger and harder to take down if we wait much longer."

Rage cocks his head. "What kind of timeframe are we looking at? A few months?"

I shake my head. "Nah. Weeks and that's being generous to get this girl to help us. Much longer and they'll have the ears and connections that will make them untouchable."

We've kept our eye on these thugs as they've climbed up the ladder. At first, we didn't see them as anything other than low-level threats. As long as they paid their dues to operate in our city in the districts, we designated all was well. And then almost overnight they shot up.

Rage's grim expression matches mine and we get down to business as the other men file in. They usually disperse between the couches and chairs spread out around the room, but they take up positions along the sides of the table this time around. Riot walks in first with Devil right behind him.

I look each of them in the eye. "We secured the hacker. She'll be here within the hour."

"And?" Rage grunts, his brows high on his forehead.

"What the hell is that supposed to mean?" I narrow my eyes on him. Ordinarily, he doesn't question me, so his tone grates on my nerves.

"There's something else."

When I only grunt, he reads my dismissal as an invitation to push on.

"There always is with you. You want us to guess or are you going to tell us?"

"The Volkovs want a partnership."

While the brothers are forging connections with some dirty government officials and some high rollers with enough money to buy their way through life, they know we are a strong force they'll have to go through eventually. The Volkovs can establish ties that will make our life hell, true, but in the end the ones we have are older, deeper and the rolling cash we have backing us speaks louder than theirs. We'll have to count on that when the time comes.

Huffs and grumbles work their way through the men and it's Rage who holds a hand up for silence.

"Interesting," he states flatly.

"I didn't say shit about taking them up on the offer. But I am considering it."

"We're working to take them out from the root. Why the hell would they think we want to partner up with them?" Devil didn't spend a lot of years on the police force before finding his way to us. A handful at most. Enough to give him a taste for doing good but his fucked-up past with an abusive father and doped-out mother left him scared and an at-risk cop on the street with a chip on his shoulder. He had a hard time not wanting to pull the trigger every time he had to do a drug bust. They gave him his walking papers when one of those busts went sideways. A "friend" on the force gave me a call and he's been part of our crew for close to five years now. Patched for two. Under my care, he's a little less hotheaded but still impulsive.

"Shut up and learn, boy." Rage has more than one problem clogging his pipes. A prominent one is with Devil. Because of Devil's issue with his mother, the pup views Rage as a weak link with his addiction problems. One Rage takes insult with.

I shake my head. "Haven't you learned the whole point of tonight is to keep our enemies close? You can't see what they have planned unless you have a good way in," I answer. "Why do you think I just spent a week with them basically up my ass?"

He begins to give some smart-ass remark, but then wisely shuts his mouth with a nod when I cut a hard look his way.

"They have armed guards at every entry. I counted about fifteen just inside the waiting area outside the auction floor. Some tried to blend in, but most looked inexperienced and green."

"Easy pickings."

"Even an inexperienced asshole can pull a trigger," I deadpan when Devil pipes up again.

I grab a piece of paper off a desk we keep down here and start mapping out every table, door and possible weak spot we'll run into in the event of an all-out takedown.

"The bar is on the side. The man behind it carries and they'd be fools not to give him a loaded shotgun as well. Here, here and here are the exit points that lead to other parts of the club. They have the auction side hidden and you're only getting back there with an invitation."

The men take over with rapid-fire questions.

"And the Society?"

"The governor was there. A couple of well-known faces we've seen from the Silver City. Others are the closet millionaires and billionaires."

"Anyone recognize you?"

"Apparently they all did and kept a wide berth around my table."

"Eighteen point five million." Riot, the club treasurer who sits beside Devil, crosses his thick arms over his chest. Eyes pinned to the wall over my shoulder, I know he's mentally working the figures. He finally drops his gaze to mine. "We can move some numbers around and make it look like a legit business purchase. I'll have the move covered by morning."

"*Spasibo, moy brat.*" Thank you, my brother.

Devil grabs a couple more glasses from the bar. I pour them all around and everyone takes a deep breath after the million-dollar vodka hits the back of our throats.

"Think she's worth the dough, Prez?"

Each of my crew comes from a hard life. Money never came as abundantly for them as it does now. Because of all the shit they've gone through to get here and for trusting me with their lives they receive an even cut of everything that comes through the Asylum and Aurum. It keeps them happy, well-paid, and loyal. I'm not sentimental in thinking they stay by my side due to our similar pasts.

I take out my phone and shoot off a few pictures I snapped of Volkov's place to Devil. "Get those to Bear. Tell him to print them out and leave them in my office." I'll add them to the spread of information we've gathered later.

Bear is an honorary member older than dirt. He and his wife Fergie are longtime friends who pulled me out of a dire situation that had a strong possibility of landing me cold and in a grave before I turned thirty. Let's just say I managed to get out of the mafia life as a hired gun because of them. And now I have my own crew, my own family. So, I opened my doors to them the second I bought this place and they've been here ever since. Bear is the only other person outside of Rage I trust blindly.

"This girl was down in the basement for a while before being brought up. She has a good insight into how many men they are using and how many women they are moving. Either way tonight was just the first step to cutting the Volkov brothers at the knees. We either do it the violent way. Take this to the streets and get innocent people killed in the process or be smart. Use our wits and erase them from the game another way."

"Understood."

"Now cut the party short and get out on the streets. Put your ears to the ground. See what you catch. They had a lot of buyers there this evening. But no way in hell they sold their entire catalog. Find out what their next plan is by any means."

Everyone stands except Rage.

The evening is dragging but we still have another half hour or so before my purchase is set to arrive. "Any word from Dragon?"

No one has anything, which I half expected. "He'll check in soon, Prez," Devil offers, half shrugging.

I appreciate his attempt at easing my mind over our brother still out in the field. "Devil, get to Asylum and watch who comes and goes. Keep me in the loop." Our high-end bar pulls in some high rollers. Someone from the auction is bound to be there. It took a few years to establish the reputation of a safe zone where the authorities never step foot. And a lot of money. Anyone can be bought. It's a hard fact of life.

"On it."

With that Rage and I are left alone in the basement nursing the remainder of the vodka.

"Now spill it. What the fuck are you not saying in front of the other men? I know you. The real you. Now tell me or I walk."

I crank an eyebrow up and peg Rage with a look that screams *fuck you*.

His *don't give a shit* attitude dies along with his playful attitude and I see the man from years of walking beside me emerge.

He plants his palms on the table and anchors himself in. "I'm not risking my life for lies. We started this with one solid rule between us. The truth or nothing, man. Don't pull this prez shit on me either. I told you when you patched me in as your second—"

"For God's sake are you going to shut up long enough for me to talk or just keep mouthing off and crying all over good vodka?"

"Depends on what you have to say next."

No one ever gets over pain or grief. They just learn to live with the oppressive weight on their chest. I carry mine as a reminder of why I'm walking this earth. It's also in my veins. "The Volkov brothers know. They're baiting me. Seeing how long I'll play to keep my secret."

"Jesus Christ. That's not good." He slides his weight into his chair and props an ankle over a knee. "How long before you think the shit hits the fans?"

I shrug. "Volkovs are working an angle by not outing me at the auction." I pause around another mouthful of vodka. "The new prospects and our crew won't trust me if they find out I've been lying to them this whole time. We've all built this club on the backbone of honesty and taking down people like my family. What will they do when they find out I'm one of them?"

Rage stands and clasps me on the shoulder. "It's really fucked we don't get to pick our family. You're an Antonov, Ares. Bratva blood through and through. Doesn't mean you have to be *like* an Antonov. Maybe it's time you just tell them. The men will either stay or go."

"We need them. Our club will die if we don't get more blood in and soon. We're getting weaker while the Volkovs are amassing a hell of a lot of muscle."

Fergie, in all her leather glory, floats down the stairs, her customary Red hanging from her lips completely unaware of the lead sitting in the pit of my stomach.

We both turn to her. "She's here, Ares."

I join Rage in standing and take one last swallow. "Let's deal with one problem at a time, brother."

FIVE
ARES

I'm out of the basement and at the foot of the stairs in a few strides. I watch my men and Fergie shuffle my new bride up the stairs. It's hard to believe the level of arrogance the Volkov brothers possess by delivering my bought bride straight to my door like a freaking package, yet there she is. All her raging, ruffled glory. Even with a bag over her head. I swear to God she's more beautiful with clothes on than standing naked in the middle of a room.

The men and I've been planning this moment for a couple of months now. Not the purchasing a bride part. But getting Nova on our side.

The way I envisioned having Nova Masters in my home went something like convenience or pressure her into offering her hacker services, pay her off and then go our separate ways.

Not me buying her at a fucking auction.

Turns out, I wasn't the only one with eyes on the same woman. And I'm not too sure the Volkov brothers are smart enough to realize who they had in their possession.

Getting into the auction wasn't as hard as I thought. I let them believe I was ready to finally take them up on their invitation. I've steadily declined for several months rolling. They were all too happy to throw the doors open for me.

I feel like shit Nova found out the hard way there are few friends in this world. My crew and I dropped the ball on letting that fucking prick Jacob down at Diablo's dive bar where she works shuffle her off to the Volkovs. A mistake he'll pay for.

But at least I have her now.

I leave instructions with Rage to care for Avery, the other woman's freedom I secured and head up two flights of stairs. I pass Fergie in the hallway. "Keep everyone on the main level. This might get loud."

"She's got fight in her, Ares, but she's scared too." I stop and turn and get a sharp red nail in my chest along with a key. "You hear me? I don't like this."

I know this rattles her morals but none of us are saints here. "I know, Fergie. I know. But this was the only way."

She waves a wrinkly hand through curling cigarette smoke. And says in a voice raspy from her pack-a-day habit, "You're wrong. But like all stupid men, you'll have to learn that the hard way." Only Fergie takes me head-on and I do nothing about it but stand there and take it. And with that I'm left looking back at her as she leaves me on the third floor with trouble in a white dress on my hands.

I slip the key Fergie gave me into the lock and make sure to slam the door behind me giving my bride time to accept my presence in the room. She jumps where she stands on the far side, making her dress sway around her legs. It's an ugly behemoth at best and my fingers itch to lower the zipper, slide the thing off her, and put her into something I paid for.

I move across the room and the closer I get the stronger the urge I have to rip the Volkov brothers limb from limb.

"Stop. Don't come any closer. Leave me. I'll kill you."

I smirk. She's got a smart mouth, that's for damn sure. She can't see me through the thick sack over her head so she's jumping around like she's done a few lines of coke in the past hour.

"*Da*, my little she-devil. I believe you. Given the chance. But that's big talk for a woman who's tied and bagged." I reach for the black bag and yank it off her head. Fiery blue eyes laser in on me through a curtain of white hair. Solid iron pierces my heart and for a moment, I don't breathe. This close I can appreciate the beautiful unblemished porcelain skin that matches the light hair. A spattering of freckles splashes over her bare shoulders. Perhaps not the most favorable aspect in a woman's opinion, but I find them irresistible to look away from. The flush of red to her cheeks brings out the hints of deep blue specs in her eyes. The contrast between the two shades is every bit as hypnotizing as music to a cobra. Kissable full lips blush a deep red probably from biting them on the ride over. I want to nibble at those creamy shoulders to see if she's as sweet as she looks. It's all I can do to stop myself from stripping this dress off to see all those curves again under a new light.

No part of me doubts she'll be more than a handful in and out of bed.

Damn if I don't love a woman who makes me work for it. And she's beautiful.

Therein lies the problem. Too beautiful. I'm tempted to let her walk. She doesn't deserve the shit she's gone through. I can find another way to take down the Volkov brothers. But my options are few and far between. I reconsider each of them, but no. I'm on a timetable which means she's in this whether she likes it or not. We both are. I don't have time to rework my angles.

She stays.

Carpet cushions my steps as I slowly make my way closer. She jumps when I reach for her tied hands.

"But I don't plan on giving you that chance, Nova Masters."

She must have given them hell with how tight they knotted the rope. I loosen the knot and slowly unwind the rough length from her wrists and halfway up her arms. Welts pucker her perfect skin.

Son-of-a-bitches marked my property. I clench my teeth at the direction of my irrational thoughts. Ire hits me head-on for the pain she must have felt. I get to the final knot and drop the rope on the floor unceremoniously, her defiant glare locked with mine.

In that second I realize my error.

Piercing Xena warrior cries tear through the room and a force of grit, determination and all-woman power plows into me.

Her bellow of rage catches me off guard and so does her next move. I receive a dainty but pretty damn strong shoulder right beneath the ribcage and the next ten seconds are punctuated with a searing pain that leaves me blind.

Lamps, magazines, bowls of loose change, and about thirty other items I keep on nearby tables all go crashing to the floor. Sparks and an electrical hiss tell me I'll be lucky if the house doesn't catch on fire.

I grunt, double over and we both tumble. A look of almost comical horror dashes over her flushed face. I tuck her smaller frame and the masses of her wedding dress into me and roll our combined weight, taking the unforgiving edge of a nightstand to the ribs. I've always wanted to visit space and right that second there are so many stars dancing across my vision it's like I took a direct flight.

"Humph." The carpet is not as forgiving as you think. We both land with a thump and I grit through the burn of pain shooting through me. We come to a rolling stop in the middle of the floor, her pinned beneath my substantial body. My arms are still around her and I know my weight has to be crushing her but fuck if I can move.

"Hold the hell up, woman," I groan as she wiggles and thrashes under me. "Keep moving like that and we are going to have a completely different problem."

Every inch she rotates those hips puts her core in direct contact with my cock. I'm only human here.

"What the hell is your problem? I just paid so you could get out of that place. Now you want to go back?"

I'm talking into her shoulder and my words are muffled.

She sets off on another wave of fighting and scrambling. I shoot up but keep her locked in place by crouching over her. Creamy legs wrap around my middle and well, to anyone looking on it would look like a totally different scenario happening here.

Parts of her dress fall over her face and she wrestles it back to reveal her mouth pulled back in a sneer. Much more and she'd be foaming. "You have to let me out of here. Don't let them leave without me; I have to go back there." Beautiful eyes widen with anxious fear.

Panic and that same fear tear across her expression. It doesn't faze me. She has to be out of it. No way in hell this chick knows what she's asking for.

"Get off me. I don't know who you are or what game you're playing but I swear if you don't get off me and let me leave I'll stab you in the heart." Her dress falls back over her face, diminishing the heat of her glare.

I clutch my fists around all her damn dress and pull it back off her face. "With what?" I challenge her and she immediately has an answer to my surprise. And possibly my untimely death.

She bucks her hips and dislodges me enough to reach for the ends of her dress. With lightning-fast moves, the she-devil snatches a heel from her foot. The spike on her stilettos is pretty serious looking.

She swings and I bat her hand away, knocking the shoe to the floor beside us.

For a moment she stares up at me dumbfounded but the surprise doesn't last long. She plants a foot firmly on the floor and lets another hellish war cry out. We roll and this time she's on top, those hips spread wide open.

I'm just enough of an asshole to be getting hard at the sight of her all fired up and hell-bent on kicking my ass.

The straps of her dress hang off her shoulders and she's breathing hard like we just spent an all-nighter together. Hair hangs in her face. She looks seriously pissed off. I smile. I have to admit. All that creamy skin is an unmeasured distraction.

Her beautiful mouth pulls back in a sneer. She lunges, kicks, and fights to free herself from my grip.

Three bouncing steps and she's out the door I realize I failed to lock behind me.

Devil's question comes back to me. "Yeah, she's worth every last penny I spent for her freedom and then some."

Nova

I run for it. I kick off my other shoe and hit the stairs at top speed. "Faster!" I scream mentally and almost break my neck in doing so. I cry out when I slam a shoulder into someone coming up the stairs. I don't stop to offer up an apology.

Floors whizz by as I descend. There's no such thing as breaks in this scenario. Only full throttle. If I hurry maybe, *maybe* I can follow the van that brought me here back to my sister. Heavy pounding on floorboards sends my heart thundering. I can't tell how much ahead I am and I am NOT going to stop and look.

I fist my dress and bound down yet another flight. Why the hell I am wearing a wedding dress is anyone's guess but I'm not about to stop and ask. I guess it's better than going Full Monty but come the hell on. Ruffles? What the hell kind of joke is this.

I don't stop until I hit the last of a million and come to a sketching halt. A man wearing a leather vest with an ugly skull on fire is standing by the entrance. To his left, I spy the front door wide open. He turns, beer in one hand and a phone in the other.

Perfect.

I take my chances and grab the phone, leaving behind a startled dude who looks to be in his early seventies and way too amused.

"Thanks," I yell back and keep trucking toward the front door. I try for the emergency dial option on the phone but I'm jostling too much to hit anything on the touch screen.

"Where the hell did you come from?" he shouts after me.

"Grab her, Bear!"

Goosebumps sprinkle over my skin instantly. I throw a look over my shoulder when I hear a string of Russian tear through the space between us. A bull of a man thunders down the stairs ricocheting off every inch of wall and hand-carved banisters in his rush to reach me. His dark eyes track my every move and he's pretty nimble for a man of his size. Tall, wide as a door, and the size of a bulldozer fueled by...panic? Odd.

But yeah, no thank you. I've dealt with enough crazy in my life. Pass!

There's an aura of power and strength with strong undertones of danger about him that makes the hair on my arms stand on end. He's rugged, probably pumps Volkswagen bugs for weights at the gym, and looks like he's been in several brawls with a bear. And lost. He might know how to fill out a pair of tuxedo pants with all that rippling man meat, but so do thugs, murders, and all-around bad guys. I learned that the hard way. Not gonna fool me again. I deal with the shady-ass people all day long. True. But it's all done under an alias and from behind a screen. Does that make them any safer? Newsflash to self. None of them know my real name nor are they currently chasing me.

Maybe that is what all this is about? Maybe one of my client's enemies found the hacker behind their money disappearing or a million other black hat *operations* I've performed. Don't judge. I have my reasons.

My internal danger-dar whirrs to life with flashing red lights and sirens. *Get out!*

I dash around the old man and don't stop until the soft pads of my bare feet hit sharp gravel.

Dead ahead the blurry shine of red taillights fades in the distance along with my hope.

"Argh!" I push through the stabbing pain and pivot directions. Frantic for a way out of here, I run before looking which has me skidding to a bumpy and sudden stop when I finally realize my catastrophic error.

"No, damn it!" Hummers, cars that look no bigger than wind-up toys and a couple of pickups. All of them scream drug-dealer money which means they probably come with fancy apps on phones to start them.

Phones.

I feel my palms start to sweat around the one I'm still clutching. I can either forfeit my lead time trying on a phone I can't unlock or go to option B.

I perform a one-eighty and spy a line of shiny bikes opposite the cars. Bingo. "Plan B, it is." Now those might be a possibility.

It's kind of hard to concentrate on the finer details like I've never ridden a bike before, but it can't be rocket science if this thug can manage it. Because I know one of these belongs to him just like I know my window of escaping is swiftly closing.

I don't spare the bull a single glance and keep on pumping my legs.

"Wait a damn minute, woman!" he growls around a mouthful of more Russian and fancy R rolls I don't understand. Doesn't matter. What does matter are heavy footfalls crunching on gravel and the fact they are getting closer. They send me gripping for my dress and I do a mean knees-to-chest movement my younger self would be proud of.

Using my years of outrunning my uncle to my advantage I break record speeds reaching the bikes what feels like the length of a football field away.

I swing my leg and pounds of dress over the seat of the nearest one so impossibly shiny I can see my panicked expression staring back at me. I try to crank and twist anything I can to start the damn thing.

"You have to ask permission to ride bitch on my bike."

My lips pinch together. It's not like I can match his strength with mine but for once I'd really love to have a set of brass knuckles. Either way, it doesn't mean he's not going to get the fight of my life.

Weighed down by this stupid dress I don't get an inch before beefy arms wrap around my middle and I'm plucked off the bike and dropped in the gravel feet first.

"Oh! You unholy bastard!" I crumple to my knees from the pain but I don't get a chance to see how bad the damage is. Those same arms are around me again and I'm swung over a massive shoulder, my ass in the air and the fight in my muscles coming to life.

"Is there any other kind of bastard?"

I rear back and drive a solid elbow blow right over his shoulder blade. He snarls, gives me a good shake so I do it again only this time I put more weight into it.

"Stop that! It's your own damn fault. I told you to hold the hell up, did I not? Maybe I should let you see how far you can get barefoot and in that dress. Or I should really send you back and get a refund. *Da*. I'm starting to like that idea."

I pound on his back to emphasize my words. "Yes! Do that! I dare you." My goading doesn't help. He only huffs out and I can practically see he thinks I'm a loon with how hard he's shaking his head. The mumbled Russian has a tone I understand too.

The fucker.

"The faster you learn to do what I say, the easier your life will be. Don't and see what happens." His tone turns mocking with a twist of dark humor. "Or you can continue to fight me and see how that goes. Maybe you like being tied up."

I swallow past a knot of fear lodged in my throat. Remember, I'm not nearly as brave as I act. That's all it is. A panicked version of myself trying not to get killed before I can save my sister. Deep down I'd rather hide behind a computer screen and let my typing do all my fighting. But here I am. Thrown over the shoulder of some mafia biker Russian dude slash drug dealer. I mean look at this place! Money oozes from every corner of the manicured lawn.

I don't know. I'm spitballing here. But something tells me I'm not far off the mark, if at all about this guy.

My captor fights with my dress and just as a cold wind hits my ass, so does his open palm.

"What the hell?" I squeak. His touch lingers on the part of my ass cheek he smacks. Strong fingers grip the fleshy globe, working in the heat of the sting.

I try to wiggle free but it only earns me another. Rage, the kind that festers and explodes out taking everyone with it, fills me. "Do that again and see what I do!"

"Still want to fight me? Okay." Those fingers dig into my flesh and the touch is no longer a suggestion of danger, but a threat of possession. "You're mine to do with what I please. Push me, little girl, and you'll see how far I'm willing to go to get what I want. You might even like it. Begging for it when I'm balls deep inside you and feeding your sweet pussy my milk."

I flex when his fingertips skim over my ass and down the sensitive skin of my thighs. He's playing with me, wanting me to take the bait. It takes everything in me not to give in to his taunts.

"Not a chance, mafia man. Touch me and I swear to God, I'll cut your dick off."

"You won't be saying that after you get a taste of me on that filthy tongue of yours."

"I'll never want you!"

"Yes. You. Will. But keep telling yourself lies." The feel of his fingers is back on my body. "But your body tells me another story. I feel those hard nipples pressing into my shoulder, *malyshka*."

I press my hand on his shoulder and try forcing my way off, but his grip is stronger than steel clamps. "Put me down!" I manage but the fight in me wanes. Tired and aching, the feeling of defeat wants to take hold. All that rage bubbles and blisters but that's all.

In a deadpan tone, his accent deep and thick, he grumbles, "You know what, *malyshka*? I wasn't going to lock you up. But you've left me no choice. I don't have time to play with you."

Dread locks my fingers into tight fists against his back. A handful of nearly naked gawkers gather around us and my heart crumples into a shriveled mass inside me. What kind of new hell hole is this?

Some wear smirks while others hold me with contempt in their eyes. Well to hell with them. Like I asked to be here inconveniencing them with my little show of rebellion or something? When they should be helping me fight against this brutish bull.

A woman in a mohawk looks on with a stupid grin on her face and winks at me when she should be helping. So much for women sticking together. My heart races, and I pound on his back. He only tightens his hold around my middle.

"I think you can use some alone time."

Normally alone suits me but I don't like the sound of finality in his tone. Like how alone? And did it involve a shovel and a hole? Maybe some lye?

Spellbound by fear, I can't do anything but work my mouth at first. "No, please. Don't. No," I croak. God help me. Not another basement.

In half the strides it took me to flash down the stairs he's standing on the third level and throws the door open to the same room I just escaped.

"Oh, hell no!"

"Oh, yes."

I rear a knee back and nail him as hard as I can. He stumbles forward and we topple onto the bed. I quickly realize I'm right back where I started, only instead of having the freedom to move around I'm now pinned to the bed with his massive body overtop mine and my dress a mound of fluffy white between us.

68

Through yards of hair in my eyes, I spot something metal and glittering in the overhead lights.

My heart explodes into chaos. I buck and throw him left and right but it's no use. Before I have a chance to scramble off and take another run at escaping I hear the grate of metal grinding and the all-too-familiar sound of cuffs locking. I yank on my wrists but it's no use.

We're face to face. His body warmth settles over mine. His full lips peel back in an arrogant smile and I swing with my only free hand. It's no surprise he catches it before my palm can land with his scruffy face. He pins it over my head and leans in. I hate there's a chance he might be right. But I hate more with how the evidence of my body's betrayal stands out between us.

He reaches out and flicks the tip of a hard nipple and chuckles darkly when I shudder.

"Bastard," I seethe through a clenched jaw.

"*Da*," he says flatly and my little knowledge of Russian extends to that one word. Yes. At least he knows what he is.

"But none of that, now, *malyshka*," he continues unaware of my inner war of finding his sharp, cool steel eyes as piercing as his arrogance to the fight inside me. I can't believe I'm even admitting this, but if it weren't for the fact he bought me tonight I'd say the sick monster crouching over me right now is freaking gorgeous. He moves between my legs and I feel it. The full length of his shaft is obviously aroused. He surveys me and twists his mouth into a semblance of what I think might be *intrigue? Fascination?* Or he might be calculating the size of a barrel he'll need to stuff me and my dress in once he's through with me.

My gaze zeroes in on his and I buck against him.

Wrong move. *Dead* wrong move.

Glints of wickedness flash at me and his smile grows. All smugness shifts to desire.

"Don't promise something you don't plan on keeping, *malyshka*," he drawls out in that sexy accent of his. Shivers flutter up my spine and chill my skin. I can't stand to look at him another second so I turn my head.

"I'd rather die than let you use any part of me. I want none of this. Of you."

A finger under my chin brings my eyes back to his smug face. Bastard knows he owns me. And I hate him for it.

"Be careful what you wish for. When you get it, there's no going back."

His wild eyes never leave mine. We stay locked like that and I don't blink until strong fingers wrap around my wrist. No matter how hard I yank, pull, kick and scream the inevitable happens.

"Fuck you!" I snarl. His lack of concern fuels my rage further. Heat builds when his hips connect with mine, where his hands pin me, where his gaze keeps me fixed in place.

He lowers his face and his warm lips brush over mine. "Maybe next time," he teases and then there's one final click of metal. My heart pounds so hard I strain to hear his words through the thundering booms in my ears.

"When I stretch that hole and make no mistake, Nova, I will have you wrapped around my cock. You'll be screaming my name and begging me to drive inside that pussy over and over again. That's a promise, *malyshka*. A promise."

I bite the insides of my cheeks. Oh, God. My body betrays me. Flaming heat of embarrassment hits my cheeks. Warmth pools between my thighs and the hard tips of my nipples might as well be open invitations to tease and suck them. His gaze falls to them for a moment, causing them to harden further. But the deep chuckle, the sound of his pleasure at seeing my reaction to his bold threats, that is my undoing. An inferno builds inside me and I can no longer tell if it's for him or my flaming rage.

Holding my gaze, he reaches out to take a tip between his thumb and forefinger. Degree by degree he pinches and squeezes until I fear his words might come true. I might beg him for everything he's promised.

But not tonight, if ever.

The thought of him being right sends another wave of anger through me. "I'll never ever want this. I'll never want you."

His eyebrows rise and those gray eyes of his pin me to the mattress with a look of victory. He reaches out and fingers the satin of my dress, letting his hand fall to my quivering chest just above my breasts. "You're already in my bed. I'd say that's half the battle won."

My prison keeper walks away, leaving me cuffed to his bed.

I've hated a lot of people in my life but nothing like what I feel right now for this man.

My life just went from bad to worse.

SIX
ARES

The next afternoon, sunshine drifted into a late spring cold front and the somber gray weather fits my mood as the city's outline comes into view. We take a left and roll off the main drag several blocks before finding the dingy warehouse Rage set up for our meeting with a trio of new clients from Chicago. The Genesis men. Not much is known about them except they have deep pockets. That's all that matters in the end. And we owe a good club friend for sending clients our way on more than one occasion. I twist the throttle and glide down the road a little faster. I agreed to this meeting before everything went down with Nova. The longer I'm away from her, the more time it will take for me to work her over to our side. My dick still aches for a taste of her sweetness, but pushing her to find her limits has been more than one kind of challenge. I for one find it hard to resist her tempting curves and soft skin.

But like I've said, when I take her she'll be fully willing to take every inch of my hard cock.

After a thirty-minute ride to the city Rage rumbles in beside me and we both kill the engines to our bikes. Silence surrounds us and we sit like that for several minutes.

"You couldn't have picked an underground garage or something?" My breath is an angry, gray mist in front of my face. My friend doesn't deserve my irritation. It's not his fault events rolled out last night the way they did. All I need is her to calm down enough to listen to reason, but that doesn't seem likely any time soon which puts our timetable in jeopardy.

"Since when does the cold bother you?"

I shrug. "Shit has me on edge is all, my brother. I half expect those twit Volkovs to make the mistake of trying to ambush us. The smarter one hinted as much back at the auction the other night."

"The men locked the area down as usual."

I force myself to relax. The last thing we need is our new potential customers to see me hotwired. They sense one thing off and they'll back out. And we are not in the business of losing money. I force myself to visualize Nova, on my bed. Instead of wearing that damn dress, she'd only be wearing my cuffs with the masses of her hair fanned across the black cotton sheets. The idea has me calming the hell down and fast.

Beside me, Rage drags his helmet off and slides it onto the handlebar. I do the same.

"The Volkovs are not smart, or should I say stupid, enough to try and off us. Not in broad daylight. It's not their MO, brother."

74

I give him another shrug. "You're not wrong on either account but you don't have to be smart or clever to know how to point a gun. If it was a prerequisite, we'd be out of business."

"True. So when are you gonna say what's really bothering you? Because I know it's not the brothers. We're handling that shit just fine."

"Are we?"

I cup my hands in front of my mouth and blow on them. "I tried talking with her this morning and ended up with a solid foot to my solar plexus. She is worse than a rabid animal. And now she's had a chance to sleep and plot for hours. Makes her twice as dangerous. I figure another day or two and she might be willing to calm down enough to where we can talk. But do we have that time?"

"Do you blame her? Wouldn't you be pissed as hell if someone cuffed you to a bed AFTER purchasing you?" Rage stops and scratches his beard telling me he's contemplating his next words carefully. "Ever consider just letting her go and letting her make her own choice?"

"That's how she got away from me last night. Not making that mistake again." I rub at the kink in my left shoulder and work the muscle. I've had deep tissue massages before but she reached new levels last night with her fucking ninja moves and my chest still feels tight when I breathe.

Rage throws his head back and rips a roar of laughter. "'Bout right."

It takes him a minute to calm down and I sit there with my hands shoved into my pockets trying not to freeze my balls off.

"So we're sitting out here on our damn bikes with icicles hanging from our balls all because you have a woman in your bed and you can't get her to talk to you."

I hate it when he does that. Strips shit down to its barest form. I nod. "*Da*. Something like that. She's determined to fight me every chance she gets."

Sitting astride our bikes, I roll back a few feet so the pillar to my left catches the brunt force of the wind coming in through the spaces where windows used to be along the east side.

"Have they reached out? The brothers I mean."

Rage fishes his phone out of his front pocket and flips it around for me to see. "Felt the message come through on the ride over. Seems they want to meet."

"Ok. Set it up as soon as possible. The more we give them a reason to stay put the easier it will be on us. They can't buy arms if they leave and there is no way they will let those girls out of their sight until they are paid for."

"Smart."

"Hold them off a couple of days. Give me some time to work with Nova."

"Got it." Rage punches out a message and I watch him hit send. "But are you really considering the whole partnership angle? Ever consider just going to the authorities and washing our hands of this?"

That brings my mind back to the evidence I have on my phone. I like to have all my bases covered even if I don't end up using half the information available to me. I'm more of a hands-on kind of guy who likes having control of every aspect of his business. Bringing the authorities in on something they have no business in isn't the right move when it would shine a spotlight on our less-than-aboveboard endeavors. "Not yet," I say matter-of-factly. "Leave them as a last resort."

Rage tilts his head to the side and waits for me to elaborate in my own time.

"We've been at this for two years and we've only just started to scratch the surface."

"Think they would do any better with all their red tape?"

"Probably not," Rage concedes.

"We're one step closer to having the Volkov brothers where we want them." I pull out my phone and bring up the recording I took of the night of the auction. Phones were not exactly allowed but no one had enough balls to ask the god of war if he wanted to hand over his phone. Not something I call myself, but the name settled after I took New York City as mine a few years back. The reputation stuck.

"There's something else you need to know. Take a listen." I place my phone on the bike and I hit play while we wait and Rage's face turns more incredulous the longer the oldest Volkov speaks.

He gestures to my phone. "Again, why not go to the authorities and just walk. Get back to just living life?" He rubs at the back of his neck, the creases overtop his brows grow deeper. Years of addiction show when he drops his guard and reveals the man behind the mask he wears for the rest of the crew. But when it's just us, the man who lives with a daily struggle comes to the surface.

I understand my friend's irritation with this whole situation. The more stressed he is the more he's tempted to fall back on old habits to help him handle his stress levels. People judge him for his weakness, but they know nothing of the man's past either.

I clasp a hand on his shoulder. "We've got this, brother." A look of doubt crosses his face but I double down and make sure he's really listening to what I say.

"There's no one who can do this for us. The Volkovs need to be stopped before it's too late. The Savages are all that stand in the way of them raping this city and leaving it in ruin. We let the badges in on this shit. We're better off taking out the trash alone."

"Even if they blame us for shit we're not doing."

"Part of being the gatekeepers. Any other way and we might as well turn in our cuts and ride off into the sunset. I don't think you like the idea of letting them win. You know sure as I do, those men will devour this city, our territory, and the innocent inside the city the second we step away."

"You're right. Damn, I know you are...it's just."

I look on as his fingers grip the handles of his bike. He's torn. I get it. He knows his limits and fears pushing himself too far. But he's stronger than he knows. I just need to remind my brother of that from time to time.

"I fear we won't be enough to stop them and we won't be able to save all those women. We should have laid waste to them the second they dared step into our territory."

"At first they were good business. We all agreed," I point out.

He nods.

"And then someone injected millions and made them powerful overnight."

"But not smarter," I add. It's on the tip of my tongue to ask him if he wants to take the back seat on this mission; I guess it is. Fuck. I don't know anymore. More like a calling really. We all have our reasons for being part of the Savages. Justice is the main driving force. But who puts labels on wiping the board of the douchebags of the world?

"True." He scrubs both hands over his face and I see my old friend come back. "So why didn't you share this with the crew?" he continues, his voice strong and in control.

I say nothing, just sit there for a minute weighing my answers. I've never lied to Rage and I don't have any plans on starting now.

Before I can say it, he's already reading my mind.

He jerks his chin toward my phone. "Who is it you don't trust with that?"

"Just a gut feeling. Not sure. Maybe I'm just a fucking paranoid motherfucker. Either way, we have the twins where we want them. Our contingency plan is in place, but I do not want to use it if we don't have to, understand? We need to know who is backing them. Without that, whoever it is can cut ties and find more stooges to use if we don't play our cards just right. And we have our golden ticket currently back at the clubhouse."

"Aren't you calling victory a little early? Her being cuffed to your bed hasn't given us anything yet."

"I'm aware. I just need her to do her hacking shit and trace the money to the source. With that information we can finally cut them off at the knees, find their backers, and clean our territory of their filth."

"Does she know yet?"

I know what he's asking but I still ask the question. "Why I bought her?"

An eyebrow jacks up as he surveys me. "The whole shit and caboodle, Ares. You literally let her get kidnapped with two other girls and did nothing. I think buying her is the least of your sins in her eyes, brother."

I can see the irritation taking hold in his expression. I don't have all the answers. Hell, not even a handful. Especially where the angel-haired woman is concerned. "Not exactly how it happened and you know it, brother."

"Shit, I know man, but she's not going to see it that way when she does finally come around to talking to you. She'll see it exactly how *I* said."

My cock still throbs from how she rotated those perfect hips and curvy ass over me. The feel of her soft skin under my rough hands nearly had me giving in to her demands. My gaze rakes over the cracked and broken windows of the warehouse. I don't know what I'm looking for. Maybe something to anchor my senses back where they need to be in the current situation, but she stole my sleep, my bed, and now my concentration. I force myself to forget those few precious moments where her gaze landed on mine. Rage would call me a pussy for thinking it, but the woman grabbed hold of something inside me when I clicked those cuffs onto those dainty wrists. "I'm working on it. Let's get this over with so we can get back," I gruff out and leave it at that.

My eyes latch onto the north side of the warehouse. Our conversation is cut short when the purr of an expensive motor cuts into the eerie quiet of the abandoned location.

A Rolls-Royce aptly called the Ghost with black tinted windows glides to a stop in front of us and I exchange a look with Rage. I know the make and model because I have the exact same car under a tarp in my underground garage. Arriving to a meeting in that makes a strong statement.

I speak to Rage without turning my head. "Ready for this?"

"Just don't die before I do, brother." I grin when Rage repeats our mantra. We can dig at each other day and night but when it comes down to it, we'd give our last drop of blood for the other. We both swing our legs over our bikes to stand in front of them as the car eases to a slow stop several feet from us.

"When we get back to the club, I'm going straight for the hottest shower of my life."

Rage spreads his feet wide and locks his arms over his chest. The leather of his cut pulls tight overtop a long-sleeved sweater that does a good job of showing off his love for a gym.

"What do we know about these assholes anyway?"

"They're friends of a previous client and come recommended. They're looking for arms. Small numbers but willing to pay our prices."

That sounded like only one person we know. "Reaper?"

Liam "Reaper" Black is president of his own club. Or would be if he would buck up and take over for his ailing father already. But my friend for over a decade swears the MC life isn't for him. He's a roaming nomad between clubs which is a contradiction. I just think he's scared of stepping into the shoes of his grandfather and father. Who wouldn't be? They did well by their town's community. But not all they did was above board either and the Savages have done enough business with the Dirty Sinners of Haven, Tennessee to know where some of the bodies are buried. And they've helped us. Reaper is former special forces. I'm sure he's battling his own demons. Taking on more isn't an easy decision.

"He finally took over for his father?"

"Looks that way. Or is about to. The man was giving me a major case of anxiety with all the back and forth on the matter. But he did say he'd see this as a personal favor to him if we go through with helping these gentlemen out."

Normally we don't do anything under ten million. With all the government payoffs it's not worth it otherwise. But there are on rare occasions when it benefits us to do the smaller local deals. We'd gone over the potential client's information before, but with everything going on the brief overview helps refresh my memory.

Right. It's coming back to me. "Chicago. Something about a turf war between them and a rival family trying to muscle in and take over. It's getting bloody is all I know."

"Something like that. Goes deeper, but not our problem; that's how I see it."

With Reaper's endorsement, I see them as potential future allies and this little meet and greet also tells me they are in short supply of support on their end which might work to our advantage. Why else would they be stepping into another family's territory eleven hours away to make a deal of this nature?

"Why the hell couldn't we have done this at the Asylum?" Rage asks without turning to face me.

I chuckle lowly. "Because I wanted to see them squirm a little," I admit. "Keep them on edge and see how they handle it."

"You're a sick bastard, Prez."

Three doors open and as many men step from the flawless white car. One turns the sides of his coat's collar up and the other two look like they live for the brute force of the freezing wind coming down through the gaping hole in the middle of the roof. All have easy gaits and the casual confidence of being the most powerful men in the room is apparent.

Some would take this time to measure dicks and remind everyone of their positions on the ladder of power, but I like my allies to handle themselves like they know what the hell they are doing.

"Lovely day for a get-together." The one with the deep tan and easy smile takes in the dreary warehouse with cracked cement and gang tags. "I thought Chicago was blistering cold." He tries to break the ice and only gets a blank stare in return but he doesn't shirk. If anything, he stands a little taller and curls a lip in an arrogant grin. He's got a deep baritone that makes him sound years older than the mid-thirties he appears.

"Ignore Santi; his ass is always cold. Frankly, I don't know how the Latin blood in him hasn't frozen solid yet."

"Fuck you, Harlon. We can't all be made of ice." Harlon. I roll the name through my mental database.

"You the son of Constantine?"

"Yes. Is that a problem?" His gaze is hard and challenging like he's faced shit recently for being the son of a notorious mafia man who went away for life about five years back. His girlfriend at the time got a little nosy and wondered where all the millions came from. Turns out she was an undercover cop looking to take down the organization from the inside. All she managed to do was shift the power from one Constantine to another.

"Good to know." Is all I say and he seems content at leaving it there, too.

Their fraternal camaraderie reminds me of my crew and I feel the energy coming off them as something sincere and familiar.

I drop my hands to my side, my fingers lax, and let the three men close the few feet between us. We're all about the same size but their long wool overcoats make them look bulkier. I'm sure they're also packing under those coats. Going toe to toe with them, I'm not sure who would come out on top. By the looks of their polished exterior I want to say me. I have no issues playing dirty in a street fight. But the scars over their knuckles and Harlon's jaw tell me they'd be hard to eliminate.

They take in our bikes and cuts and I don't mistake the appreciation for our machines.

My phone vibrates in my pocket but I ignore it knowing it's probably Riot or Devil messaging with business.

"We have a mutual friend." Harlon has broad shoulders, silvering hair around the edges and enough creases along the corners of his eyes that tell me he's hitting forty. The other two appear younger, but not by many years.

"So I hear."

"Reaper sends his regards. Says he wishes he could be here but has his hands full with family matters at the moment."

I nod and take the hand he offers in a tight grip and he returns it in kind. Solid, strong and unafraid of another strong male. I like that.

"Name's Cassian." The man in the middle offers his hand next. Rinse repeat down the line. All have strong grips and have no trouble holding my gaze. Small details like these let me know they might be dressed to the nines and like they walked out of a fucking photoshoot but they don't step away from a fight. The calluses on their hands also tell me they put some sweat into climbing the ladder of Chicago's underworld and dear old daddy didn't hand it to Harlon. Respectable in my book. How the other two fit into the equation I've yet to unravel.

"We've been known as the ruthless kings, the men of Genesis and undertakers by the few who have crossed us."

Harlon's dark eyes hold mine.

I read the undertones for what they are meant to be, a warning to most and a show of strength to others. To me, it's white noise.

"Thanks for taking a minute with us," Harlon continues. "You come highly recommended at keeping your mouths zipped and delivered with no questions asked. I hope that's still true. I believe Reaper filled you in on what we are looking for?"

"He has," Rage offers without missing a beat.

Small arms. Semi-automatics. Untraceable.

My phone goes off again, but reaching for it right now is bad form. My crew will get an earful when I get back to the clubhouse.

"Gentlemen," I look each of them in the eye. "You can call me Ares and this is Rage. I appreciate your candid nature. Let me return the favor. We can supply what you need if you can meet our price."

Harlon seems like the leader of the trio with the way he stands apart from the other two slightly. Almost imperceivable but I grew up learning to read body language and exploiting it to my advantage and this man is the one who will be making the deal. The other two are important but Harlon is the one who handles shit when it hits the fan.

Hair falls in his eyes and he easily brushes it away. In doing so I notice the gold ring on his finger. A married mafia man in the middle of a war. All of them wear bands. I file that information for use if I ever need it.

"I was informed you would go directly to money. I like that. It's why we're all here, right?"

"I'm reaching for my phone." Harlon offers and opens the side of his coat slowly. I spot the butts of two Smith and

Wesson .40s with silver inlay hanging in their holsters. Not my choice of weapon, but powerful enough to get the job done.

Harlon pulls a phone from his inner coat pocket, taps a couple of times before he flips his phone around. "This is just one of our bank accounts. All you need to do is give me the coordinates and I'll make sure you receive your amount in full right now. Deal?"

I exchange a look with Rage. We don't have to speak to know what the other is thinking. He knows what we need most right now so I let him fill in our new clients. "Keep your money," Rage drawls in a casual tone. "We want something else."

Their cool expressions of confidence falter for the briefest of seconds. "Something wrong with the deal, gentlemen? Did I just not prove we can pay your fee and then some?"

"We're not after money. We're looking for something more valuable."

It's like their expressions were connected in some way. All three pinch their brows and rock back on their heels with curiosity in their gazes.

"We're listening," Harlon offers.

Good, I have their attention.

"We're after connections. We'll supply what you are looking for and in return when we need a favor just give us your word you'll be there. Do that for us and I think we can have a long-running relationship that will be mutually beneficial." Three sets of keen, dark eyes watch us intently and I can see the gears working as they each consider my offer.

"The Savages and the Genesis men. If we were to form a union between our families we could control a lot more than our current territory."

"We could do a lot. And prevent a lot more," I offer tentatively.

My phone goes off again and I know something is wrong this time.

"Exactly." The one named Cassian nods and clasps his friend on the shoulder. "This anything to do with the Volkov brothers?"

That piques my interest and I ignore the vibration in my pocket again. I turn the weight of my full attention on him. "What do you know about the twins?"

"That they are pieces of shit with growing power. Don't seem so shocked. We make it our job to know potential threats and rising powers. We're not fools. State lines and territories don't mean shit to them. What is your problem today, is our problem tomorrow. You get my meaning?"

"You should know they've been in contact with us. They're looking to move merchandise through our city and soon. You can see why we mention them. Five days tops. They're throwing your name around as backers. This true?"

That's Santi.

I grit my back molars half expecting them to do shit like this. "Not exactly."

Harlon, Cassian, and Santi don't seem like men who take people at their word. They consider my curt reply for a few seconds. I expect more questions, more suspicion or at least a show of mistrust.

I get none of that from the trio. Only nods. "Reaper told me about your crew. Your true objective. I think you'll find it aligns with ours."

I pull the conversation back to where it interests me most. "What did you tell the Volkovs?"

"Out of respect for you and this being your territory we told them to clear it with you first."

"Good man. Set it up. Keep us in the loop. We'll be in contact with the products you need."

Harlon breaks rank with his men and steps close enough I can see the reflection of the graying light in the black of his pupils. "Our city is yours to do what you need to do with the Volkovs when the time comes. All you need to do is call. Our city, our club, our resources are all yours. The brothers need taking down and I hope you give us the opportunity to help."

He clutches my hand, slipping a card into it when he pulls away and they leave.

The second the taillights of the Ghost disappear I pull my phone out and read over the various messages from Fergie.

"Fuck. Let's go, Rage."

"What's up?"

"It seems our little hacker is also an escape artist."

SEVEN
NOVA

I've got a problem. I lick my lips and crack them open with a snarl. *Problem* is actually an understatement.

"Don't touch me," I say viciously but my words are better off being screamed into the void of a black hole than at this old broad. She just looks down at me with a surly expression that reads she's so over my flavor of trouble.

Wads of black cotton mix with the white satin and mesh of my wedding dress to create my own personal tangled hell wrapped around my legs.

A gray-haired version of Christine Lahti stands back and straightens her leather skirt, her made-up eyes sharp and calculating.

Well, shit.

Clicking her tongue, she pulls out a phone from between her ample boobs and I look on as she shoots off a message. Something I noticed she did the whole time she sicced her men on me.

After working for hours, I finally managed to slip one hand free of the cuffs my captor failed to secure tightly enough. A little digging in the nightstand drawer and I found a key for the other hand.

I got three-quarters of the way downstairs when granny here found me heading for the front door at break-neck speeds.

Needless to say, I didn't make it past the centurions standing guard by the entrance.

Siren red lips purse in that *don't tempt me little shit* way grandmas use on heathen grandchildren they don't want to be stuck babysitting. Or that's what her expression looks like in my experience.

"Try that again and I'll personally see you are knocked out until Ares gets back, young lady," she huffs. "Maybe now you'll see fighting isn't the only way to get what you want."

Bullshit.

Two men wearing leather vests with matching skulls engulfed in flames kneel over me and their grip on my arms is bruising.

Some days—most days—I wish I were the meek and soft cuddly type. I would have gotten in this world a lot easier, I'm pretty sure. But nope. Not me. I'm the spitting image of my mother inside and out according to my piece-of-shit uncle. And I pay for it every day of my life.

I tell myself to get a grip, to calm down a little, but it's not working. "Give me a fighting chance, old lady, and I'll show you just how much fight I still have in me."

I wiggle and dodge the cuffs, roll left and then right before they finally get a good hold on my wrists, and lock me back to the heavy wooden headboard.

A tangle of black sheets wraps around my legs tighter, restricting my movement. Hair is everywhere and I'm breathing heavily. My heart feels like I've run a twenty-mile marathon and my palms begin to sweat.

"Move my hair. Please. Move my hair from my face." I feel the edges of my vision begin to blur and when everyone freezes at my odd demand I start to jerk my head side to side to get the long-ass lengths off my face.

"I can't breathe. Move the hair. Move the hair!"

Finally someone with enough brain cells to understand plain English brushes away my hair from my face and I begin to breathe a little easier.

"Devil, tighten that cuff a little more. That's it."

Brown eyes meet mine and I think I see a hint of remorse staring back at me before he moves off the bed and checks the work of the other man.

A river of debris litters the floor between me and the door. Nothing I can't jump over or use to my advantage, I determine with a glance. The turned-over chair and lamp would serve to slow down these two brutes.

Granny lights up another Marlboro Red and puffs on the end a few times until I see her visibly calm down through her cloud of cancer fumes.

She points the fiery end toward me and shakes it like a witch casting a spell. "Ares deserves the ass whooping you want to give him but when he comes back, you need to listen to him, little girl. We don't have time for your petulant attitude."

She works the ends of the wedding dress I'm still wearing until it's no longer wrapped around my waist and leaves me in an empty room without another word.

I must have lost my fight against the adrenaline crash that hit me after everyone left the room and accidentally fell asleep.

Early evening light casts eerie shadows over the room. To my left a coat rack looks like a warped fanged monster; to my right a jacket hanging over the bedpost a longhaired hag.

I slam my eyes closed and shove away the nightmares that chased me into adulthood. No one my age should be afraid of the dark. Just another scar I carry with me. I breathe through the rush of adrenaline pumping into my veins and force my heart to settle into a steady beat I can count. It's almost hypnotic. "What a real badass you are, Nova Masters."

You changed your life. You no longer have to live in fear. You are in full control.

I say my mantra over and over, but who the hell am I kidding. I crack my eyes open and look around. There's nothing I control anymore.

The burning sensation returns and I wrestle with the tears before they can fall. Momentous efforts go into sweeping them back into the pools of despair I reserve deep inside my soul. One day, when the cement breaks open, I fear it will sweep me away with the waves of pain I've kept buried behind a dam.

But today is not that day. I hold onto that truth and let it be my life raft.

I try my wrists again but this time the locks are so tight I can barely feel my fingers much less wiggle free of the clamped metal.

I flex and extend each digit trying to work blood to the tips and it works for the most part. At least the tingling fades to a muted irritation.

I've been up here hours, a full day? Two? I don't know. I could have slept for an hour or a day. Judging by the weary aches running through my body, though, I'd bank on only a short while.

I latch onto details of the room that looks nothing like a dark, dank dungeon as he'd called it last night. I'm spread out on a four-poster bed with midnight black satin sheets and a matching spread with gold trim. The comforter matches the drawn curtains. Everything else is either gleaming wood or crystal. Nightstands on either side of the bed hold lamps. Or did before I happened to them.

Not exactly your typical biker decor but a high-profile mafia man fit in here just fine.

It would actually be homey and comfortable. Maybe even pretty if it wasn't my prison. But a dungeon it isn't. More like a decked-out attic with a view. He seriously needs a dictionary if he thinks this place should be called a dungeon. I've been in plenty of modern dungeons—aka basements—to know what one looks like. This is the man's bedroom, his sanctuary. Not the dungeon.

That said, the man had enough money to own one. Serious money. The walls appear off-white but upon focusing I notice the finely woven brocade design of golden flowers on white. I used to study interior design magazines and pore over all the lovely details the rich and famous used in their homes on nights I felt nostalgic for a home of my own. Unlike all those pictures on the pages of the magazine, not one single photograph or artistic painting decorates the vast amount of painted space nor do any decorate the dresser or nightstands. Then again, they could all be on the floor smashed under my efforts at escape. Who knows? What I do notice is the walk-in closet to my left and the rows of neatly hung clothing. A mix of suits and jeans.

Soft lighting illuminates rows of shoes like I would stack books on a shelf. A center island showcases what I think must be priceless watches with how they are under lock and key. The gleam of the fancy wrist pieces catches the smallest amount of light.

I crane my neck to the side and spot a familiar orange book with a bold title across the front: *How Not to Give a Fuck.*

I snort. I'd say that's not going so well for him given my current prisoner status.

The man granny called Devil strolls through the door, breaking up my thoughts. On the one hand, he's holding a pan of water and hair ties. In the other is a brush. There is a God.

I track Devil's slow, even steps as he silently moves across the room to the side of the bed I'm cuffed to. He places the pan of water on the nightstand and starts wordlessly cleaning my wrists.

To get free, it took hours of twisting and pulling to get my thumb to work free of the cuff. Red puffy marks and a few scratches were left in the process. They match the ones on my ankles from the auction house.

Devil whistles low and turns my hand this way and that. He looks sincerely worried over my injuries. His touch is gentle and not at all as harsh as his appearance. He gives the term liking tattoos a whole new meaning. The only place I can see he doesn't have ink is his face. Ripped jeans, white cotton pullover, and again the same leather vest all the other men are wearing complete his look.

And then the answer to one of the million questions swirling in my brain pops out. No one lives in this city without hearing about the Savages. I'm only surprised it took me this long to put two and two together.

"Savages?"

He continues cleaning for a few seconds before tossing the sullied rag back in the pan and moves to help me sit up. "Was it the skull on the back of my cut that gave it away?" he grunts and hefts me up until he has full access to my ratty-feeling swaths of hair.

"Took you long enough."

But it still doesn't make me understand what is going on any better.

An easy smile pulls over Devil's lips at his sarcastic remark.

"Look, just let me go and I'll disappear. You can say I got away."

He starts whipping the brush through my hair with even strokes. "Ares arrives and sees you in a mess after telling us to care for you; he'll kick my ass into next week before I get a word of explanation out. Stop moving."

"Then let me go. Problem solved."

"Not happening. But nice try." He hits a tangle in my hair and bends over it, feverishly working the knots loose until the long lengths fall loosely around my shoulders again.

"Why the hell did you have to try and escape? Look at your wrists, your dress. The hair. What a fucking mess, woman. I stand corrected, Ares sees this shit and he'll go from wanting to kick my ass to straight-up putting his blade through my chest." He laughs but there's not a drop of joy in the sound.

Devil continues to comb my hair until it's straight and off my face. The tension inside my chest lessens a fraction. When he starts to twist and weave with a bizarre smoothness I can't help but wonder.

"Why are you braiding my hair?"

"I had a sister once. She didn't like her hair in her face either. Mom never put in the effort to learn how to braid and my father was the reason she hated her long hair. He'd yank on it every time she didn't obey his commands on the spot." I feel the darkness in him curl around the edges of my own energy before he continues. "So I get it." And he leaves it at that.

Perceptive.

"Thank you," I whisper, not liking the uneasy feeling of gratitude I feel for his small show of kindness.

"You're welcome, Nova."

"Where's your sister now?"

"Dead."

His softly spoken reply brings about a stinging pain at the edges of my eyes. Why did I have to agree to a girls' night out? If I'd gone straight home and stayed there instead of giving in to my little sister's wishes we'd all be safe right now and my best friend would be alive.

I reach for my cuffs again frantically. "Get them off me please. Please."

"Hey, hey, whoa, there." He takes my hands in his and I feel his calmness take over me. He wraps arms around me and I don't know why but I calm down enough to stop tearing at my skin.

God, he must think I'm a lunatic. But I don't know how much longer I can stay like this and keep any level of sanity. I turn my thoughts back on the hard facts. They drive my tears away and bring me back on task—getting someone to free me.

With the softest voice I can muster I say, "Ares? Who is he?"

"Yeah, the prez." His hands go back to fussing over my hair.

That doesn't mean much in my world. I know jack about the MC life and all the slang and names. I work at another angle. "Is he the one…" I work my throat faster to fight back the panic at the truth I'm about to voice for the first time. "The one who bought me?" So I know who to shoot the next time I get my hand on a gun. Or stab. I can do knives, too.

"You mean the one who saved you." He looks into my eyes with a hard glare and I suddenly see why people would run in the opposite direction if you ever saw him walking down the street. He can do intense like nobody's business.

Instead of doing the smart thing and shutting up I, of course, do the opposite of what my internal survival instincts scream.

And with the decision goes all attempts at being soft and sweet. I pucker my lips in disgust and growl, "How can you say that? Save me? He's going to be the one who kills my sister and me!" I slam my mouth shut hoping he doesn't catch on to my slip up. I jerk on my hands and use the strength I built up overnight to shake his hands loose from my hair.

He steps back and narrows his eyes on me but I refuse to meet his questioning gaze. I do and that opens up a conversation I don't want to have.

The girl who was transported to this hell hole with me comes into the room just then. "I'll be back," Devil grunts, leaving me alone with the girl. She's near my age. Maybe a year younger. Last time I saw her there were circles under her eyes no amount of concealer could completely hide and a heaviness about her.

I look at her now and gone is the caked-on makeup, the feeling of dread and in its place is an airy feeling I don't compute. Her hair is loose around her shoulders and she's wearing jeans half a size too big, but the smile on her face looks at home. And so does she.

I watch Devil's fleeting back as she enters, bringing with her the smell of food.

Thank God! Finally someone who will help.

"I need you to get the key." She'll help me. I know she will. I lock eyes with her and see hope. Like real bona fide hope. What the heck? None of that fake shit I used to plaster on my face for my sister's sake, either. This girl looks…happy? When I'd met her she'd been naked, cold and coming off a night of pleasuring men. I could smell the sex on her. Twisted and as screwed up as that sounds, there is true calm in her eyes now.

I guess this is a step up in her eyes since she has real clothes that don't involve netting, chains, and leather. But one hell is no better than another.

"Oh man, they got to you." I shake my head and question the food on the plate as she slides my way. Not that I can pick it up and feed myself. I shake my cuffs to make that point and she smiles sheepishly.

"The key. There has to be another one around here," I try again and she only slides onto the bed instead of, you know, rummaging through the drawers to find something to pop these locks. She has to be around my sister's age. Barely hitting twenty if that. She fidgets with the ends of her shirt. I practically see little butterflies flying around her head; she has such a sweet demeanor.

She hasn't seen or lived through the horrors thrust upon me. Good for her. Truly, but bad for me. They must have brainwashed her at the other place. Someone this pliable is easy to control. But not me. I'm not weak.

"You need to eat," she insists all but ignoring my current state.

I'm tempted to kick the food off the bed, but she doesn't deserve my wrath.

I back up toward the head of the bed, my chains rattling and shifting as I move to push my back against the headboard. "Yeah, I think I'll pass."

"You won't be strong when you really need to be if you don't eat."

My stomach unceremoniously grumbles at the smell of pot roast, carrots, and fresh, warm bread.

Damn. She does make a strong point.

She scoops up the bowl and uses the bread as a spoon. Savory herbs and the softness of moist bread wake up my senses. I take the next bite and another chomping at the food not caring in the least about the dribble of broth down my chin.

Her expression settles into one of concern as she watches me scarf down my first meal in… I don't remember when I last had something to eat. And that's speaking before I was shoveled into the back of a van.

"I saw your sister," she starts in the whispery-soft voice of hers. Like she doesn't have the confidence to speak her mind. Or someone beat it out of her. Right then I make a silent vow to take her with me if I ever break out of this twisted mess.

But right now I have to focus on the one of us who needs me most. My sister.

"At least I think she was your sister. She said your name and that you were sisters. She kept asking me about Ellie when I was down in the holding chambers helping serve food. And I've never met another Nova so…two and two."

I stop chewing. "Where are the holding chambers exactly? How do I get back there? You have to help me. Tell me everything."

Avery holds a hand up for me to slow down. "At the auction last night. I'm sorry I didn't get to talk to you sooner. Not that it would have done any good." She looks pointedly at my cuffs. "I just wanted you to know that the last time I saw her, she was okay."

"Avery, you have to help me get out of these cuffs. I have to get to her. Someone needs to help her."

"Ares. When he comes you need to talk to him. He'll listen."

I start to tear at them and bang the locked metal on the wall. Anything to make the locking mechanism jam, break, or whatever. "So he can lock her up here? No, I'll get free to save her myself."

Warm hands take mine.

"It's going to be okay, Nova." She locks our fingers and Avery feels the tremble in mine.

"You don't need to be scared. He's not like the other men. I don't know why he has you like this and not me. But…"

Yeah, he's much worse, I tell myself.

My heart lodges into my chest because just as she sings her praises of her bastard master the bedroom door, or rather my cell door flies open and smashes off the back wall.

I forget about the food, my sister, and the fact I'm still cuffed. Adrenaline surges through me and I feel like the fucking Hulk! Muscles from my head to my toes tense and prepare for a fight.

Storm-ravaged gray eyes slam into me when the bear stomps in with a heaving chest. "Get the fuck out," he roars.

The meek mouse of a girl I wished I could be like for all of two seconds scampers out of the room without a backward glance. So much for him being different from all other men, huh? That girl is going to end up in a landfill if she doesn't grow a backbone.

But that is the last thought I can spare for the girl because I have to make sure I don't end up there first.

Devil comes in on the heels of his friend, *boss? Overlord?* I recall the term Devil used. *Prez?* I have no clue what that means. Hands stuffed in his pockets, Devil leans his impressive weight against the door jamb.

Ares' eyes move from mine to my wrists and the rage he had when arriving triples in an instant.

"What the hell happened to her, Devil?"

"I tried to stop her but she kept going on about needing to get back to where the auction happened." I narrow my eyes on Devil for ratting me out, but the effect I'm going for comes off more as a pesky prisoner rather than the death threat I'm arrowing his way because he just smirks and shakes his head.

Go ahead. Let them all underestimate me.

Ares says something in Russian I of course don't understand. All the while he never takes his eyes off me as he speaks. He puts a hand on Devil's shoulder and gives him a couple of pats.

"I brought what you requested. It's by the door, Prez."

"Thanks, brother. I'll take it from here."

Alone with Ares I watch him stride fully into the room and pull a small key from his pocket. A spare I'm guessing since the old lady took the one from the nightstand. Why he has cuff keys in his nightstand drawer, I don't know but I can take one wild guess.

I send a nasty look at the ugly dress wrapped around my body. "You in the habit of buying brides and locking up innocent women to your headboard often. What kind of barbarian are you?"

He takes my chin in hand. "The bastard kind."

He places the key on the nightstand as if teasing me with my freedom.

"Just the one. And you're going to give me what I want right now."

EIGHT

NOVA

My throat goes bone dry. I scoff in his face and yank my chin from his grip. "You haven't even told me your name. No way I'm going to fuck you." I don't care how good-looking he is or how good he smells. I have my hard limits.

He chuckles like I said something funny.

"You already know my name. Now we're going to talk about you and you are going to give me the answers I want and then you'll do as I tell you, little girl." He says that as if he actually believes his own words.

For once be smart, Nova. I measure my words, fearing his answer but ask all the same. I frown, my ire mounting. "And what is it you want from me?"

He's dressed differently than when I saw him last. A white Henley replaces the tuxedo shirt and instead of form-fitting black slacks, he now fills out a pair of black jeans that mold perfectly to every inch of his muscular body.

Over his white shirt, he's wearing the same vest as the other men. A bleached skull with a wild flame of fire wrapped around it. Black eyes stare out from the center and the morbid thing has its mouth gaping open as if in a silent scream.

Chills crawl over my rapidly heating skin.

He makes the mistake of stepping into reaching distance and I rear back and drive home the heel of my foot.

What I don't predict is him anticipating my move and coming to fall over me when I retract my foot.

Two hundred plus pounds of Russian mafia man lands on top of me and we are back where we were last night. Him between my legs and my dress around my waist. Surprise surprise, his usual grim expression across his stubbled face is practically plastered into place. A plus for continuity in that department.

A hurricane made of anger, unwanted heat, and curiosity swirl through my head. My fingers grip the metal around my wrists and I make the conscious decision to not immediately lash out.

He peers down my body in a slow glide and I see appreciation for my lack of decent panties. A lacy white piece of nothing I can't wait to strip off and burn along with this piece of trash dress.

Ares leans his substantial weight forward and braces his hands beside my head. The headboard creaks and groans under his weight.

Between my legs, I feel the familiar signs of how my body reacts when this bastard gets near me. And it pisses me off.

My chest heaves at the feel of all of him pressing into me. My gaze searches his face for any hint of what was going on here. I can fight or reason with him. Since lashing out hasn't gotten me anywhere, maybe a change of tactics will.

"If I promise…?" I trail off, unsure of what I'm willing to do to get these damn things off me. Screw him. Kiss him.

"Measure what you say next. You don't exactly get to make the rules here."

I freeze at the feel of him pressing against my core.

"Try *none* of the rules."

He rocks his hips and I involuntarily groan at the feel of his arousal brushing over the thin material of my thong.

And suddenly his voice is low, gravelly, and very much a whisper in my ear.

"Don't worry, I have plenty of pussy elsewhere, *malyshka*. What I need from you is another skill set that doesn't involve the exchange of bodily fluid. Unless you want it, that is. Are you ready to beg for my cock?" His voice turns husky and his accent rougher.

"As if!" I croak between heavy breaths. Maybe in another life. Maybe, I admit to myself.

His little tease hangs between us and I am not about to reach out and pluck it from the air. Maybe if he had never cuffed me I'd be a little more open to the idea, but yeah, I tend to hold a grudge.

I swallow thickly.

"Wha…what is it you want?" Every deep breath he takes makes my puckered nipples brush against his chest.

Puckered because of the adrenaline jacking my system, not because he smells of the spring wind and the very essence of freedom. Nor the fact his warm breath on my ear is a weakness no other soul on this planet is aware of.

I stiffen through a rolling shudder as to not tip my hand. But he sees. Those piercing gray eyes notice everything and there's not a part of my body his knowing gaze doesn't caress.

The bodice of my wedding gown hangs low over my chest and hints of my areolas peek over the fine white edge. His gaze brushes over them, causing the hard tips beneath the satin to push against the thin material harder.

His eyes narrow and I go still when he growls in appreciation but doesn't move to touch me or make nasty suggestions as I expect.

No, not this man. I'm quickly learning he likes to make people beg before he gives them anything and I suspect that includes anything that goes on in the bedroom.

He bends over me and we're face to face. "Tell me why you want to go back to the place that did this to you. Tell me the truth and I'll uncuff one hand."

This man can hurt me, kill me, force me to do anything he wants yet he hasn't. But for some reason I don't understand, he wants to barter? Why?

"Asshole," I grit out and I mean it.

He knows I do because he arches a brow and offers a humorless smile. "Or not. Your choice, Nova Masters."

"Stop saying my name like that." I move my ass over the sumptuous covers hating the softness of my prison.

"Nova. Masters. Why? Does it bother you?" His hands simultaneously move up my bare arms and settle over my wrists. *Close, so close, play nice.*

I slam my eyes shut and push through hearing my full name on his lips and the knee-jerk reaction to lash out with venom. It's not the same as when my uncle used to say it, I realize. This is different. Ares is most definitely not my uncle.

"Someone I despise used to call me by my full name."

I don't realize my face is in a scowl until he takes the back of his thumb and rubs at the creases in my forehead.

"You're too pretty and young to be so jaded."

"Yeah well." My shrug isn't as effective as I'd like it to be.

Ares backs off and considers me for such a long moment I start to get uneasy. "What?" I finally ask. My fingers itch to smack the smugness—or is it arrogance—from his face.

"This man. Is he still living, Nova Masters?"

My brows furrow again this time in pure confusion. "What? Why?"

He shrugs. "Because if so, I'll put him in a grave for you. Give the word and his address." The promise of murder rolls off his lips like he has no problem making other people's issues disappear. Good to know. I'm closer to being dumped in that landfill than I originally thought given I'm *his* issue.

His words stun me into unfamiliar silence. I grapple for something to say to that but surprise and disbelief render me mute. Lump after lump works its way into my throat every time I try to swallow. Breathe. Just breathe.

Ares looks at his watch. "We can get back to that. Tell me why you want to return to the place that did this to you."

My gaze flits from one irrelevant item in the room to another. I'm so shocked I can't return his gaze until a gentle finger beneath my chin drags my attention back. His eyes are hard, but the creases around the edges speak of a softness he's yet to show me.

"Answer me, *malyshka*."

I don't know what the word means but the way the soft vowels roll off his tongue in a soothing tone, I can't fight the urge to tell him the truth.

At this point he has me and he knows it. Worse, I know it. I have a decision to make and I can feel myself playing tug of war over the finer details. I can fight, wait for a chance to get away, and turn these people over to the authorities. And get nowhere. Or I can make it appear I'll play ball. Get him to buy my sister for anything he wants from me in exchange.

"My sister," I begin slowly. "She was taken the same night I was. My best friend, too. I already know her fate. One of the beasts…" I pause. Swallow. Force the painful tears from my eyes. "They had two beasts handling all of us. The beast with the IQ of a donkey forced an overdose on Ellie. She didn't make it. I'm not sure if that is a curse or a blessing at this point."

My eyes fall to his chest as I speak. "She was disposed of like trash while they prepped me to go out on the stage." I force my gaze to his. "So I could be sold to you."

I don't see any evidence of concern on his face. It's a stoic sheet void of expression which makes my hopes of helping my sister dwindle to nothing.

He removes himself from between my legs and the warmth of his body goes with him. I didn't realize it helped ease my anxiety and heartache but now that I'm left without it, I find myself wishing he'd return.

My mysterious captor drops his chin to his chest and momentarily shuts his eyes. His lips move but make no sound. But he looks like he is grappling for patience only not with me.

"I am sorry for this outcome, *malyshka*."

I find myself softening at the sincerity in his tone. But not enough to forget the crimes committed against me and my only family.

He rises to his full height and several things compete for my attention at that moment. All those bulging muscles flex with irritation and coiled anger. I know because it's showing all over his face and the banked fire in his eyes when they land on me sing the truth loud and clear.

The first time I saw him an aura of power emitted almost like a shield. Now that I'm this close to him it seeps into me and I can feel the energy as if it's my own.

I also notice he hasn't uncuffed me yet as promised. "Hey?" I rattle the cuff but his attention is on the phone in his hand. "You made a promise."

Maybe it's someone's darkest fantasy to be tied up by this man but all I want to do is find the nearest weapon and use it to get the hell out of here.

Ares gives me a look as if to say how dare I question him. "And I will keep it."

But he doesn't move to unlock the cuff. To his credit, he didn't leave the room either.

"Rage."

Pause.

"Brother, we have a problem."

From there he breaks out into fluid Russian and I'm left wondering if I've made a terrible mistake. His tone is dry no matter the language which makes him hard to read.

The back and forth continues when he puts the phone on speaker and places it at the end of the bed. I don't think he's worried about me listening in on the call knowing I have no clue as to what they are saying.

I look on as he takes his vest, hangs it over the back of a nearby chair, and then strips off his Henley.

All those muscles I caught a hint of beneath cotton are just as defined as I imagined. I want to look away but God help me I can't. Deeply tanned skin is marred with puckered white crisscrossing scars over his back when he turns away from me and heads toward the walk-in closet.

His physical scars match my emotional ones—layered, deep, and ugly. I don't know where that thought comes from but it sinks in and takes root. But yeah, someone in his line of work is bound to have a body that matches the job description.

Savages. The name of their gang rolls across my mind.

Fitting, I realize. He steps from the closet and pulls on a clean shirt. He tugs it down his chest and it drapes over all those planes and dips. He shoves up the sleeves, revealing his thick forearms.

The man on the other end of the call says something I *do* understand and pulls me back to the conversation. Polaris.

"What about my sister?"

Electric gray eyes meet mine.

He snatches the key off the nightstand and I tense.

This is it, Nova. Get ready. All my nerve endings are firing and sputtering. My whole body is on fire. The next seconds of my life determine if I save my sister or not. I need to remember that. Because I know myself, I bite my tongue and watch every move he makes.

My mind stutters. Truly I was ready for him to walk out the door and leave me here indefinitely.

Instead, he keys the cuff holding my right wrist, but not the other. The bed dips as he lowers his massive body next to me and gone is the man ready for battle with me and in his place is one showing compassion.

I'm thrown off balance and instead of fighting him for the key and bolting, I sit there, my wrist between his massive hands as he massages the pain away.

"What are you doing?" I ask but the ire is seeping from my tone the longer he works.

"No more pain?"

I shake my head. Not only at the idea of this monster caring for my comfort but the impossible suggestion of him not being a monster at all.

"Do not look at me like that."

His request puzzles me. "Like what?"

"Like you want to peel back my layers. I've put bodies in the ground, stolen people's last breaths with these hands, and all pitilessly. And I'll do it again. So try and refrain from looking too deeply. What you find won't be pretty."

I've dealt with shady people my entire adult life. But never a killer. That I know of. I make sure to keep my dealings with people wanting revenge against a partner, wanting to steal corporate secrets. Nothing that ever involved death and the morgue. I have my hard lines.

I can't help but wonder how many men he's taken off the field. Does it matter? Does it change my situation? No and no. But I'm curious as to why I no longer fear his presence.

"And the other one?" I rattle the wrist that is still cuffed.

"Not until you can prove to me you're worth the millions I paid for you."

His statement sends a bolt of lightning through me. Our gazes collide. "I'm not fucking you; I've made that clear."

He drops my hand, crosses the room, and pulls something out of the bag Devil left at the door. Seconds and Ares is back in front of me tossing a laptop on my lap.

"My laptop."

"I had it procured from your residence."

Disturbing. Just how far did he take his stalking of me? "And?" I ask, picking my battles. After this, I would never be going home to the shitty apartment over a lousy supermarket anyway so moot point. "Unless you're giving me this so I can contact the cops, I don't know what you want me to do with it."

"I want you to hack someone." He states it matter-of-factly.

"You want me to commit a crime." It's a statement, not a question. There isn't an ounce of hesitation in his expression or in how he pops the lid open and puts my fingers on the keys.

His eyes flicker over my face, watchful of every minuscule twitch of my expression looking for something he can use against me, I guess. Why I don't know, I've already given the information about my sister.

"Prove to me you're worth the time and effort or we are done here."

Done as in dead? Images of landfills flit across my mind.

Blood drains from my face and my palms turn sweaty. Admitting to my own crimes is never a good thing. But this is a case of pot meets kettle? Right? "I don't know what you mean."

"No lies, *malyshka*. I know what you do in the back of El Diablo's bar. The black hat shop you've set up for yourself has earned a nice reputation along the black market. Your name has traveled well. I've been watching you for weeks, *Reina*. Queen. How do you think I knew of you?"

There's a bigger story behind all that but right now I focus on the more pressing matter. Hearing my handle on his lips is startling. But it's his last words that I hang onto the most.

"Excuse me? You've been watching me?" I recall the feeling of being watched several times. Polaris and Ellie called me paranoid but it turns out I had been right. I should have been more careful.

"Who all followed me? And was it all the time?"

"Regrettably not as much as I should have. And it was either myself or Devil."

My heart thuds at his admission. "What does that mean? Did you watch me get taken?"

He looms over me and brushes a thumb down the side of my face. He's taking a risk getting this near to me and he knows it. But he still chances a good punch to the balls to simply reach out and touch me. But why?

"It means had I not called Devil off you that night to take care of other club business you would never have been snatched off the street. You and I would be having this conversation over dinner instead of my bed."

"So it's by pure design I'm not getting passed around in some rich fucker's perverted party like a Barbie bride sex toy."

Ares faces me, locks our gazes. "And luck. Had I not been able to score an invite last-minute…" he trails off but I get his meaning. Or I thought I did.

"I would have gone to war to find you, Nova Masters, so let's just say everything turned out for the better. Bloody streets don't make for good business in the long run."

My fingertips clutch the metal casing of my laptop. Okayyy. Whatever that means. "I do this, what do I get in return? Wait!" I throw up my free hand and push off the bed. I'm dizzy at first and he shoots a hand out but I dash it away. It's a little awkward but I like to have my feet under me when I'm negotiating. Sitting on my ass gives him all the power and I'm so over feeling beneath him.

I narrow my eyes. "I'll tell you what I want. I want out of these cuffs. Completely. And you have to promise me we will go in and find my sister. That's my offer."

Ares gives me a look as if questioning my sanity. Large hands settle on my shoulders and I'm back on the bed, and back on my ass. And my laptop right back where he placed it to begin with.

"Again. You speak as if you have options. My world, my rules. You can learn the hard way or the *harder* way. Your choice."

I sit silently taking in the truth of his words. I hate every second because I know he's right.

Shit.

The screen blares to life. He keys up a black window with several rows of numbers with one big one at the top with over seven digits.

He pulls a paper from his back pocket. "This is the account I want those funds transferred into. You have forty-five seconds or what you want won't matter much at all."

A hand on the back of my head turns me to face the screen when I don't move. "Tick-tock, Nova Masters. Your sister's fate depends on those fingers moving faster."

"Well, do you have the authorization sequence?"

"Forty seconds."

My heart pounds.

My fingers glide over the keys. I open three other dialogue boxes and start typing out back door codes some of the best hackers don't even know about. My own creations I've used to crack some of the most highly encrypted sites and we are not talking just banks. If the government ever got their hands on my coding they'd bury me under the prison and probably steal my codes for themselves.

"Thirty seconds."

"Not helping I am doing this single-handedly you know."

"Twenty-five."

"Fucking bastard," I say between gritted teeth. "Hold shift," I bark. "Again. And now." He does as I instruct wordlessly.

"Five."

I hit enter and watch the numbers on the account tick backward until the whole amount is replaced with zeroes just as my time runs out.

"Good girl."

"Fuck you. I want out of these cuffs, Russian. I did what you asked. Twice. Or are you going to leave me hooked to your headboard and alone in this room for another night?"

His lip quirks into a half-smile that makes me want to drive my fist into the side of his face.

"You're definitely sleeping here tonight, *malyshka*. Nothing is changing about that. This is my bed, my room. And I won't be spending another night on the couch because of you.

But whether you're wearing my cuffs or not is entirely up to you and if you run again."

I don't embarrass easily, but the way he says that has my face filling with heat. "You have such a wry sense of humor."

Muscles tick in his jaw as if he's biting back more than just his deadpanned response. "Who is joking, Nova Masters?"

"Oh, don't you dare act like this is any of my fault."

Steely eyes meet mine.

Change of subject before my mouth gets me into deeper trouble.

I arch a brow. "Whose account did I just bleed dry? Some mom-and-pop business you want to take over and strong-arm? Some poor soul who didn't pay for your protection and now you're extorting?" What a piece of work this one is. I'll use him to get my sister and then leave this town behind like I've done so many others. Maybe Rio or London. Polaris would like a change and I need as much distance between me and this monster as possible.

"Mine. You just gave five point seven million dollars to the local children's hospital. Congratulations."

My mouth falls open.

All the boiling anger leaves my blood. I want to hate this man, drive a blade into his fucking beating heart for what he's done to me. But every minute I spend with him I find it harder to want to see him dead.

NINE

NOVA

He keys the remaining cuff and the second my hand is free I bolt for the door with fifty pounds of wedding dress in my wake. Inches away from shoving the slab of wood open, I find myself stopping cold, turning when I hear what he says in such a calm voice I almost think my sleep-deprived brain must be hallucinating.

"You go; your sister dies. I told you. You can learn the hard way no one goes against my word. Or you can make this difficult and I can lock you to the bed until I am done with you."

"What did you say?"

He stalks toward me, his impressive size shoving my smaller frame. Two-thirds of me is all dress and it's no match for the hundreds of pounds of muscle he's hulking around.

"You heard me, little girl."

He plants his feet and crosses his arms over a wide chest as solid as a wall. Unmoving.

"You leave, I won't lift a finger to help your sister. She dies the death you were meant to die as well. At the hands of some cruel master who will use her, fuck her virgin body, and then dump her when he's through taking everything she has to offer his dark appetite."

My hatred for this man solidifies. "You fucking bastard." Let him do his worst to me, but my sister. No. I'll save her myself.

"Tell me you don't already know this." His lips peel back and his anger matches mine. "Tell me, Nova Masters. Tell me I don't speak the truth."

His face is level with mine. My heart is thumping out of my chest.

My hand twitches and I do the unthinkable. I aim high and take the best swing of my life and hallelujah holy shit, does it hurt! I hold back a groan of pain when my knuckles strike the hard bones of his jaw. With my chest heaving and heart racing.

"Don't ever threaten my sister again. I've never wanted to kill a man, but for you, I'll make an exception."

Storms roll behind thick black lashes. He unhooks his arms and I brace for the inevitable blow for striking him. As if nothing just happened, he takes my right hand and pries my fingers open one at a time. "Next time go for the Adam's apple. Palm open, thumb flexed. Strike with your body behind it. You'll take anyone down with that one move. Have no mercy."

Noted. I don't think a two-by-four would dent this man's hard face.

When I don't reply, he gets in my face and uses the calmest voice I've ever heard on a man just punched in the face. "Just when I think you'll fight to the death you turn this lovely shade of red and look meek as a mouse."

What? "I am not meek or weak." I slice a hand between us. "You have no idea what you are talking about."

He takes my shoulders and turns me around, pushing me toward a door opposite the one I want to exit as if I'd not spoken.

He throws it open and behind the highly polished oak is a lustrous bathroom in all white, gold and black. Just like the room. Towels, a glistening shower stall, and a deep jacuzzi all beckon me closer. I catch a glimpse of myself in the mirror. Dark shadows ring my eyes and Devil's braid is long gone. My hair is in another matted mess. I also see the blush on my cheeks.

Ares steps up behind me; his presence is all-consuming and powerful. A man who thinks the world revolves around him. Such arrogance.

Rage. Frustration and an unwanted amount of defeat shadow the fight I have in my heart.

How can such a beautifully rugged man be cruel yet tender?

My heart stutters and trembles in my chest. I'm on the verge of tears as I hold his gaze. I fucking hate my life. Knowing I have little to no control over anything right now, the fight in me fades to a whisper and leaves my muscles feeling weak. No matter what I said before, I feel like a throttled mouse.

"Strip, *malyshka*."

"Leave," I shoot back.

He gives a low sexy laugh. "Not happening. I guess you like it the hard way."

"Hands on the sink."

When I don't comply, he makes sure I do. We stay like that for a moment. His hands locked on mine; his body warped against my backside. Through this dress, it's almost impossible to feel a damn thing, but his hard cock against my ass is unmistakable.

He makes a sound of approval and nuzzles my neck. The spot right below my earlobe and my second weakest point.

"Am I free to go now? I did what you wanted. Just let me leave now."

"That was only an audition. You still belong to me." Smooth, warm lips drag over the pulse point. "Mine," he husks.

I don't know how to respond to that and it doesn't seem Ares needs my help to continue his torture of me.

"Come."

When I stay planted in front of the sink, he wraps his arms around my middle and cups my breasts from underneath, pressing them high through the satin of my dress.

My nipples instantly harden into tight, tortured, greedy peaks.

I lie to myself and refuse to acknowledge the buzzing I feel deep in my core has anything to do with his touch.

Ares' nostrils flare and his gaze meets mine in the mirror with the force of a blazing inferno.

"You can do as I say, or I can make you. Your choice. But I will get what I want."

Strong fingers find the zipper to my dress and it's in a puddle at my feet in less than three seconds.

"As long as you are in my care you will not wear anything I haven't provided for you."

"Do I have a choice?"

"No."

I'm in nothing but this dreadful thong but I can't bring myself to care. Every inch of my body is suddenly beyond exhausted. Over my shoulder, Ares drinks in my fully nude body and he slowly wraps an arm around me just below my ample breasts. His dark hair hangs over a section of his forehead and gives him a softer look. He's a good foot taller than me in those biker boots.

Standing like this I fit directly beneath his chin. Remnants of his morning aftershave linger and I draw in the masculine scent.

"Step out," he gruffly instructs and I do. No questions. When he moves me beneath the hot water of the shower, I feel a wave of life pull me to the surface. I didn't realize how cold my body was until the jets of warmth seep into my muscles.

I grab for the shampoo bottle but he takes it from my trembling fingers.

"Under my care means just that."

The last remnants of pride wash away with the soap suds. My true reality is setting in. No matter how hard I want to fight it. My life is his to do with as he pleases. For now. Let me catch a breather. A shower, a change of clothes. Maybe something to eat if I'm lucky. I can kick ass and run better in my boots than I can in that dress anyway.

He loosens the braid Devil put in my hair and works a deep lather, massaging my scalp until I would admittedly agree to do anything this man asks of me at that moment. He applies the conditioner and rinses my hair fully before moving on to the rest of me.

I want to dredge up fits of fight and wrangle my rebellion back from the sidelines, but it's not happening. Two days of pure adrenaline cranking through my bloodstream has left me washed out.

"You've done this before. Come on. You can tell me. How many women have you bought and kept here as pets?"

Surprise surprise the mafia monster man doesn't answer.

He moves to the soap next and at this point, I just don't care about modesty. He grabs for a body gel and smooths his rough hands over my arms, shoulders, and down my sore calves. Years of callus build-up feels better than any plush bath sponge I've ever purchased.

He takes his time washing my feet and inspecting the few cuts and bruises from my fruitless attempts at escaping last night.

He's back to standing and moves his hands beneath my breasts, taking the weight expertly. My head falls back against his shoulder. He caresses them, massaging and working me with his long fingers. Under his captivating touch, my nipples turn rock hard. With a far gentler touch than I expect from a man of his nature, he turns me to face him. I look on as he squeezes out more soap and gently takes the weight of my breasts in his hands again and this time he rubs those palms over my nipples.

"Let me wash away the bad memories, *malyshka*. Just close your eyes and let me do this for you."

He moves lower and stops halfway to the apex of my thighs. I try to stifle a moan but what's the use. This feels good. I'm here. He's got me right where he wants me and there's not a damn thing I can do. Might as well enjoy it right? What that makes me I have no idea. I don't exactly know what to do.

"What is this?"

He brushes a soaped-up thumb over black ink placed just above my pelvic bone.

"A tattoo."

"*Da, malyshka*. I know that. What does it say?"

"My life, my death. My way." I'd gotten the words in Latin done the same year I took control over my own life. Right now they feel like a slander staining my skin rather than a life mantra.

"*Ty sil'nyy angel moy.*"

His words brush over my skin and leave a wash of goosebumps in their wake.

"You are strong," he repeats for me in English. "Let me take your burdens. Just for a little while."

I smooth my hand over his intent on pushing him away but he slowly places both of mine over his shoulders, uncaring that I'm soaking his shirt through.

"Fuck you, Ares." But my words are cold, powerless as my resolve slips. He smells divine, irresistible, and wrong. So wrong. I know better than to think these things yet the feminine side of me who enjoys the idea of a strong man caring for me gives in a little more.

He gives me a look of pure, raw, soul-scorching lust.

"No, Nova. I'm not fucking you tonight. But this pussy is wet for me all the same." He sweeps the pad of his thumb over my clit and my knees give out.

"Pozvol'te mne dostavit' vam udovol'stviye segodnya vecherom, Nova."

His soothing words lure me under his spell and my lashes slowly drift to touch my cheeks.

He presses his thumb hard against my clit, swirls the nub and in that one move, I'm done. My mouth gapes open and I moan deeply.

Ares throws my leg over his shoulder, uncaring of the water soaking him through. Angling my hips toward him, he pulls me in closer, devouring every inch of my pussy with his greedy mouth.

Strong fingers grip my bare ass and I'm suddenly lifted like I weigh no more than a book. My back presses against the shower wall and both my legs are now over his shoulders. Those fingers of his inch closer to places I've never felt a man.

"Ares," I warn, but he's not listening to me.

Hungry lips latch onto my clit and suck on the throbbing nub.

Hot liquid drips from my core as my insides quake with my release. He probes my pussy with the tip of his tongue and rims my asshole with a finger. The combination works as a sensory overload and I tense but can't believe the messed-up thought that enters my head.

I want him.

"Mine," he says in a husky voice so low I strain to hear him over the sound of jetting water.

He eases me down the wall until I'm settled around his waist now and not practically sitting on his shoulders.

The truth is I've always wanted to belong to someone like you see in the movies. Be so completely taken by someone the rest of the world doesn't exist outside that tiny bubble. But that is a fantasy. One I cooked up on nights when I killed the lights as my sister slept. It's been just the two of us for so long. Two girls against the world. Most nights were hard. Still are. I fell prey nightly to my own weakness of feeling lonely with no one to turn to for help. Usually the next morning those fanciful ideas died along with the rest of my dreams. But hearing Ares say that I'm his stirs up deep feelings and desires I wish I could drown.

I put my hands on his hard chest intent on pushing him away. I try, but he's unmoving. My captor only stands there with me curled around him, his eyes searching my face for God knows what.

"Let me down," I say, but he's not listening. He presses into me until there's no space between us.

"No. You stay where I put you. And right now I have my white-haired angel where I want her."

His words are equivalent to being struck by a bolt of lightning. Powerful, burning, and utterly lethal.

I can feel his body, hard against mine and I have no control over how my softer form curls around his. The rough material of his jeans is delicious torture against my clit. He rolls his hips sharply and hits my quivering core with just the right amount of friction to have me shuddering in his embrace.

"Ares, don't," I beg him and he chuckles so deeply it strokes my libido instead of sending me running like it should. The cords of his powerful body flex and ripple under my thighs. Perfection and yet wrong. I know this but I still let my eyes drift open to drink in the way our forms connect.

He murmurs more Russian against my lips.

"What?"

"You're the devil's weakness. A fallen angel."

Tugging my lips up he captures my mouth in a heated, consuming kiss. He slants his mouth over mine and plies my lips open demanding entry. His wicked tongue brushes over mine.

I breathe in his exhales and he does the same with mine.

And that is when I break.

I give in to him. Thighs, belly, breasts, I stop holding back and meld against him until there's not a single inch of my body not touching his.

I kiss the man who bought me, cuffed me to his bed and held me prisoner.

And I kiss him hard. The more of his taste and heat I consume the less of the last horrid hours plague my mind. And it's freeing. If just for a little while, I concede.

I wrap my arms around his neck and go with him when he pulls me off the wall, taking my full weight in his arms. With my core pressed to the outline of his hard cock and I wantonly rub my clit, dry humping the mafia man.

Controlling fingers grip the ample flesh of my ass and he stops me from moving over him.

"When I say and how I say," he gruffs and I'm back against the wall. This time he places a foot on the floor of the shower and his head is back between my legs.

I grip handfuls of hair. His answer to that is to tunnel two thick fingers into my dripping core as his tongue snakes over my clit.

He is utterly controlling me and it's infuriating as much as it is a turn-on.

I'm flipped around and put on all fours.

Water crashes over us but he doesn't seem to care.

Hands grip my ass and I'm on my knees. "When I take you, feed you my cock for the first time, Nova; this is how you will look." Hands slide up my ass, over my back, and return possessively. "Giving, begging, and dripping for my cock."

Sweet. Agonizing. Torture.

"You can't do this to me."

I tremble uncontrollably under his caresses.

A claiming bite sinks into flesh. I arch, press into him. "No."

He spreads my thighs farther and I swallow a moan as the tip of his tongue lavishes my core so sweetly.

"Yet your juices are sweet on my tongue. I told you no lies, *malyshka*."

His mouth is back on me and those curious fingers of his have my ass cheeks spread wide. He growls like he's in heaven the longer he eats my pussy. He circles a thumb over my back entrance, causing me to gasp from surprise as much as curiosity.

I'm falling in mere seconds. My whole body at the mercy of his touch. My screams are muffled by his tongue as he flips me, and in one swift motion has me against his chest, my legs wrapped around his middle. Kneeling in the middle of the shower, he feasts on my cries and whimpers. Sweet tangy remnants of my releases coat his lips and tongue. He feeds it to me like honey.

Steel gray meets ice blue. "*Moy. Tol'ko. moy.* Mine. Only mine," he translates for me.

Ares, the god of war, the man who purchased my body now wants to claim my soul.

I fear I'm weak enough that he just might.

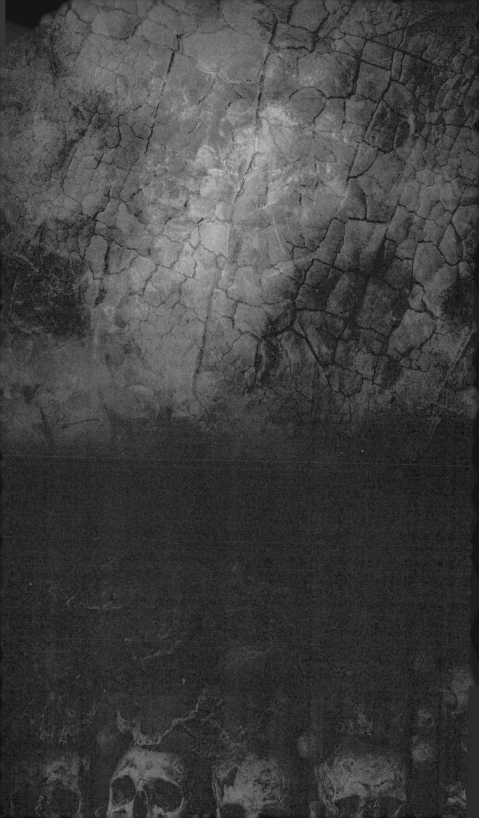

Ten

Nova

I don't know how I am expected to function like a normal human being after a shower of that magnitude. But fifteen minutes later Ares passes me a shirt that costs more than a month's worth of food.

"We need to talk." Leaning a hip against the center island of his walk-in closet, I lift my chin and force determination into my voice.

"Later. Right now my crew needs me downstairs."

"I'm not going down there in this." I hand him back the shirt. When he doesn't take it I toss it over the watches and turn on my heel.

I'm brought to a stop abruptly with hands cinched around my waist.

"You have a hard time following instructions. Let me spell it out for you." He taps me on the end of my nose. "Since I do not have anything else that could possibly fit you, you will wear this shirt. If I had it my way that is all you would wear. But I don't like the idea of my crew seeing what I've purchased."

And there's the asshole.

A moment of silence passes between us. This is about power. He might have had it in the shower, but if I don't make a stand and show him I'm not about to let him walk all over me there will be no end to his arrogance.

It doesn't work. The naked Russian reaches out and yanks off my towel, tossing it on the floor. My gaze drops to his cock and the glorious thing bounces between his legs, thick and ready. Thickly veined. I force myself to breathe.

Pre-cum wets the tip. I admit, at that moment I'm tempted to take him in hand, stroke him until he shoots his release. See how he likes his control taken away. It's obvious this man knows nothing about me or how far I'll go to get what I want.

Before I can decide, Ares steps over my towel and turns me around to face the mirror that takes up the back half of the closet. His eyes dip to the apex of my thighs.

Dome fixtures rimming the large room bathes us in golden hues. The dimness casts his face in hard shadows.

I suck in a harsh breath. Our eyes catch. Ares' scent fills me and the electric tingles draping over my body cause me to shudder. He has my body on constant high alert. The look on his face is one of hunger. His lips are parted but it's not his mouth that has all my focus. It's the way his hard shaft so easily settles into the crack of my ass.

"I meant what I said. Until I permit you, you will only wear what I've provided."

The low timbre of his voice should infuriate me; just being this close to him should have my fingers itching for a blade. But every syllable he utters zings straight to my sex and fills my head with all the promises he made in the shower.

My chin lifts, our equal amounts of stubbornness pitting for dominance. I can pick this hill to slay dragons on and ultimately die or wait and fight this battle another day.

He runs the tips of his fingers over my bare arms until the lengths of my hair are in his hands. He brushes it to the side and drapes the fine Italian dress shirt in its place. With his arms around me, I watch as he buttons each closure until the very last one is in place.

Smooth, cool, and not a single wrinkle. Through the thin material, you can just barely see the dark tips of my nipples.

He flicks them causing my eyes to widen and other parts of me to respond. "*Malyshka*, you better cover those, or I'll spend my evening fucking you."

From the smirk etched at the corners of his lips he thinks he's won. I shake my head, unable to link the events of the past days to the myriad of emotions this man forces me to feel.

"You'll find several pairs of jeans and freshly purchased undergarments in those drawers. Shoes are there."

I follow the line of his gaze.

"I'm not wearing anything you bought for another woman."

"I purchased them and had Fergie stock the drawers while you slept earlier."

Oh. I consider myself a light sleeper so that surprises me.

I quickly undo his work, strip the shirt, and layer myself with as many garments as I can find. Minus his shirt. Bra, camisole in black, black panties, black jeans. I'm getting a feeling this man likes black. It works for me too. A pair of mid-calf boots in black with a low heel sit off to the side. I rub the material. Real leather. Of course. I shove my feet into them and want to moan at how gloriously they fit.

"How did you know I like boots?"

"From watching you wear nothing else. You are a peculiar creature of habit, Nova Masters."

Right.

By the time I finish, Ares is fully clothed and leaning against the frame of the door, a dark look shining from beneath his hooded eyes.

"There is nothing you can do to keep me from what I want. But I like watching you try." He passes his shirt back to me and stands there until I pull it on and button it into place.

"Happy?"

"Getting there. I like you wearing my things."

"Come." He turns. My fingers go involuntarily to the design on the back of his vest.

"What does this mean?"

"More than we can cover on the way to the party."

I follow him but can't help giving the bed one last glance on our way out the door.

Ares draws up and I nearly run into him. "What's wrong?"

"Let me make this perfectly clear. I can lock you up or you can join me downstairs for a drink and some food. Those are your two choices."

Another threat to lay at my feet.

We pass a couple making out on the stairs and I spot Avery standing off to the side of a crowd getting rowdy. None of the people look like they have any interest in helping me find my sister. My anger renews. I didn't pay much attention to the finer details the last time I stood at the base of the stairs, but this time around I take it all in.

The massive front door is only a handful of feet away. And this time no one is guarding it.

I also see there's a rack of FOBs for the cars outside. A detail I missed. Nice to know.

To my right is a massive open room and Ares leads us in that direction. Avery waves to me, that hopeful smile splashing across her face.

Everything is laid out to accommodate a huge gathering of people. Large couches are pushed up against the back wall. A pool table sits in front of a roaring fireplace and every available surface either holds a bottle or a body getting fucked.

Someone cranks up the music and an electric guitar competes with a thumping bass to fill the house with so much noise I can no longer hear the girl with the green mohawk screaming her release from the far corner. To the right of me, a man with a nose piercing that matches the one on the tip of his dick. His fly is open and his cock poised at the mouth of a redhead while a brunette holds her ample breasts out for him to feast on.

The erotic scenes flash heat through my body. Heat Ares stirred inside me less than an hour ago. I try to keep the surprise off my face, but it's hard. It's not like I'm some sheltered little fucking flower, but damn. Some hardcore porn seems sweeter than this. There's no love involved. Just bodily needs, I guess.

"Later," Ares promises darkly in my ear as if he can read my thoughts.

I mentally roll my eyes. Not likely, I tell myself. No way in hell I'd let these people witness me at my weakest.

Ares presses against my back and I feel the contrary to my thoughts hard against my ass. But I know his game. He's letting me know I won't get far without him right there to stop me and proving he has something I want. Pure arrogance. As if to drive home the silent message, my captor winds a possessive arm around my middle and drags me closer still.

A girl in cutoffs and bare tits bouncing seductively walks by, dragging Devil wearing a wicked smile in her wake.

"Hey, baby. Glad you could join us." Devil, decked out in tattered jeans, a light sweater, and his vest, looking every bit his namesake. He comes in fast and plants a kiss on my cheek, earning a growl from Ares. He elbows a grinning Devil away but the exchange goes off with Devil throwing his boss a rueful smile.

Ares leans into me, an arm laid across my shoulders. "Don't pay attention to him. He fucks anything with a wet hole."

Jesus Christ. This man. I straighten my shoulders, slip some steel into my backbone while I'm at it. "Ass. You realize that's an insult, right?" I burn him with a pointed look of disgust.

The scowl I'm learning rarely leaves his face is firmly set. And it's on mine the second he pins me against the nearest wall. All his party-goers pass paying us no mind. He pushes in on me and presses his lips against the shell of my ear. "He tries anything with you and my brother will be dickless before a night can pass. No one touches what's mine."

Mine. There's that word again.

Now that I'm fully dressed I feel stronger about what I'm saying. "I'm not a piece of meat, Ares. My life, my death, my way." But my words fall on deaf ears. A man with long black hair pulled back in a haphazard bun with a helmet under his arm strolls through the door.

My heart turns to stone.

I recognize those high cheekbones and that black leather jacket. But I can't be sure. The rooms were dark and the two beasts occupied my attention. I could be wrong.

Behind me, I feel Ares physically stiffen as well. Ares cuffs my wrist with his hand and wordlessly drags me to the edge of the room where Avery huddles by the door alone.

"Watch her," he says to the girl and turns to me with, "behave and we will talk after the party. I have business to tend to."

"Who is he? I might have seen him there. Or at least I think I did that night. At the auction. Why is he here?" I hate the quiver in my voice. Is he here to take me back? Check in on me? If he's here he knows where my sister is. Right?

143

Ares considers me as if he's contemplating his options but ultimately decides against whatever went on inside that head. "He's no one you need to worry about," he finally opts for. "Stay here. I'll be back to collect you from this same spot when I finish. You move from here I'll be left with no choice but to cuff you back to my bed."

His threat does not sound empty.

I don't answer him. I don't care what he says; I have my own agenda. And that's landing in the back of whatever vehicle that man came in. I can't think of any faster way to get back to my sister.

He raises an eyebrow like that is all it will take to scare me off my path. With the music blaring he puts his lips close to my ear. "I can see your gears turning. Don't be foolish." He retreats and taps the side of my head.

I throw his hand away. I can't believe I let my stupid fantasies carry me away. I nearly slept with the enemy because of them. How stupid can I get? What the hell have I done? *Pull yourself out of this daze, girl.*

I stand straight and meet his stormy glare. "Whatever, Ares." I know I'm standing on the world's thinnest ice. I haven't forgotten I arrived here tied up and hooded after being bought.

I'm hit with the full force of his unwavering attention and it weighs a ton. Seems he doesn't like my answer. I push on anyway. "Look, have your party. But I don't have time for this. You gave me your word."

With each word I speak, his expression darkens further. He dwarfs me by a good foot which dents my ego more than I care to admit. "Your sister will be fine. Trust me on this. I know what I am doing." A hardness steals over him; that tick in the side of his jaw does a cool twenty miles an hour. "There won't be any movement with the merchandise—the women—for another five days. Let me deal with what just walked through my door, and then what is needed of you will come. Everything in its time."

Ares' next move is so fast my eyes can't track where his hand lands until it collars my throat. His nostrils flare. Those strong fingers of his aren't choking me but they are tight enough for me to understand his message. He's in control whether I like it or not.

"You will not put yourself in danger nor disobey my orders. There's nowhere for you to go. You are to stay in this spot until I collect you. I won't be long." I feel each of his fingers against my heated flesh and to my utter shame the clamp of control around my neck makes me wet enough to feel the moisture between my legs.

Unaware of my internal plight he lowers his mouth to within a half-inch of mine. "You are too stubborn for your good, *malyshka*." If fire could shoot from eyeballs the man would be toast at my feet. Since that's only a current fantasy of mine, I have to settle on him reading the hatred I have for him through the narrow slits of my eyes.

He chuckles.

My lungs burn for air.

All I can think of right now is to do whatever it takes to get what I want. Shift in plans. I plan on taking him down along with the trash who kidnapped me and sold me.

One by one his fingers loosen and though he takes his hand away slowly I can still feel the weight of his grip on my throat as I watch Ares walk away. Another man, I think Fergie called him Rage, steps up beside Ares. They exchange words then descend a flight of stairs.

A cold, calculating gaze finds mine one last time before he moves out of sight.

I need my head examined after I get my ass out of this situation.

The arrogant smirk he's wearing tells me that man thinks he has full control over me. Ha! I have no idea what gave him that idea or why. Because he gave me a couple great orgasms? Foolish man. He thinks I won't try to run with all these people here. I scoff. Nowhere for me to go? I grin.

A woman passes with a tray and I snag a plastic cup of something when Avery leaves to help a girl who's had way too much whiskey already.

Poor Ares is about to find out just how much I don't like to be controlled.

I turn to a random woman with too much kohl liner and not enough clothes. "Who are all these people?" The last time I stood in this spot I only saw a handful of these faces at best. I want to make sure none of them will get in my way when I head for the front door.

"Locals who like to party. People the Savages have helped, others who have helped them is my understanding. Those two over there, are prospects. You know, men working to prove themselves to the Savages before they can be patched in."

More MC lingo. I nod and act like this is the most fascinating information I've ever heard.

146

"The one with the crewcut is Blaze. Former military. Just got out, in fact. Less than a year."

Not that I care, but I keep up the small talk while scanning the area for exits and guards. When coming down the stairs with Ares tonight I noticed two offshoots toward the back of the mansion. One goes to the open-style kitchen which is visible from my current position. I bet near there has to be a library, home office… something with a phone and internet connection.

I can run upstairs, grab my laptop and try to connect, get a message out to a friend or call. Seems faster to call with Ares' promise of not taking long with whoever he's meeting with.

"The other one with the sexy tatts around his neck and down his arm is Casanova. Bear's boy. He's gotta dick piercing too that hit the spot if you know what I mean."

Way too much information.

I bump her shoulder with mine. "Yep."

Casanova is working his charm on a chick with purple hair pulled up in a high pony. She favors black lipstick and shorts that might as well be panties.

I suck in a surprised breath. Whoa. That man is not shy. I hide my surprise at the view by the pool table behind the lip of my drink. Vodka on ice. I welcome the sizzle and burn on the back of my throat. "That can't be his real name." I work to keep the conversation light.

The kohl-rimmed eyes of my new friend turns to me. "Who Casanova's? Nah, he has that name for a reason and I'm about to take full advantage of it."

Given he's currently balls deep in another broad I'm thinking she doesn't mind sharing.

"Is Bear here tonight?"

"Nope. He and Fergie don't like the party scene too much. Bear is a recovering alcoholic and Fergie respects that. They'll be here in the morning though to make sure no one got stupid and died."

"Are you serious?"

"Sorta. A year back a man OD'd right over there. Since then, the Savages laid down the law. No drugs allowed on Savage property."

"But they'll sell it out on the street. Hypocrites."

"You got that wrong. Listen, I don't know where you got your deets, but the Savage crew, they don't get mixed up in drug runnin'. They do a lot of other shit, but not that."

Admittedly I haven't been in New York City long enough to know more than their crew name. It got thrown around a time or two among my clients but that's about as much as I know. A fact I am about to change.

"Hey, I'm going to find a bathroom; hold my drink?"

"Sure. Second level. First door on the left."

I give my new acquaintance a nod of thanks and lose myself in the crowd of booze, smoke, and sex.

With a key FOB in hand I shuffle through a fresh crowd of newcomers looking for free liquor and zero my attention on the front door cracked open enough to show me there's no one outside looking to stop me.

"Hey, baby, where you rushing off to?"

Focused in one direction, I forget to check my peripherals.

Devil clips an arm around my neck and hauls me against his side. We're suddenly heading in the opposite direction my feet are pointed. It's obvious this man gets handsy after a few too many. I pry myself out of his grip and he easily lets me go.

"Maybe you should give me that."

He grabs for the FOB in my hand. I've moved before I think better of my action and bust a solid right hook against his jaw. Not my finest moment. Acting before thinking has always been a weakness and one that I might regret soon.

"Wanna have a go at it, Devil?"

Nova, what are you doing? Do you have a death wish?

I hash out that thought when he steps in, pushing me deeper into a corner. Left or right is nearly impossible unless I truly want this to break out in an all-out brawl with a man over twice my size in every definition of the word.

Those dark eyes of his are sharper than they were a minute ago. He narrows them and I feel him analyzing the hell out of me. Something tells me far too many people have underestimated this man and paid the price.

Rubbing at the place I struck, instead of anger, he rolls back on his heels and bellows out a hearty laugh. "Nah, baby, but if you didn't already belong to the prez, I'd take that hit to the face as a personal invitation to bend you over the nearest surface and fuck you all night long."

Making eye contact with him and holding it I deadpan, "Lovely."

He drags a cigarette from a silver case in his front pocket and flicks a Zippo to life with the other. "Pure fucking poetry, baby," he says around a mouth of spiraling smoke. He grins and pulls a passing woman to his side and she deepthroats his tongue.

"You two have fun."

I edge around them cautiously because I don't care how preoccupied Devil seems, that man notices everything and I don't need him running to find Ares. As if reading my mind he drags me back to him, points to the FOB, and says, "That's biometrically activated, sweetheart. You have fun with that."

Crap.

"You wanna fuck with Ares? Take those precious keys he never lets out of his sight to the old Chevy truck parked in the garage." I've seen devious intent written all over a person's face before, but I am starting to see how this man came about his name. He was the Devil in human flesh. "Like I said," he purrs. "Have fun with that."

I rethink my plan and head in the direction of the kitchen. There's another hallway that leads to the right wing and I head that way. Several closed doors greet me but the one at the end of the hallway with the light spilling from beneath it calls my name. I edge cautiously closer but hear no voices.

Reaching out I slide a hand over the mahogany door and try the handle to find it unlocked. Inside there's a low fire in the hearth.

I risk a glance behind me. When I find no one, I take a breath, enter and quietly shut the door behind me with a click.

Papers of various sizes scatter across a massive desk that takes up the back portion of the spacious office that doubles as a library.

Rich leathers, dark carpet, and a fully stocked bar all clue me in on this being Ares' office.

"Bingo, baby."

I rifle through the papers. Bank statements with amounts circled with the name Asylum printed across the top don't tell me much but that fact they are on his desk is good enough for me.

Others have more numbers from a place called Aurum. A casino. Ares owns, I'm assuming. I don't have a degree in forensic accounting, but the Feds do and I bet they'd love to see these papers.

I shuffle a few pages together, fold and slide them into the tops of my jeans securing my long shirt over the top. I guess something good came of wearing this thing after all.

To the side of all the papers, there is a small note with the word Genesis circled and a date beneath it.

"That's five days from now."

Ares' words come back to me. He said the merchandise wouldn't be moved for five days. I haven't the slightest clue what genesis means but I file that information away for later.

Given the messy state of the desk, I don't worry about reorganizing anything. Instead, I look for a phone. There's nothing but a landline. I grab the receiver and dial in the only number I know besides my own and my sister's.

Someone picks up. "Hey, let me speak to Jacob."

"Not here."

Crap. My brain hiccups before spitting out a reasonable backup plan. One that might land me in Ares' cuffs again. If he catches me. "Tell him Reina will be there tonight."

I hang up the phone and slip out the office door to find the hallway abandoned. Music blares and everyone is either screwing someone or about to. I hit the stairs and come to a sudden stop on the second landing. There's a huge opening that gives me a direct view of the party below.

Ares is surrounded by women all fawning over him and the fucker looks like he's eating it up.

Let them have him. Our eyes connect but I flick away the come-hither gesture he aims my way. Holding his gaze with a feverish glare, I opt out of the party. *Yeah, not into groupies. Thanks.*

I turn and with that my thoughts fall back to my plan. There's more than one way to find who I am looking for. It was Jacob's bar they kidnapped us from. Someone needs to warn him his clients are being targeted. And the proof I need to take down these fuckers is on his security feed. All I have to do is get to it before *they* do.

Should be easy.

Eleven

Ares

The raging fire inside that woman rivals the stubbornness she harbors for anyone who doesn't see life through her special-colored lens. And I know it's my fault too. I haven't exactly come clean about why she's here. I'd planned on doing that tonight, but the woman pushes me to my limit and I'm only human. Resisting her tempting body proved far more difficult than I anticipated. The shower acted like gasoline on the fire of her fury. One second she's a fire I can control and the next she's an inferno of grit and fight.

Only thing that kept my dick behind my zipper and not in her sweet pussy was the fact I would have given her all of me. Taking her bareback would be my personal heaven but I don't need the weakness that comes with it. Anything my enemies can use against me is a weakness I can't afford.

Admittedly, the revelation about her sister still being back at the Volkov compound threw me off balance and why I had Rage pull Dragon back in tonight.

I'm about to take her back upstairs and teach her the demon inside her holds no sway over the one inside me when the person I need to see walks through my door, bringing with him the fires of hell.

One look at Dragon's worn face and I know it's bad. What he has to tell me in private reveals my deepest fears.

"I found her. She's alive but the friend isn't. Me asking around might have set off some alarms. Sorry about that, Prez. The Volkov brothers are more than a little spooked."

"Fuck. How the hell did we miss this shit?" I throw a hand up. "Never mind. I know how." I'd called Devil off her that night. We'd had a fire down at Asylum and I needed all hands on deck. What was one night, right?

Dragon, looking worse for wear falls into a seat at the table and throws an ankle over a knee.

"You need to do whatever it is you're gonna do and fast, brothers."

Rage grabs a bottle and Dragon throws his hand up. "I'm good. I can't stay long. They sent me on a scouting run."

I cross my arms and rub at the stubble covering my chin. "That's new."

"I've been promoted apparently. The two thugs working the basement killed a girl and they won't let them anywhere near the merchandise, sorry, women, anymore."

Dragon scrubs a hand over his face and looks ten years older since the last time I saw him. "I don't know how much longer I can do this shit. They have me talking like them. How much longer before I'm like them?"

Red eyes meet mine.

"The things they do to these women, Prez. The degradation they go through at their hands. It's hard to not kill them all and walk away."

"The sister?"

"Alive is all I can say. They seem to like their virgins untouched in every way but one."

I straighten at that news.

"Details."

Dragon's expression turns stone cold. His eyes take on a glassy haze. "There's more than one way to break a woman. You know this."

I do. I lived through the horrors of my mother's life. And her death at the hands of my father. That night I vowed to see him into an early grave. Growing up in the home a Russian mobster should have warped my mind the way it did my brothers'. My blood brothers. Boys who turned into men as bloodthirsty as the man who fathered them. Who all betrayed me all for the sake of our father's approval. And greed. I can *never* forget their greed.

Seeing Nova's fighting spirit makes me think of the strength of my mother.

On nights my father flew into a rage I would beg my mother to hide, but she refused. As a kid, I didn't understand her stance, but now I see she was the bravest woman I knew.

The noose around her neck was taut from day one with my father. Somehow she found it in herself to teach me compassion for others. The second I was old enough to know how to point a gun and pull the trigger my father worked diligently to erase her teachings. I don't think the things he wanted to stick registered in my head the way he preferred them.

The man who fathered me took enslaved women in front of her, beat them all if anyone dared to fail in pleasing him in the manner he desired. I swore off sex most of my younger days because of the cruel, unnecessary vileness I witnessed. Only when I learned to control my bitterness and anger did I dare trust myself around the softness of a woman.

Seething anger boils through my veins for the past I can't shake. So much so it turns into ice in my veins. "Get back and keep tabs on the sister. Let us know if you catch wind of the next auction being moved."

I finish with Dragon and climb the stairs to find Nova not where I left her. Damn infuriating woman. Any other woman wouldn't have dared disobey my order. It amuses me. Most of the time. But tonight I'm not in the mood for games.

I spy the mass of her white hair and the blue embers of her glaring eyes.

Piper finds me as I pass the kitchen heading for the stairs.

"What's she got that I don't?"

"Not tonight." Piper and Kendra both sidle up close, one on either side. Their hands go straight for my junk.

I don't have time for this shit. Over the top of their heads, I jerk my chin in the direction of a prospect. Piper leans in and I can smell whiskey on her breath. Nothing new, but it's her blown-up pupils and the familiar mark in the crook of her elbow that forces red into my vision. I brace an arm between her and me and signal Blaze to come get her. "Take her to her room and make sure she doesn't leave." I point to her arm. "That shit stops here."

Kendra backs off at the tone of my voice.

"Got it, Prez."

I pry the drink from Piper's hand. "Tomorrow see to it she's in rehab. I don't care if this is her first time shooting up or her fiftieth. She does it again and she's out on her ass."

"I'll call Fergie in to sit with her."

"*Da, moy droog.* Good man."

I pull my phone out and flip over to a private app that pings any phone being used within my compound.

Bingo. I take the stairs two at a time and strip my shirt off the second I hit the third-floor landing.

I haven't spent a lot of time with the hacker in my room, but I'm aiming to change that right now. One Nova Masters is about to find out when I give an order it's obeyed.

Nova

The clock on the nightstand reads two-thirty in the morning and the thump and grind of music from the party downstairs only grows. I've barely managed to slide under the sheets when the door opens at my back. I force myself not to move at the sound of clothes, belts, keys hitting the floor. I smile.

A cool brush of air enters beneath the sheets before a warm body replaces the cold draft. As much I try to stop it, my body trembles. As much as he arouses me, he also terrifies me. Not of what he'll do to me, but of what he'll bring to life inside me.

"You better have clothes on," I lash out picturing the smirk I *know* the bastard is wearing on his smug face.

"Why when you have on enough for the both of us."

He moves in and I edge away.

When I rushed up here, I found the room back in order. Overturned lamps, tossed books, coins. All are back in their original spots. Someone came in and straightened the mess, leaving behind a fresh vase of flowers. Like I'm staying here as a guest and not a monitored prisoner.

I ruffle the edges of the papers I stuffed beneath the mattress and count my blessings, few as they are. I have a fraction of the proof. One more piece and the recipe will be complete to hand over to the authorities.

And my laptop. I tried to connect but someone changed the password. I wonder who that could have been.

"Aren't you supposed to be downstairs with your girls?"

"You jealous of the club candy?"

The low timbre of his voice is next to my ear.

"Club candy? Seriously. What the hell is it with all these weird names? Prez?"

"Answer my question."

He rolls me over, the press of his fingers finding my neck. He's nowhere near choking me, but I feel the shift of power between us all the same.

"Arrogant bastard." The thudding of my pulse fills my ears but I still hear the gravelly timbre of his deep voice over the rush of blood.

"Not an answer. I'll give you one more try, *dorogaya moya*, before I feed that naughty mouth my cock."

I'm aware of just how little clothing he's wearing. The truth is evident when he rises over me and the sheets pool at our waists. The dark, thick outline of his shaft teases my hand to reach for it.

Suddenly I'm all too grateful for the fact I've left my clothing on. Seeing his muscular bare chest, the way the shadows cling to all those grooves and dips in the low lighting is a fine way to make me momentarily forget he's the enemy. Again.

His steel eyes flicker over mine. I feel more pinned in place by the piercing stare than I do with his hand closed over my throat.

He ignores the finely pressed line of my mouth and takes my silence as an invitation to steal a kiss. Hard lips crash into mine. The heat of his tongue forcing entry.

I shake my head and try to dislodge him but he's strong and has dominance over me.

Powerful and imposing. From head to toe one full-body shiver slithers through me leaving my body covered in goosebumps and my nipples puckered treats for his eyes.

Steel turns molten. His growl is hungry and on the cusp of revealing his irritation.

We both know what this is. Him being pissed at me for disobeying his direct order. Well, fuck him.

He pushes to his knees and the sheet hiding the lower half of him falls away. Lord save me from my wicked desires. The man is a decade older than me, is in some mafia doing only God knows what. Bought me at freaking auction, that's what. And I want to fuck him. I've got to be broken inside, right? Something damaged in my earlier years that makes me want to ride him and kill him in the same breath?

The muscles, the scars, the scruff of beard along his jaw. It all works in tandem against my self-control. Around him, I'm not the version of Nova Masters I know. The one ushering my sister to college, making sure she's in bed by midnight. Making sure the laundry is folded and keeping my line of work and the people I have to interact with far from our home.

But here, inside Ares' room. Surrounded by his heat, his touch, and that cum-dripping cock, I'm just hungry. Hungry to live.

I shiver, heat pooling through me though I struggle to wrangle my inner demons. Ones he's stirring awake with the devilish stroke of his thumb over my pulse point.

"Ares, don't." I don't know if I am pleading more for him or myself at this point. He takes this too far, farther than he did in the shower and I won't be able to stop myself.

Ares withdraws his hand from my neck to drag the pads of his fingers down the length of my chest. The brush of heat from his touch might as well be pokers laced with the fires of possession. The invisible scars he leaves behind sink deep. The pools of gray in his eyes arresting.

I whimper in embarrassment; the shame of my forbidden pleasure at the hand of the enemy splashes across my cheeks, leaving them flaming red.

Ares searches for the buttons on the shirt I borrowed and when he finds them, the grin on his face is beyond wicked.

Right when I think he'll take his time undoing each and every one of them, I quickly discover the man positioned over me is nowhere near as patient as I once thought.

One fierce pull and the tiny white buttons ping off walls and lampshades. He does the same to my camisole. The small V of the neck gives him the right amount of leverage over the material and it parts like butter being cut with a branding iron.

My bra, a scrap of matching lace and silk doesn't stand a chance. Those beady little tips puckered high on my breasts begging for his touch know what they want.

And they get it.

"Don't what?" His voice is a harsh pull on my libido. "You tempt me beyond reason and for no other reason than you make my dick hard enough to pound steel beams, I'm going to fuck you."

Warm lips encompass one nipple, his tongue a swirling force I can't resist. He moves to the next his strong fingers squeezing the ample flesh until I feel breathless. His teasing is both hot as a flash of lightning and equally slow-burning. Waves of pleasure and pain roll through me.

I smack at him, push him away. I'm aware of him gripping my wrists with his larger one and holding them over my head. But I'm powerless to stop him.

But what infuriates me most is the hot liquid dripping to wet my panties.

He moves his massive body between my legs and drags the teeth of my zipper down in a hiss of a promise; this isn't going to stop until he says. With little effort, he frees me of my jeans. He eyes the black panties and in one swift breath, those are on the floor with my pants.

He pulls his eyes to mine, his hand sliding to my thighs. Between us his heavy, veined cock bounces with angry need. The bulbous head drips with pre-cum. He fists the length and works his shaft. "Watch me," he rumbles. What he doesn't realize is he doesn't have to demand a thing. I can't take my eyes away from him anyway.

Cords of muscle bulge and ripple as he works his cock between my legs. He's not even touching me there and I feel the walls of my pussy contract, protesting that fact.

Hot juices spill down the crease of my folds, wetting the sheets beneath me. There's no way I can hide the reaction my body has to him.

Unable to stop myself, I reach for him, stroke a thumb over the bead of pre-cum dripping from the slit of his cock, and bring it to my throbbing clit. I rub his juices over the tender nub. Once. Twice. My hips begin to rock but he's not having that.

Fire shoots through those gray eyes and the depths of them turn so hot we stand the risk of catching fire.

The crown of his cock pushes my hand away and he begins to swirl the fat head around my clit. This is wrong. I should be fighting him. Beating him off me. But none of that is happening.

He increases the pressure and I'm right back to rocking. He growls something I don't understand, reaches for the nightstand, and rips open a box. In a breath he's back over me sheathing his cock with a condom.

"Hurry," I plead. I trail my fingers over my quivering stomach and swirl the pad of my finger over my throbbing clit. I buck into my hand but my touch is not the same as his.

"Will I hurt you?"

I know what he's asking and I shake my head. "No. But make me forget those bad memories, Ares. Just for tonight?"

Hair slips over his forehead and I brush it away.

"I'll make you only remember me."

I'm so slick, wet, and needy that when he poises the tip of his shaft at my entrance and thrusts home, he slips through my juices to the hilt in one swift glide. Ares groans and proves he has no intentions of letting my body grow accustomed to his thickness.

Fire flashes through me. I claw at him like a mad, wild animal. He falls over me, pulls out, and sinks balls deep into my core so hard, so fast, I lose control. Not that I suffered from any illusion I had any to begin with.

My orgasm is instant. White heat and soul-gripping spasms ripple through me, leaving parts of me broken. I knew giving in to him would be far from soft and tender. But the way the power crackles and shifts in the room is palpable.

Ares groans deeply and slides his hands beneath my ass. He moves back and pounds into my body. He pumps into me in slow strokes dragging my honeyed arousal with him when he pulls free of my body.

I grip the sheets and then him, looking for any kind of purchase before he drags me into his world. One I might not survive. "Ares!"

Cool steel turns smoky gray with intent. Hold my gaze, I look on as he falls between my legs and devours my juices. The pad of his tongue teases over my asshole before driving into the hot slit of my pussy.

I thrash against the bed and him. Untamed, hungry, and desperate. I'm all the above. Strong arms pin me in place. He groans deeply and drags his tongue over the swollen bud tucked between my folds. His breath teases me and finally, that wonderful mouth of his settles over my clit. Sensitive from my first orgasm, I cry out when he sucks it between his lips. I'm gasping for air when he moves his attention to my dripping slit and drives his tongue deep, *deep* inside me. Like a starved man he feasts on my juices until he's tongued me deliciously; I forget to breathe.

"Oh, God—"

He groans deeply and I swear it's my name I hear on his lips. "There's no God here, *moya prekrasnaya*. My beautiful. Just His white-haired angel. One I'm taking for myself."

I believe him. He could make sinners out of nuns.

"Do you remember what I promised you in the shower, *malyshka*?"

My eyes widen. No! I inhale harshly, cling to the sheets, but my fight is useless. I'm no longer lying flat on my back, but on my stomach. Hands on my hips bring me to my knees, my ass in the air for him to do to me anything he wishes.

My head is on a swivel and I peer at him over my shoulder. Vicious words hang on the cusp of slipping from my lips.

He blows a stream of air over my puckered entrance, his fingers lingering close by when I moan. "Ares, what are you doing?"

"I'm going to make you come again." Using the pad of his thumb he drags my juices to coat my asshole. He repeats the movement and I'm ready to give him what he wants. He pops the tip of his thumb inside the tight rings.

"Ares," I moan, pushing my ass into his touch. I've never taken a man there. This will be my first. Heat settles over me from that thought and I want to roll away before he can deliver on the delicious promise his forbidden strokes give.

"But I'm not going to give you my cock until you are on the edge of that orgasm and begging me for every inch."

Another inch of his thumb penetrates my ass. Slow torturous strokes push me close to the edge.

His tongue is back at my pussy. He pushes my back down, forcing my ass higher. In slow glides of his tongue, he moves between my greedy clit and teasing the entrance to my pussy. He never lets up. Fingers my ass, his lips and tonging me relentlessly, I'm finished.

Expensive satin strains to hold my cries. I know he's going to shatter me, leave me in pieces.

Ares growls as he leans over my ass and trails the warm pad of his tongue over the round globe of one cheek, then the other.

Any thoughts of my fight dissolve the second a thick finger drags through my juices. I dig my nails into the sheets and bury my shame in the pillows. Moans fall from my lips, cries.

"Please. More." *No, Nova, don't beg.* "Ares, please." *Those can't be my words, my voice.*

He sinks one finger and then the next into my sheath and the walls of my channel clench around him.

"I want to hear you beg, *malyshka*. Beg and I'll consider giving this sweet cunt my cock. She looks hungry. So hungry."

She is.

And if I want to be honest, I crave to feel the pain his cock will bring me. The burn. Anything to strip me of the pain I feel so deep inside me no other human being has begun to touch that darkness.

"Ares, please!"

"Please what?"

I fist the sheets and cry out. So hard I know someone somewhere in this fucking mansion hears. But they don't dare check to see if their Prez is murdering me softly or fucking me to death.

"Ares, please. Please fuck me."

A thick, hard cock sinks into me and I'm so close to the edge the second his balls slap my clit I'm not close; I'm done.

He fists my hair, angles my head to the side, and devours my screams. Inhales my cries. Fucks me hard. So hard the metal of the frame thunders against the wall. Paint chips and wood cracks. And yet, he's not done with me.

His eyes flash with raw power. Pinning me in place, he drives into me. Wedged between my legs, his thumb tortures my asshole as he mercilessly fucks me into the mattress.

Biting my earlobe, he pulls a rasped cry from my lips.

"Deny me all you want. Curse me until the day I die, but your body, malyshka…your body wants me fucking it until we're both dead."

He controls the direction of my head with a twist of my hair. He kisses the corner of my mouth, taking my throat in hand as he sinks one final time into my core. His harsh breathing is loud in my ear, jacking up my own.

My walls clamp around him, hold him as tightly as he's holding me.

And then I do the unthinkable. I shimmy my hips, suck his length deeper and pull his milk into my womb.

"Fucking minx. You wicked angel. You want me?"

He pulls out and thrusts so deeply inside me I rock forward, feeling the burn on my knees.

Holding my hair in his grip he drives into me several more times before his cock swells with his need for release. He shouts through his release, muscle upon muscle clenches and ripples.

Heat crackles between us. Ropes of his cum spill into the condom. With each pulse of his release more of my sanity and control slips away. He consumes me. Utterly and completely. There's not a part of me his body isn't touching.

He releases my hair and withdraws the cuff of his hand around my throat. Drawing in deep gulps of air I move to my side. Ares, breathing harshly, pulls me to him and we both collapse in a sweaty heap in the middle of the bed.

I go to move but his arm clamps down. "Stay put."

I watch his naked form move across the room to the bathroom. Those scars on his back are a stark contrast to the shadows consuming the light.

Thirty minutes later Ares is breathing heavily beside me. I slip from beneath the covers, pull on another of his shirts and then toe on my jeans and boots. Music from the rager downstairs muffles my shuffling around.

I try all the pockets but find nothing. With the lamp in a low setting it gives off just enough light that I spy the keys on the nightstand. Beside it is a silver and gold switchblade with letter engravings down the side of the handle.

Bingo, baby.

The only drawback—both lay four inches from his face.

Shit.

I eye the clock and it's marching closer to closing time down at Jacobs.

Double shit. I skip looking for a jacket and head straight for my target. Enough adrenaline churns through my system I'll be warm at the top of Mount Everest anyway. The keys to the old Chevy parked among the expensive Jaguars and whatever the other shiny ones are. Not my forte; I just know Ares would probably cry if something happened to them. A terribly wicked idea comes to mind. One the devil himself will drag me to hell for.

My heart in my throat, the knife in my back pocket, and the keys in my hand, I don't stop running until I'm standing outside.

Knees to chest Olympic runner style I vault like a gazelle over gravel and manicured lawn until I hit the door to the garage. "Unlocked. Thank you, baby Jesus."

I work the blade open and bury it inside three cars' worth of brand-new tires. Some of them have white walls. Those I know are expensive. Burn. Maybe he'll reconsider using cuffs on women from now on. I drive the blade a little deeper on the last tire and take great satisfaction at the pop and hiss.

For all of five seconds, I consider the Harleys lined out front. But see a light spring to life on the third floor. I jump in the old truck luckily parked along the side of the garage and key the ignition. Metal grinds and creaks. Custom black leather, polished everything, and an old-timey radio dating back to the original date of the truck gleam with pride. Which makes this all the sweeter.

I pat the big steering wheel. My stars must all be sitting pretty and in alignment or my guardian angel is working overtime keeping me alive. Either way, I don't have to gun the ignition and bust my way through the iron gate of the

Compound when I reach the end of the drive. Some unlucky moron left it wide open and I ride right on out. He'll be getting a piece of his ass handed to him when Ares finds out. Probably Devil.

I slam on the brakes and consider my options. South takes me to the city where I'll find Jacob. West I can ride until the gas runs out.

I accelerate and throw my hand out the window with a middle finger salute.

"*Do svidaniya,* Ares." Goodbye.

TWELVE
NOVA

"Jacob! Jacob, come on! Open the fucking door. What the hell is wrong with you?" I ball a fist and pound on puke-colored metal. Nada.

Cars whizz by both exits of the alley. New York springs are damn near as cold as winter. The last few days have been brutal. Wishing I had taken the extra thirty seconds to grab a jacket from Ares' closet I raise a fist and pound again. Above me hangs a single bulb encased in a metal cage and does little to chase away the crawling shadows of the back alley.

"What the hell, man? Open up!" I'd go around front if they hadn't already locked up for the night which is weird on its own. Friday nights are usually the busiest for a guy who sells beer and whiskey to the local blue-collar workers. Given the customers only cared about not seeing the bottom of their drink no one paid a lot of attention to the random chick or dude ducking into the back room or hacker misfit who used a stack of crates as a desk seven days a week. There's a lot of money to be made in the underground economy if you have the right connections and clients willing to see the value in what you have to offer. Lucky for me I have a good source who has a knack for pulling in the high rollers in need of my special skill set. Enough to put my sister into college, feed us and make our two-bedroom apartment not look like shit though the location could be better.

The last time I stood out here I was being shuffled inside a van by a masked asshole. Albeit it was in the front parking lot and not the back entrance to El Diablo, but not much difference. The thudding of my heart and the hair on the back of my neck drive home a feeling of urgency to get inside.

My body grudgingly reminds me of the fear locking my knees and sending my heart into a stammering rhythm by repeating the same reactions now.

Had it only been a few days ago I'd stood here, knocked a couple of times and the door would swing open? Jacob is a paranoid type and never left a door unguarded. Not finding someone there to immediately let me in is odd, but whatever. I'm here for one thing only.

Another round of pounding gives me a head with dark hair popping out the door.

"Finally."

Accusatory eyes turn surprised when they land on my face.

"Nova?" Jacob pulls back. Eyes narrow on me but that's nothing new. The man considers everyone like they want to either beat the shit out of him or rob him. I consider the personality flaws remnants of his childhood growing up poor and always on the wrong side of the law until he pulled his shit together in his late teens. We met half a decade ago when I saved his ass from a guy who thought his head would look good rolling on the floor. Some smooth talking in the middle of this very pub landed me a backroom to operate, my first client and Jacob as a decent friend. Just don't ask him for money.

I step over the threshold and have to work myself in through the small slant of an opening.

"What's with you? Didn't you get my message?"

He ignores my question and comes at me with his own. Looking a little pale he asks, "What are you doing here?" The fugly door clicks behind him with a solid thud closing us in. My heart rate drops to a respectable thud knowing I'm safer in here than out there.

"No *where have you been for the last three or four days,* Nov? No asking *hey, you doing okay?* And don't look so shocked to see me. It gives a girl a complex."

He doesn't say anything, just moves to the other side of the backroom, peeks out, and then slams the door. That should have been my first clue of how the evening is about to go, but I can be a little narrowminded when I get hyper-focused.

"You can't be here?" He looks at me exasperated but then again, that's Jacob for you.

I lift a brow and close my arms over my chest. "And why is that?" I make my way to the door he just slammed and pop it open. "I don't need long."

I move through the hallway toward the front of the bar and notice the shades drawn over the front windows and all the tables taken up by burly dudes with more beard than face.

I come up short, realizing he might be right about me needing to leave. But Polaris needs me to be here right now so I swallow my surprise and their less-than-welcoming glares at my intrusion. I silently curse my narrow-sighted tendencies and push on. Hopefully, Jacob doesn't catch my split-second hesitance.

None of my business anyway.

Jacob is hot on my ass. "Look, you need to know some assholes are using your bar as hunting grounds."

I make a right down another hallway. This one is less welcoming than the last with its nonexistent light and stale air.

"Slow the hell up, Nov. Where are you going?"

A heavy hand lands on my shoulder and pulls me back. I stumble, losing my momentum forward.

"Where are you going? You need to leave the same way you came in. Now."

Jacob's already whiny voice kicks up a few notches. Hissing really isn't a good sound on any day. The way it comes out of his mouth mixes with the creepy vibes from just being here again and my arms break out in goosebumps.

"Are you listening? I just need to see your security tape from Tuesday night and then I'm out. Promise."

"What? No. You need to leave." That hand is back on my shoulder.

I shove it away and let myself into the security room. Inside the small ten by ten room, I aim straight for the CCTV and pop out a thumb drive from the drawer. My motions are fluid and come from a solid year of doing this every night. I leave no traces of my dealings. An understanding between the man currently breathing down my neck and myself for a twenty percent cut of my profits.

Pricey but it's not like I can work out of my house with my sister there. Like I've said, I keep her and my shady friends as far apart as possible. Only thing she needs to focus on is getting her degree in psychology. Not getting killed in the middle of the night from a deal gone wrong or an unsatisfied customer. Although hindsight might have helped us fight off our attackers instead of taking all three of us by surprise.

"I said there's nothing for you to see, Nova." Jacob's voice hardens but instead of sending me fleeing in fear as I pretty much think he intended I do the exact opposite.

I stop cold and turn on my heel. "No, you said I needed to leave. There's a difference." Curiosity pulls my eyes to his and away from the gray and white still image of the front parking lot.

Knowing how well my next question is about to go over, I ask it anyway. "What are you afraid I'll find, Jacob? Got something to hide?"

Four fat knuckles swing out and narrowly miss my jaw. I grab the nearest thing and throw it in his face. I only wish the cold coffee would have done more in stopping him from fisting the knot of my ponytail and using it against me.

With more force than I realize he has, Jacob throws me through the door and I land with a thud against the back wall of the hallway.

"What is it you don't want me to see, Jacob?" I say viciously. He's looking rather sweaty and pissed when he charges. I catch a shoulder to the stomach and I can't fly but I do a nice job of tumble ass over feet. Not so much as instinct rather than pure unfiltered rage drives me to reach for the blade I procured from a sleeping Ares.

With all of my non-existent experience at fighting, I drive the four-inch blade through my friend's thick boot and hear a gut-wrenching crunching.

Oh shit. I scramble back when he howls in pain.

Behind me chairs screech over the hardwood flooring.

"Jacob?" a random voice booms into the back hallway.

Damn.

My back shoots straight up and the whip of fear slashing me locks my knees.

"I'm going to kill you, you bitch." He sounds set on committing to his promise which has me swallowing the lump of fear choking me.

Furious black eyes latch onto me and yes. He is very much set on wanting me dead. Okay, so perhaps it was a little rash of me to slash all of Ares' tires and an even worse idea coming here. Alone. In the middle of the night. During some kind of bro get-together with the city's ugliest dudes.

Fog starts to clear around the idea I might have stepped into the deep end of the pool here.

Sometimes I really do wish I had even a dash of luck on my side and even better fighting skills. A gun would be nice too. As it stands, neither is in my possession at the moment and my only form of defense is currently buried in my former friend's foot.

Jacob glances at me and then back to the knife sticking out of his foot like he reads my mind.

Good or bad, I'm here now and there is no way in hell I'm leaving without what I came for.

"I'm going to need that back." I wrap a hand around the knife and yank. I don't look back as I dive over him and lock myself in the security room.

Peeling screams slam into the door a few seconds before real fists make contact with the wooden panes. If he decides to put all two-fifty plus pounds of his weight into getting through that door, there won't be much else between him and me making good on his wish to see me in the morgue. I slam the thumb drive into the USB slot and pull up the recordings from that night.

"What?" There's no way. Why? My gut hurts at the idea of my friend betraying me. No, he'd never do that. Right?

"What the hell, Jacob." I find myself yelling for the tenth time.

"Why couldn't you be a good little bitch and just stay gone. You've fucked everything up now. The Volkovs will be here in a minute." Another railing against the door.

Panicked, I say, "You let this happen to me?"

My heart hammers. Nerves make working the keys a little difficult but I hit rewind and play it back again. Only instead of seeing Monday evening roll over into Tuesday, it jumps straight to Wednesday. A full day is missing from the files.

Dread sinks in and my palms become sweaty as I hit rewind and play. Rewind and play. "What the hell are you into, Jacob?" In all my time here the man never gave thought to the security system. And now the specific time I'm looking for is erased?

Deep down the bitter acid burning a hole in my stomach tells me I already know the answer to my questions. And that makes getting out of this room all the harder. The second I throw that door open he'll have me again. *Think, Nova.*

My sister. Maybe this is how I get back to her?

Back at the door, I hold my palm over the wood and start with the first words I think.

"Jacob. Where is she? Where are they holding her? Tell me and I'll walk. You'll never see me again. I won't call the cops."

Hysterical laughter is my answer. "You think there aren't any in this town on someone's payroll? Naive bitch. You're not going anywhere except under my basement floor." His muffed answer is what I expected.

"That is a little cliche, don't you think? Even for you." He's a wanna-be Soprano only without the pinky ring, expensive suits, or Italian accent. But by the size of his gut, I'd say he has an unhealthy relationship with carbs.

"Look, we've been friends for a few years now? Does that not count toward anything?"

Nothing.

His silence is a good sign shit is about to hit the proverbial fan but it is the deafening crack of thunder right outside the door followed by all-out hell releasing inside the bar that drives the point to my feet. I shoot a look over my shoulder and spot familiar bikes in view of the surveillance camera; their riders nowhere to be seen.

Oh shit.

Fingers trembling, I force the lock open and swing the door wide, bracing for I don't know what to expect really.

But it's not Devil toting something that looks like a shotgun forged with a Glock. He stops in front of me and speaks without looking my way. "I see you found the Chevy keys."

"Yeah, thanks for the tip."

His lips pull into a wolfish grin. "It'll be fun to see what Ares does to you for taking his second baby." And there is the truth.

"You set me up." Dread fills me. Why I don't know but the way Devil grins like he's set me up for the perfect fall gives me instant heartburn.

He shrugs. "Thought maybe we could kick the ant nest. Get behind me and try not dying, before I get you to the prez."

"You planned this."

He neither confirms nor denies my allegations. Just takes my hand and says, "Here."

Cold metal meets my fingers.

"I don't know how to use that thing." A disadvantage at the moment but it is what it is.

Devil looks at the bloody knife I'm clutching in my other hand. "My guess is you're a quick learner. Just don't shoot me in the back unless you mean it."

When I make no move to take it, he grabs a hand and curls my fingers over the rough handle.

"Safety's off and there's a bullet in the chamber. Point and pull at anyone who isn't a Savage. Got it?"

I nod and see my life flash by in the glint of light off silver. I plaster myself to the wall just as a wooden handle swooshes by the tip of my nose to make a sickening thud in flesh.

Devil grunts. I don't hear it more than see his shoulder hunch and his chest cave from the force of the knife flying through the air. A flash of grit hits his expression a split second before he aims and pulls the trigger.

My ears stop working from the deafening boom and right before my eyes a man in a leather jacket and spiky black hair topples to the floor.

I'm frozen to the spot.

Beside me, Devil wraps a hand around the grip of the knife sitting several inches inside his shoulder and pulls, the heavy weight clatters at our feet, blood splattering on the tips of my boots.

I watch for signs of him fainting, but I guess I'm the only one seeing dots in front of my eyes. Which is a good thing. Truly. Between the two of us he is definitely the one going to survive and maybe save my ass.

My entire mindset about doing anything it takes to save my sister just got a real dose of reality. People are out here getting hurt because of me. But none are innocent, I remind myself. Not even Ares.

Ohmygodwhatthehellisgoingon is all my brain is screaming when I fall in behind Devil and let the man be a shield for my rash, compulsive stupidity.

"Let's see what Ares has to say about your midnight adventure. If you wanted to paint the town red, you should have told me. I would have loaded you on the back of my bike and taken you myself."

His voice is muffled in my half-deaf ears.

Ares. Shit. He's going to kill me if we make it out of this. How the hell did he even find me?

I grip the back of Devil's shirt and follow him back the way I came. Before we hit the back door that leads to the alley, we make a left. The short hallway opens up into the public side of the bar. And where the rest of Jacob's crew of misfit kidnappers are getting as good as they are giving.

Riot, Rage, and Ares are in the middle of the bar. If it isn't nailed down, it's in someone's hands. Tables, chairs, and beer mugs are all being used as weapons.

I'm not sure how the chaos started; all I do know is, Devil's the only thing standing between Jacob and me getting his wish right now. Wherever he ran off to.

Standing in the middle of the entryway, I take a look over my shoulder and realize I might not want the answer to my question, but got it anyway.

It's the shock of blond hair I spy first and then the gun. Standing at the opposite end of the hallway. Jacob aims down the barrel of his Glock. I see a muzzle flash before the wood over my right shoulder splinters. The crack of the bullet leaving the chamber never registers over the grunts and glass shatters from the end of the hallway.

"Oh, shit! Get down!" I hear myself scream and then everything hits fast forward.

What used to be a long spread of glass with large neon signs is now gaping holes, the flashing lights glitching remnants of their former ugliness. Dingy beige shades hang in tattered flutters of cloth.

Fists, chairs, ball bats fly through the air and the random thud of a high-powered rifle going off reverberates through the bar. It's so loud the sound waves penetrate my chest and jack my heart rate up to match the amount of adrenaline filling my bloodstream.

I take in the crowd but can't spot Ares at first. But when I do, he looks like the real god of war standing in the middle of the bar. Eyes wild and muscles bulging. He swings left, right—anyone unfortunate to fall prey to his wrath crumbles to the floor. In a blink, flames engulf the back wall and lick up the sides of tables until they've encompassed Ares. Smoke rolls and rises so I hit the deck and do what I was taught long before gods of war, Russian traffickers, and bikers. Stop. Drop...and crawl.

I shriek when beefy arms snake around my middle and jerk me to my feet.

Pings of empty bullet shells falling to the floor and particles of wood splinters flying through the air keep my head down and body tucked behind the wall of muscle blocking my view.

Broad shoulders, flaming skull, and an aura of rage all tell me it's one very pissed-off Russian playing human shield.

"Ares."

He swings his head around. Gray eyes turn to impenetrable steel. "Shut the fuck up and stay down. I'll deal with you later."

Devil's prophecy. Shit.

Ares wraps his digits over the lips of a table and I tuck and roll behind the slab of wood just in time for it to take several slugs down the middle. Thin wood cleaves in two. We dive for another table, this one thicker than the last but not by much.

Ares takes a knee, rounds the table, and pulls the trigger. Round after round pings off and the vibrations of heavy bodies hitting the floor feed through the palms of my hands. Hell is in my future at the joy I'm feeling as these men meet their end, but I take solace in knowing they'll all be outside the devil's gates before me.

"We don't have enough men," Ares calls out.

"No shit! We need an army!" No sooner does one hit that ground does another pop up seemingly from nowhere. "How many are on Volkov's payroll?"

Ares' mouth quirks a degree but I realize it's not me he is talking to but Rage who slides in beside us, the chamber of his gun cocked back telling me he's out of ammo.

"I'm out!" Rage yells, his face a scrunched-up version of Eastwood's son. It's kind of eerie at how similar the two look.

"Here." Like we are not in the middle of a freaking shootout, Rage produces a phone from his pocket and punches in numbers before passing it over to Ares like some multitasking pro.

My eyes swing to a man coming in fast behind us, low light from the overheads glinting off the metal of a ball bat aiming for Ares' head. He must have seen my wild expression because Ares pivots on a knee, aims and puts the man on the ground in less than two seconds—his lifeless eyes empty doors.

Smoke burns my eyes. Flying embers sprinkle across my shirt leaving behind little scorch marks like black stars on a white canvas. The phone Ares had pinned between his shoulder and ear clatters to the floor. I swipe it up. Sweaty palms make it nearly impossible to keep my grip on it, but I manage. "Hey, yeah sorry. Kinda busy right now. I don't know who this is, but you'll have to wait," I yell.

A muzzle flash and another man, this one is in greasy jeans and with a mug no one can love falls at my feet. There is no use in trying to control my breathing or my racing heart.

"Nova, down!"

I forget about the phone, smoke, and embers. A big hand in the middle of my back shoves me to the floor and I'm suddenly under hundreds of pounds of pissed-off Russian. Above us chunks of plaster, glass, and wood rain down from where a freaking grenade goes off.

The worst part is the silence that follows. It wraps around me blocking the sounds of male grunts and guns. The only faculty working right now is my eyes and they are full of grit and dust. Through that pain I see Ares. Gun in hand.

But it's not doing any good. Too many of Jacob's men rush us and Ares is forced to move from being my body shield to mano a mano. And the men coming for him know how to take a hit. They keep coming.

I roll. What kind of fucking crazy ass people throw a grenade! Air finally rushes back into my lungs and my hearing eases in with the sound of bullets spraying the wall behind us. If we were pinned down before, we're in deep shit now.

Ares feeds the last two men who don't know when to quit two bullets each.

Ohmygodwhatthehellishappening starts all over on loop in my head.

What the fuck did I just witness?

They die or we die. I repeat to myself knowing it is true. Did I come here tonight for this? Am I not willing to put a bullet in Jacob? I am.

I clamp a hand down on Ares' shoulder and he whirls wildly on me. Using his free hand, he checks me over. "You hit? Tell me. I need to know. Are. You. Hit?"

I shake my head. "No." The fear in his eyes at me possibly being hurt shocks me. No one ever cared that much about me. Except for my sister and Ellie, that is. But others? They rather hurt me for their own benefit. I tuck this little bit of information away to analyze later. Like when I don't have bullets flying at me.

"Are you okay? Look at me. Are you okay?" Hurried hands take my face.

"I said I'm fine. I'm not hit."

I see Ares' lips moving but my ringing ears don't let me hear his voice over a muffle. I give him one final nod and he seems to be satisfied with that because he moves into action. Plaster dust clouds the air and through it I spy Ares reloading; his hand is a blur of movement over the metal weapon.

My hearing comes back full in time for more bullets to pepper our last remaining shield. From my vantage point, I can see there's no other table but this one. Shit. What have I done? We're all going to freaking die in the middle of a dingy dive bar on the trashy side of town.

Ares snatches the phone from me. "You said you wanted a chance to prove you are on our side."

There's a long pause I feel goes on forever before Ares speaks again.

"I'm turning on my location. Ping it and meet us in the back alley and don't let red lights stop you from getting here as fast as you can. We'll need to set a reservation with a crew who can work fast. Maintenance on this will need to be thorough before the law gets involved. Fire is eating most of it but there are other aspects to secure."

Another silence and then Ares ends the call, tossing the phone back to me.

Ares pulls a cartridge from his pocket and tosses it to his friend. Together they work to clear a path toward the back entrance.

"When I tell you to haul ass and get outside, you run and don't look back."

Maddening tears burn at the back of my eyes from the idea of leaving him to deal with my mess while I get away. It's the smoke and not from frustration, I tell myself. Pure frustration.

What the hell am I in the middle of?

"No." From the corner of my eye, I lock onto my target. "You can leave. I came here for something."

Jacob is standing across the bar, reloading a gun that looks like it can level this place in less than ten rounds. Through the chaos I never let the gun Devil shoved into my hand go. One silver lining I am not about to waste. I raise my arms and aim down the barrel. Jacob needs ending. God only knows how long he's been hurting innocent women.

My heart explodes into thundering beats. My hands tremble. But all those girls I will be saving...I take a deep breath and squeeze the trigger.

A blow to my hands has the bullet hitting the wooden floorboards fifteen feet away.

"What the hell, Ares?" I'm so angry hands are shoved down before I can bury a bullet in Jacob's back.

Riot and Devil are pinned down, each fighting back a new wave of men. Where the fuck do they keep coming from?

"Not happening. You will not get blood on your hands. Never. I will take that burden. At this rate one more asshole's death might actually earn me some brownie points." A dark part of me wants to laugh at his admission, but the reasonable side of me who still cares for other humans feels horrified at his admission.

Ares disarms me, tucking the weapon in the band of his pants.

"You don't get it. I don't know how it all works but he's the reason I was at the stupid auction. Why my sister is there now, Ares? You owe me this."

"I know," Ares grates.

My brain stutters. He knows what?

He doesn't get a chance to clarify. Pellets from a shotgun determined to finish us off bury themselves in the wood of the table we're tucked behind and the wall over top of my head. Beating back the assholes trying to end us is now all-out fight or die.

Ares and Rage both peel around opposite sides of the table. One. Two. Three pops and as many bodies fall.

Clattering of metal on wood stops. I jump over the table. I might not have a gun but the chair in my hands makes a sickening crack when I break it over Jacob's back.

He drops his gun and Ares is on him before I can palm the gun at my feet.

Ares rears back and levels Jacob to his knees with one blow to the face.

And then the raging bull is gunning for me. Ares turns, grips my hips, and hoists me until our gazes are level. A rush of Russian hits my ears before he breaks off in words I can understand.

"Are you okay? Are you hit? Are you fucking crazy?"

"No. I don't think so." I pat myself to make sure. The way he's looking at me makes me feel I should have at least a dozen holes in my body.

A rough hand on my chin jerks my attention back on him. "Your life is in my care, *malyshka*. Do you understand me? Why do you keep risking it for this piece of trash?" He turns his eyes on Jacob for a moment.

"I have to. I have to do everything I can to protect what's mine," I say frankly.

He dashes away my answer. "Never put yourself at this level of risk, any level of risk again and…" His words drop off, he puts me back on the ground. With everyone either subdued or bleeding out on the wood floor, he spouts orders off to Devil, Rage, and Riot before he takes my arm roughly. "The Genesis men will be here in a minute; when they arrive, make sure this looks like inner warring. And him," Ares presses the muzzle of his gun to a trembling Jacob's head. "Bring him out back."

I'm dragged out the back. No sooner do we step out of the door does a white car pull up. Three men step out and everything about them and their ride screams money and power. The shadowed smug looks on their faces send another message. One of death. They must be BFFs with my captor.

All three pin me with dark gazes that yep, look just like Ares'. They look like the type of men who end problems and make sure they stay buried. "This the hacker who kicked the hornet's nest?"

"Me? You want to blame me for this?"

Metal hits brick behind me. Riot and Rage shoulder through the back door. The pressure shifts from me to the sack of shit they are carrying.

They toss the bleeding asshole on the cracked cement at Ares' feet. Jacob pushes to his knees his expression void. I've heard rumblings along the dark web of the Savages being ruthless assholes. Men who keep their territory clean. I never thought anything of it until tonight. I mean, really considered the hushed reputation no one ever spoke about in normal tones. I always thought men like them would never cross my path and now I'm surrounded by them and my life is in their hands. In one particular Russian's hands to be exact.

And if it were not for Jacob I wouldn't have had a million bullets aiming my way tonight. My sister would be getting ready for her finals.

I don't think, I act. Which is half the reason I'm in this situation, but I can't let this moment pass. I ignore the pain radiating up my wrist to my shoulder when I bury my fist in his face. I welcome it, rear back, and do it again.

"How could you?" I seethe. "How Jacob?"

Blood drips into his eyes from gashes over his eyebrows and a few other nicks along the side of his face. Good, he deserves those and much more.

"For the money," I continue when he does nothing but spits blood. I can feel Ares come up behind me. He's still, as are the other men, but all serve as a force of strength.

"Did the time I held your head out of the toilet while you puked your guts out after a drunken binger when your sister died mean nothing? Or how you crashed on my couch because you couldn't face going home and being alone that first week?"

"You fared better than she did. What the hell is your problem?"

I stumble back. "What did you say?" I swing my gaze to Ares' and then back to Jacob in disbelief. His dead eyes look at me but I'm not sure he's seeing me. His face is void of any emotion like he's waiting for the reaper to appear for his soul any second.

I clamp a hand over my mouth, gutted and sickened to my core by his admission. "You sold your sister?" I whisper harshly.

"Half-sister."

"Blood is blood."

Jacob's breathing is labored and the bubbles in the blood dripping from his lip says a lot about the state of his ribs. I can't find it in me to care.

"You know what those Russian brothers wanted and you let them take me. And you were in on it? How much did they pay you and your crew of trash?" My chest tightens. Wailing alarms go off in my head. The problem I'm standing in the middle of goes deeper than just me and my sister. And Jacob is feeding the underground economy with innocent souls.

Blood bubbles through swollen lips and a sheen of red across otherwise white teeth is evident in the low light. "What are you going to do about it? Nothing. You're just another bitch. These pricks kill me and the Volkovs will retaliate. I doubt these fuckers want war." Jacob spits a mouthful of blood at Ares' feet.

"I trusted you!" I can't see the bloody face in front of me for the angry tears swimming behind my lashes.

He shrugs. "We all need money. You think you are the only one who can do under-the-table shit and get paid for it? It worked out for you. You think you're all high and mighty, Reina?" He slurs my hacker name, sneering it with disgust.

"I don't see you any worse for wear." His face splits with a macabre grin.

I force myself to keep my fists at my side and not buried in his face. I doubt it would do much damage to his already battered appearance. "What about my sister? And Ellie. She's dead because of you. But what the hell do you care, right? You sold your own flesh and blood."

"Virgins get more. They'll keep your sweet little Polaris alive until they find a buyer for such a young virgin piece of pussy. She paid back the debt I had with the Volkovs. What I got for you and that whore friend of yours was icing. I'm here to stay. And this city is ripe for the picking. Your pussy ass boyfriend won't do shit about it either."

A muzzle flash and a sharp pop. I turn to see Ares, the Glock in his hand smoking.

Thirteen

Ares

When I woke to find Nova gone, I knew where she was headed. She did exactly what I would have done. The entire time I raced to her I couldn't help but second guess myself. What if Jacob killed her on the spot? What if she found what she was looking for and Jacob killed her before I got there?

I broke at least five traffic laws getting to her. The next time I try to play the hero someone should shoot me. The fear of her getting hurt shredded me. Worst fucked up feeling to have eating at you.

I knew Nova would do anything to find her sister. Letting her take off to find her own answers went against my gut instinct but she and I are a lot alike. Hearing from Devil she was looking for a way off the property I had two choices—cuff her or let her find what she was looking for. I figured she deserved to know just how much of a piece of shit Jacob really was. Putting a bullet in his brain was the least I could do for her. I don't feel an ounce of remorse for ending him. Same for the Volkovs when the time comes. If that makes me an unholy bastard in her eyes… well, I've certainly been called worse and that's something I can live with as long as she doesn't get the stain on her soul.

That saying about giving someone enough rope to hang themselves isn't far off base. Nova needed to see for herself, hear the words from her supposed friend's mouth. By me telling her he was the reason she was at that auction wouldn't have been enough. She's a hands-on kind of girl and I respect that about her. But the truth acts as a noose; once you hear it, it can choke the life from you. She'll have to learn the truth of this like the rest of us—the hard way.

I twist the throttle and open my baby up. Midnight has come and gone and in a handful of hours more we'll be seeing the sun touch the horizon. City lights fade until it's nothing but back roads and open fields. I don't know how long we've been riding but I don't hear her complaining of the cold wind so I keep us pointed north.

Standing back to let her do what she needed tore my fucking nerves to pieces. When I busted out of the house and aimed for my Hummer, I didn't expect the slashed tires awaiting me. In hindsight, I probably should have kept the knife off the nightstand.

I spot a familiar dirt road that leads to a riverbank I visit once in a while when I go for a ride this far north. Summer nights work wonders with easing past nightmares. A little something between me and the road. A secret cove I've never taken another soul lies ahead a few miles. At this hour it will be deserted by anyone else who might have found it, too.

I throttle down and ease the bike over the smooth dirt. Instead of killing the motor, I let the rumble of my girl work her magic a little longer. We sit there, and little by little I feel the tension sitting between my shoulder blades loosen.

Something about Nova is different. Being caught between bullets and dead bodies has stolen her light. She's too quiet. A clawing feeling in my chest tells me she's all fight and bravado when she has to be. But it's not a life choice. And not one I would pick for her either. She deserves light and sunshine. Not grit, blood, and filth. Meeting me was probably the worst day of her life. I'm not sure how that makes me feel, but I guess it doesn't matter much since we are both in this shit pool like it or not.

I cut the engine. The moon over the water is a calming view. The bitter cold has edged off a bit. Another week and this place will be blooming with wildflowers and fireflies. But not yet.

Silence falls over us and I give Nova the time she needs to gather her rattled senses. And I know she will. The shit she witnessed and heard tonight would shake anyone but she's strong. She just needs a little time. I can give her that.

"What will happen to Jacob's body?"

To my surprise, Nova nuzzles into me as if seeking comfort or support. I swear viciously under my breath at the circumstances we're in. The last thing I want to do is talk about him.

She's riding bitch, thighs wrapped around me and those hands of hers haven't left my front belt loops since we peeled out of Jacob's parking lot.

I debate lying. Discussing any angles of business outside the crew isn't something I'm comfortable with, but if I start telling her lies when would they stop? It is bad enough I can't tell her who I really am. Not without her freaking out and using the knife she still has tucked in her back pocket on me. Or worse. Lose her trust forever.

The more I chew on that the more I realize I'd rather she try to kill me than break the small amount of trust she's bestowed upon me.

"His body will be taken care of like everyone else. I knew the Volkovs had men on their payroll. Tonight we got to see just how many and that was probably not all of them." I say flatly, ready to leave it at that. I'm more interested in talking about what I need her to do. But she's not dropping it.

"Like the nightly trash?" Her tone turns bitter.

I don't say anything to that because she's not far off the mark.

I reach around and draw her from the back to sit over my lap. Sitting like that I can see her eyes and gauge her emotions. See how far too far is. Determined blue eyes meet mine.

"There's my Nova."

A crackle of energy pops and hisses between us.

"I am not *your Nova*."

"I paid for you, didn't I?"

"Fuck you, Ares!"

She smacks at my chest, pushes me to get off the bike. I just tighten my arms and hold her to me until she quiets. We sit like this for a while, her chest heaving and the tears flowing. I know she needs the silence so I let her have it.

I'm not surprised a girl with her smart mouth and spirit hasn't found a man. Most walking dickheads don't know what to do with a woman who knows her mind the way this woman does. Weak idiots. Knowing that weasel Jacob, she probably turned him down and he couldn't handle the rejection. His retaliation resulted in her being shuffled off to auction.

Never in my life have I felt good about ending another person's life. Until him.

Nova's legs are spread over my lap. The wind has wiped her hair loose from her ponytail. I reach for a few strands and rub the soft tips together, considering my next words.

"Did Jacob ever suggest you two would be good together?"

Her brows bunch together over watery eyes. "What?" She peers out at the calm water for a moment and turns away from me I get to see a side of Nova I've never seen before. The vulnerable side. Quiet, pensive. Beautiful. I turn her to face me.

"Maybe, I don't know."

I wanna press my forehead to hers, breathe in her life force and feed her my own. The shit I've never wanted to do with another woman. She damn near has me wonder what we would name our kids. Suddenly it is killing me to know who took her virginity. What her life dreams are. Does she like the beach or love snow more? I hope the snow.

I stab my fingers through my hair and let the locks fall where they may.

I take her face in my hands and kiss her. Kiss her so hard we both come up gasping for air moments later. "You need to know I am not in the business of making friends with my enemies. And I have a lot of those. The Volkov brothers. Jacob. These are people who have done wrong to others and it will catch up to them. I'm the Devil's assassin. Tonight was only Jacob's turn."

Moonlight catches on the daggers her eyes shoot at me. "And the Volkovs? How long before they pay for their crimes? How long do we wait? How many more will have to be hurt before you act? Why can't we go to the police?"

"It will all work out as I've planned. But the last thing we need to do is bring the law in on this."

"You're so fucking arrogant it's suffocating."

"I am not arrogant. I'm a lot of things but not arrogant. Ruthless. Cutthroat. Savage. But not arrogant. That gets people killed."

"I beg to differ. You say it will all work out. Like it's working out for my sister? Are you forgetting about her?

Finding out about her sister was an unfortunate turn of events. "*Nyet, malyshka.* But I can't help her if it means putting hundreds of other girls just like her in danger. I lose my shit, go blazing in, take them down, how do I find out who their puppet master is? The guy putting up the money to make this whole operation work? Because I sure as shit know it's not the Volkovs. They barely had a dollar in their bank account a few months back and suddenly they are flush?"

What I can't say is I think the man involved is my father.

"They move to another city; the cycle starts up all over again and hundreds of other Novas and Polarises are stripped from their loved ones. So, no." I say abruptly. "It ends here. In my city. My way. At my time."

Consciously or not, her hands fall from my shoulders where she's trying to push me away to settle over her abdomen. I imagine she's thinking over the mantra branded into her skin.

I take her hands and place them back on my shoulders where she slips them under the leather of my cut.

"Don't put this one on me. I don't have anything to lose but my sister, Ares. I have to do what is best for her." Her tone is quiet but her words are no less powerful.

"No one is putting anything on you, *malyshka*. We get back to the compound we have work to do. We have to do this my way. It's the only way this will work." I cup her face and take her lips in another hard kiss. I feel her stiffen around me, but her hands under my cut and her nails digging into my flesh send mixed signals.

I break the kiss and press my forehead to hers. Her sweet, hot, delicate appearance hides the steel will of a woman determined to save her blood.

She smacks me away and it's fire and brimstone I see staring back at me. "Don't fight us, *malyshka*. You won't win."

If I didn't know any better, I swear I see fear lace with excitement in those pretty blues and it's an irresistible concoction. And then she speaks.

"Like you biker types are so loyal to your women. I'm not a fast fuck, Ares."

I level my gaze on her. "*Nyet*, you're my bride."

"You're a real dick, you know. I'm not yours. Never will be. Now take me back. I have enough evidence to do what I need even without the surveillance video. You won't move on the Russian brothers, then I will."

"What do you mean?"

She's off the bike and on her feet. For being such a small thing, she can move fast.

"These." She pulls out a wad of paper from beneath her shirt. My shirt. The sight of my sleeves rolled back to reveal her slight forearms and the sides hanging open to show the sexy dip between her breasts reminds me just how fragile of a flower she is despite her will to fight.

My attention drops to the papers she is shaking in front of my face. My casino and bar's names are along the top.

"What exactly do you think you have?"

She tucks a wayward lock of hair behind an ear. The move is unconscious but tells me she's nervous as hell. "Proof you're dirty, Russian." Those plump lips press into a flat kissable line. Moonlight hits her at just the right angle to make her appear like a warring angel. All the white hair needs to be in my hands.

I give her a stone-cold stare and she tries her hardest to give it right back before those eyes fall to my chest. Damn, she is adorable when she thinks she's right. I throw my leg over the seat and step toward her. I tower over her but she's not backing down. The fight in her roars to life but I see her weight shifting from foot to foot. She's trying to analyze whether she can outrun me.

I quietly dare her to try.

"Jesus fucking Christ. This woman." I look skyward but I'm not going to find the heavenly amount of patience I need up there.

I stab my fingers through my hair and take a deep breath. I frown at her walking backward from me.

"Where do you think you're going?"

I won't let her warranted fears get between us. I do that and I might as well kiss the job I need for her to do goodbye.

Two steps and I have her and the papers. The ones Riot doctored to hide the eighteen point five million dropped on her purchase and Avery's. I snatch the papers and snap open my Zippo. Seconds later I step over the smoldering pile of dying embers at my feet.

I'm in her face and I don't let her gaze fall to my feet. I take her chin in hand and drag those pretty blues back to level on me. She needs to hear this loud and clear. "You want your sister; it's my way. You have a hard time trusting. I get that, but you'll have to start at some point. But there's no way in hell I'll take the fall for something I am working to stop."

Her lower lip trembles.

"No! My sister is not part of your games of power or whatever the hell you mafia people do to make all that money. Given the last few days, I have a pretty good idea of how low you worms will slither."

Balled fists lay into me and I take the blows of anger. "Get it out. Take what you need." When she looks ready to crumble I pick her up and sprawl her over the seat of my bike, belly down, ass up.

I reach around and release the button on her pants; the zipper cranks around my hand as I ease my fingers under the band of her panties.

She wiggles and tries to push off the bike, but I grip her hips and hold her in place. Nails claw at the leather and I just add her offenses to my list of punishments. I grab the band of her jeans and pull until I see the creamy skin of her ass in the moonlight. Fucking beautiful.

"Ares!"

Wide blue eyes track me raising a hand. She knows what I'm about to do and I can see the excitement glistening in her eyes.

I bring my hand down with a smack on her bare ass cheek. She shrieks, gasps, and gives me a sweet little shudder I'm damn sure she thinks I don't catch. That's all I need. I yank up the ends of her shirt and trail my finger down her spine. There are no words for the delicate beauty she holds.

I deliver another smack and rub at the burn. On the other hand, juices drench my fingers. I swirl a pad over her nub and deliver another blow. She moans, thrusts her ass into my palm.

"There's no escape, Nova. I'm not stopping until you acknowledge you're mine."

"Never!"

I grin. I love her fire.

"Keep it up and I'll be spanking this ass again and again instead of fucking it." I tug on the band of her jeans and lower the material farther down her delicious curves. I glide my palm over both cheeks and let her feel how hard she has me through the denim of my jeans.

I stroke the thickness of my erection against her ass and her hips have a mind of their own. They move over me looking for what I have to give.

Her pretty gaze swings around again and I swear to God those eyes, this body, I could die right now and be a happy man.

"I don't belong to anyone. And I've done nothing to you."

"We will see about that. You left damage in your wake back at the compound. You left my protection. You put yourself at risk of getting killed." My fingers tighten into the flesh of her ass with each punishable crime she committed and that little mouth of her releases a beautiful gasp.

"Think you can do shit like that and get away with it?"

She pushes her hips into me and I push right back. Her gasps of surprise turn to moans. "You're not going anywhere. Not until you learn the most valuable asset you have is your life. And who it belongs to."

Nova

Agonizing pain radiates up my body. The bewildering rush of pleasure that follows has me tightening my lips to keep them from giving him what he wants.

There's more than one kind of control. One by force and that which your body falls under willingly. Never in my life has another person held me mesmerized the way this Russian does. I don't know why, but when he speaks my body jumps on board, ready to be his to command. I find it infuriating and exciting in one breath.

I jump at the smack that lands on my ass. Burning fire and something I've never felt before at the tail end of pain warms over me. Pleasure. He slips my jeans down my ass and thighs until they are around my knees. Apparently happy with my state of undress, he falls to his knees behind me.

"Let me hear you say it."

"Say what?"

Wrong answer.

I arch off the seat and try to hold on but there's nothing to grip onto as his tongue stabs my core repeatedly.

"Oh, God! Oh, God. No... Ares, you can't!"

"Yes, I can," he chuckles darkly and continues to torture me. My skin is on fire, but the nub between my folds is pulsing so hard I'm going to come in his mouth any second.

"Say it!"

"No!" *But yes...oh my God. Yes!* My eyes flutter closed and there's not enough cushion underneath to hold onto.

My body trembles from his seeking tongue. He licks, teases, swirls and drives me crazy seeking out the sweet spot that will have me spilling juices all over his mouth.

"Ares!" I scream and buck but the hands on my lower back hold me in place. I try to free myself but the more I move the deeper, the tighter his hold becomes. One finger at a time presses open my thighs until I'm fully on display to whatever he wants from me.

"Beautiful," he growls against the folds of my slick, wet pussy.

I know I am on the losing end of this struggle.

"Ares—" I try again. Risking shifting my focus from balancing over top of the bike, I peer over my shoulder to see he's sadly still fully dressed.

"I'm taking what's mine. You have no regard for it, but I do. You don't value your life? Let me show you what you're missing." Moonlight catches on the juices coating his lips and chin.

His hands slide down my back to rub over my ass and I press into his touch, the slight movement earning me another stab of his tongue into my core.

Smack.

"You can't do this." I hear myself say but the man isn't listening. Dark hair has fallen over his forehead, making him look wild, untamed. A hungry beast and I'm all he craves.

"Quiet, *malyshka*. Since I am the one paying for the damage you caused, it's only fair I take my payment."

Yet another smack comes down on my ass cheek. This time the other side.

God, what's happening to me? I let out a low groan and struggle against the hand holding me down. "Ares! Stop," I plea, but do I really want him to stop?

Lights from passing cars touch on us briefly before moving on.

"Let me hear it, *malyshka*."

I don't realize I'm moving, rocking my hips over his face. But I do and I'm so close. The fire lit inside me will either burn me alive or release inside and consume my body and soul. Either way I'll never be the same. My knees tremble and my legs turn weak as ribbon as the climax he's stoked explodes through me.

"Bad girl, *malyshka*. I didn't tell you to come." His hands run up my back and he buries his fist into my hair, pulls my mouth around and claims a kiss. I can feel every inch of his hard cock pressed against my ass and rock my hips seeking more of everything he is making me feel.

He takes the kiss deeper. Hungry and greedy he takes and takes. His muscles ripple over the top of me and the second I try to take a little control back I get my just reward.

Smack.

I stiffen under the blaze of heat searing across my skin. And the returning pleasure sending messages to my still quacking core. "More," I beg.

"So pretty. Say it again."

"More, Ares…more," I whisper quietly.

Lips press to the shell of my ear. He's holding my hair back and inside for the first time in my adult life I don't feel a rising panic at a man fisting the long locks. I actually enjoy it.

"Tell me who you belong to. Tell me you trust me with your body."

"Yes," I whisper and part of me actually believes it. He could have easily let me die tonight. But he protected me. Shielded my life with his own.

"Now all I have to win is your heart." I hear him say softly over my moans.

To my embarrassment, the hot liquid spilling for him to savor like a starved man reveals I'm more than turned on.

He's back to eating me, teasing my pussy with his tongue while he thrusts his thumb in and out of my ass. Swirling, tasting, claiming.

Through the dimness, I see the anger he keeps in check hovering just below the surface. The finely chiseled muscles of his body contract and ripple as he shrugs out of his vest and hangs it on the handlebars. His shirt, another Henley, hugs his bulging muscles. He's a walking wet dream and it's me he's taking. Me he wants. As I tumble closer to the edge of my release, I realize he might have bought me, paid money for my body, but he won't be happy until he owns my heart, body and soul. He's an all-or-nothing kind of man.

But can I do that? Can I give him what he wants and still keep my promise to myself? My life, my death. My way? I truly don't think it's possible.

I hear the sound of a zipper lowering and a treacherous wave of heat washes through me. The padded edge of the bike's seat keeps my ass in perfect alignment with him as he spreads my dripping folds with the head of his cock.

"Fuck, *malyshka*, you're burning up. So fucking hot."

I don't get to see his cock before he's taking me hard and fast. But I can feel him just fine. The swollen head of his cock stretches me wide and prepares me for the full girth of his erection as he tunnels into me.

The night edges away and becomes a distant thought. My focus zeroes in on the hot blade thrusting into me. The burn of his hands holding my ass wide and the hot juices of my sticky pussy spilling down to wet my thighs and panties.

I claw at leather. "Ares," I groan. He drags out, drives home, and the bike rocks beneath me from the powerful force of his thrust. Eyes wide and mouth gaping open I cry out with anguished pleasure. Fingers of pain rake through me and in their burning wake searing euphoria fills me to overflowing.

Consumed. Utterly and wholly consumed. That is what this man does to me.

Angry energy swirls around the man. It's so thick I can practically breathe it in, taste it. Radiating rage, the Russian god of war craves payment and he's taking it with every stroke, every slap on my ass.

Arousal sends another pool of hot liquid to spill over his cock. My walls clench, and I can do little more than gasp and struggle with the net of tangled emotions weighing me down.

"You fucking love taking every thick inch of my cock. Maybe you slashed those tires knowing I would fuck you harder."

Lies. Risking shifting my focus from balancing over top of the bike, I peer over my shoulder to see he's sadly still fully dressed.

Dominating. Powerful. Hungry. Tonight scared him as much as it did me. I guess I learned something about my captor. He doesn't like the control being taken away from him and I did that tonight. Now he'll take it back by any means necessary starting with my body.

"Sdavaisya. Surrender to me, Nova. Give me what I want."

Inch by inch Ares stretches the tight ring of muscles of my ass, working me there as he fucks my tight pussy. My inner walls clamp around him, suck him deeper and he gives me what I want.

Any thoughts of what went down at Jacob's tonight drift to the back of my mind as he dominates my body and I willingly give him what he wants. "Let me hear you like taking my cock."

Yes! More!

"You think highly of yourself," I retort to the feel of another smack on my ass. "Arrogant and possessive."

"Mouthy and compulsive."

Ares withdraws, teases my entrance, and growls in what sounds like appreciation of the juices dripping all over him.

"Da, you fucking love taking my cock. Just like your ass will." Gripping my cheeks open, the tips of both thumbs ease into my back entrance. Slow. Oh my God, ever so slowly.

"Your body tells me everything I need to know." He grinds his thick cock deeper inside me and instead of telling him how good it feels, I show him.

I clamp down around him and shimmy my hips.

He roars an animalistic sound, causing me to shiver. Leaning his weight over me, Ares fucks me harder and faster until I think we'll either fall over or he'll break me in two. I clamor for purchase but there's nothing to grab but the leather seat under me.

"Yes, Ares," I moan eagerly.

"That's it, give me everything," he soothes in a low, husky tone.

And through it all the infuriating man continues to finger my ass. Stretch me, take me where no man has ever touched me.

"You torture me every second you draw breath and now I'm going to fuck you until your body knows nothing but my touch. I'll ruin you a little every day for any other man stupid enough to try and take you from me."

Another man? God, if I survive the days I have left with this man I'll never want anyone else between my legs again. Ares ruined me the second he cuffed me to his bed. A truth I will take to my grave.

"Come for me, *krasivaya*. Give it to me, beautiful. Push into me as I take you. Just like that. Fuck, yes!"

Ferocious fire swarms to life in my core and no other climax in my life compares to the one slamming into me with so much heat it knocks the wind from my lungs.

My Russian fucks me until everything is a blur of pleasure and pain. I welcome it, crave it even.

Ares wraps an arm around my waist and feeds my greedy pussy every inch of his throbbing cock. His balls slap my clit, sending me soaring through the shockwaves of my climax. Nothing can muffle my screams and cries. Honestly, I don't think Ares cares any more than I do about anyone hearing us in the middle of nowhere.

He's too busy roaring through his own release as his cock pulses deep inside me, his seed spilling into my unprotected womb.

Fourteen
Nova

Ten minutes later I'm settled on the back of Ares' bike and welcome the sting of cold air against my cheeks. We glide down the road toward his compound. Miles of unremarkable scenery blurs by us. Only the ache of pain in my gut has my attention. This is why I don't have friends. Give a person the chance to betray you and they will. It's only a matter of time and opportunity.

And the fact Ares' milk coats my womb. I haven't taken my pill this month. Which, hello, is another byproduct of my current situation. The first time he took me we used a condom, but this time neither of us thought of it. I can't think about what this might mean or why something so important never occurred to me.

I get that tonight by the riverbank was for me, but it was also for him. Ares doesn't like not having full control and he wanted it back. All the while demanding I surrender to him.

Sdavaisya. Surrender. Even the word sounds sensual.

But now that my body has cooled the nightmares pry their way back in before I get a chance to weld shut the hatch. I tighten my arms around Ares and duck behind him to cut the worst of the frigid wind. He settles a large hand over mine where I have it on his abdomen. Pesky fantasies of a life like this, him my shield against the harshness life brings, and me always at his side tickle the back of my mind. I let them. Because tomorrow they will be nothing more than dreams unfulfilled.

We ride this way and miles of silence pass unnoticed.

Beneath me, the vibrations of the bike lure me deep into thought. All I can hear is the sound of a bullet sinking into Jacob's head and then his lifeless body falling at my feet.

And feeling nothing as his lifeblood pooled at my feet. Nothing but gratitude for ridding this world of someone like him and all the goons inside who helped him. If that makes me a bad person, so be it, but I can't help but sigh with relief. No one else will suffer at his hands.

"Look at me."

I don't realize the bike is not moving and we are parked outside the compound until Ares' warm hand settles over my cool cheeks.

"Eyes on me," he commands in a soft, firm tone. He has his vest on again and it fits snugly around his chest. The sleeves to his shirt are forced up his thick forearms revealing a deep tan. I notice the time. It's almost sunrise. We've been out all night and all there is to show for it is violence. And time with Ares that pesky voice chimes up again in my head. Time with the man who stepped up and saved my ass.

I obey letting the tears fall unashamed down my cheeks. He brushes them away with his thumbs before pressing his forehead to mine. The fact his powerful hands on me settle the twitching of my nerves doesn't go unnoticed. And how his scent—spring air and an immeasurable sense of power—do the same. I don't know how else to consider it. Not like either really has a smell, but he embodies both all the same and it makes him who he is.

"You want to help your sister, but I need to know you're ready to do this my way. No questions, Nova. No more running off. You got your revenge. I need to hear you say it. That you will obey me." His words brush over me softly but leave me, scraping along my nerves like sandpaper.

I throw his hands off my face and put distance between us. "Just because you can give me a few orgasms faster than light travels doesn't mean I am your pawn. Big deal, no different from any other man out there. None of it means I have to be happy about it or fall at your feet like an obedient dog."

He stalks forward until I'm bowing over his bike, his nose touching mine. "No other man has made you feel the way I do. Don't lie." Furious forged steel holds me in place. "You'll learn my word is law. The easy way or the hard way. Your choice."

My chin nearly hits my chest. "Or what, Russian? You'll cuff me again? Leave me a spasming mess on your bed every time I do something you don't agree with to control me? Is that what happened tonight. I don't live my life to make others happy so you can keep your '*my way or no way*'. Hard freaking pass, Russian. I don't do good with ultimatums. Tonight wasn't revenge for me."

"Then what was it?"

"About getting information. Finding Polaris. What they plan on doing to her. Taking her? Something. All you seem to do is party and ride." I gesture to the bike.

"I have my in. I'm working on it. And I wasn't issuing an ultimatum. This happens my way. There are no other options." His lips press into a fine line of finality and oh, no. I'm not about to leave it there.

"And for the record," I jab his slab of stone for a chest with a finger. "Nothing but a black hole of regret lives in my stomach, Ares whatever your last name is. I can't believe I've fucked you twice now and don't even know your last name. Let you take me bareback. What was I thinking? And to top it all off you probably know everything there is to know about me."

It's not like a blaring siren but my admission stuns him a little. The twitch of his eyebrow quirks up and that infamous smirk of his dims. "You're not on the pill?"

"Since I've had zero control over my life, that's right."

"We'll fix that. I'll make sure you have what you need."

"You could just let me leave, forget about me."

In the middle of the freaking driveway his eyes narrow on me. "Never," he husks. He straightens to his full height. The movement puts enough space between us that I can finally breathe a little more freely. When he looms over me like before it's like my brain shuts off.

"And what if I'm pregnant? Will you just toss me away then? Maybe I should wish for it just so I can be rid of you."

"You think you'll have a little monster? Is that what you regret? You fear?"

"I've only seen the monster in you. What else do I know?" My cheeks flame with anger and embarrassment. I've given him more of myself than I have any other man. And I did it willingly. What does that say about me?

"You want a name and some backstory? Is that all it will take for you to finally trust me?" His accent grows deeper. Moonlight illuminates his beautiful eyes and reflects in the silvery pools...hurt?

"No, but it's a good start."

It quickly passes and his face is back in front of mine and his voice drops a few degrees to downright chilly. "Be careful what you ask for, Nova Masters; you might get it. I *am* a monster. I bring death because I come from death. You better remember that. I am not a man who can give you family and some pretty life your neighbors will envy. But you're mine now and you'll have to live with that."

"But you give all these people that and more. Maybe not something pretty and perfect, but you give them a place to belong." I didn't mean to say that. But now that it is out there the energy between us shifts from thundering anger to something more intimate. And dangerous. Or at least it is for me. I'm standing on the cusp of something changing between us and if I am not careful I might fall into this Russian's web never to leave.

"And yet when you look at me all you see is—"

"This isn't about you. My life, my death. My way, Russian. You nor any other man will ever take that from me." I cut him off before he can put words into my mouth. "You stole something from me tonight. I wanted Jacob to pay for what he did and you took that from me." I feel the warm wetness of a tear slip down my face. I scrub it away with the back of my hand, angry my emotions are all over the place.

"I saved you from committing a bigger mistake than leaving me in the middle of the night, *malyshka*." His voice is tight. Controlled. But when he utters that one word it's the bomb inside me going off and leaves the anger in me partially deflated.

"Stop calling me that. I'm not yours. And I'm not some perfect doll to put on a pedestal. I thought he was my friend. And then I wanted to put a bullet in Jacob's head myself. I'm the monster, Ares. Me. What's wrong with me?" I can't stop the tears from falling down my face.

"You took that away from me."

His arms come around me and I'm swallowed by his larger body. "I saved you from the nightmares, *malyshka*. You don't have to believe me now, but one day you will. You never want to be the one behind the trigger."

"You do." I force myself to hold his powerful gaze. "You pull that trigger. Why can't I?"

"For the same reason you are crying in my arms. You are too sweet a soul to tarnish it for a man who doesn't deserve your angelic heart. We are very different. *Ty svet tam, gde ya t'ma.*"

"What?"

He pulls back and peers down at me and for a moment, it feels as though our souls connect on some primal level.

"You are light where I am darkness." His hooded gaze flicks over my flushed face. His lips find mine and I savor the taste of his tongue brushing over mine.

He breaks the kiss and takes in all of me with a sweeping gaze. My nipples stand stiff against the fabric of his shirt contrary to my will. It's his rumbling voice and the heat of his body as he closes the little space we have between us.

"I am an unholy bastard. Remember that."

"True. But that doesn't change my mind."

I don't know where these words are coming from. But I keep vomiting things I shouldn't be saying. "Ares, you need to remember something too. Given a chance, I'll do it again. No one controls me. No one." I hear the lies spilling from my lips. I mean, come on. What happened by the lake can't exactly be forgotten. He took control over me and I handed it to him with no questions asked. And it felt good.

He jerks his head in a nod. "Noted."

Unforgiving fingers lock around my wrist and I'm dragged back into my prison with my captor leading the way.

And this time he's leading me to the basement instead of the stairs that lead to his bedroom. There's no music, groupie sex, or smell of liquor when he pulls me past the foyer, living room, and down the hallway in the direction I've seen him use that lead to lower levels and God knows what is down there.

"What are you doing? Where are you taking me?"

"Seems actions are all you hear so I'm going to show you my way is the only way."

Damn it.

"But first, you need to eat something."

We pass the basement door I've seen him go through a few times now and head straight for the kitchen.

The hallway dead ends where the kitchen begins. There's a large center island with several stools pulled up under the white marble ledge. Gold glints in the morning sunlight throughout the entire thing big enough to fit a feast. Behind it is a large window, its panes fogged over from the morning chill. Beyond are rolling hills of trees covered in a layer of cottony fog.

Avery is there and the way the morning rays of early light catch in her soft eyes makes her appear every bit the morning person I can only dream of being. There's a reason I went into hacking and a lot of it had to do with never wanting a boss lording over me. And the other reason is I got to pick my own hours which mimic that of vampires. Plus I can type code blind on three cups of coffee and two hours of sleep.

She sets her phone on the counter when she sees us enter.

"The crew get back yet, Avery?" Ares' voice is gruffer than the hours-old stubble along his jaw. As if I need a reminder, my body jumps in at that moment and sends me memos of what the burn from that beard feels like against the tender flesh of my thighs.

That's right. Everyone is out cleaning up my mess. But was it really mine? Or did I push Ares to act? I don't really know. But I wonder what the hell has him stalling. I mull over these questions one at a time, their taste leaving a bitter aftertaste.

His hands are still on me. But instead of gripping my wrist, he's drawn his touch around my middle. The heat of his palm against my abdomen feels possessive. And I won't lie, the way his thumb tucks inside the band of my jeans feels nice. A less jaded version of myself would think he's trying to tell me I belong to him. But I'm more of a realist. He's happy with the way my body makes his feel. Nothing deeper than that. The heart will get on board with that idea as soon as it stops trying to beat a hole through my chest.

I pull a barstool out and he comes to stand behind me, my ever-present protector or prison guard I haven't decided on yet.

Cautiously I ask, "Do you know if anyone got hurt? Devil took a nasty blade to the shoulder. He looked okay, but…" Because of me, I want to say but I leave that out.

"Devil will be fine." Cut and dry. I purse my lips, debating whether or not I should push the topic. Not like Devil is my responsibility but the man was there because of me and protecting me.

"If you say so. Maybe we should check on him."

"He'll report in when he's ready."

Case closed?

Yeah. Not for me.

"He took that blade for me."

The only sign Ares is even the tiniest bit worried about his friend is the slight tensing of his jaw and his chest rising with a deeper breath than normal. Or he could just be irritated with me.

"Da."

That one-syllable word cuts. But it seals my lips.

With a hip pressed against the counter's edge, Avery smiles up at Ares like he's a freaking god or something and a hushed voice in my head agrees. Stupid voice. We both look like we passed through hell on the way home. Gunpowder clings to us and there's more than soot and dirt mixed with blood down the front of my shirt. But Avery doesn't seem to notice. He's got something smeared along the underside of his jaw and his vest took a nasty blade. In the light of the kitchen, I can see the razor-fine cut that would have left something brutal over his right pec and down his abdomen if not for the thick leather. I trace the pad of my finger over it. Had he died because of me…I can't really follow that line of thinking. Not because of where it leads, but more so of not knowing where it would leave me. Ares has done a lot to me and I'm beginning to think it's not all bad.

He brushes my hair over my shoulder and I once again fail to realize it hangs over my shoulders and down my back. Normally it'd have it tied back but the agonizing panic attacks I get from having it hang around me don't come.

I turn back to Avery. Her shiny blonde hair is pulled back in an over-the-shoulder braid that makes her look younger than her twenty years. Her shirt is a little too snug and her jeans a little too low on her hips. The look fits her sweet innocent demeanor perfectly. Like a naughty librarian with sex appeal.

Innocent and fuckable. The same weakness my sister has. I consider Avery. She'll be a perfect lover to a lucky bastard one day. I can't help but think her submissive demeanor is what brought the attention of the Russian twins in the first place. Breaking someone like her must appeal to people like them and a trait they can sell like ice water on a hot day. My stomach churns. That she is still smiling proves the girl is stronger than she looks.

"No one has reported in yet, sir," Avery answers shyly. "I've made some coffee for everyone. They called Bear when they couldn't get a hold of you. Said they wouldn't be long. Can I get you a cup?"

"Lost my phone at some point this evening." Ares pats his pockets to double-check.

She turns bright eyes on me and bless her sweet innocent soul; this woman is going to learn the hard way being nice gets you kicked in the teeth the second she pushes to her feet. How has she not learned this yet with all she's been through? My heart falls back to someone else as sweet and innocent as Avery. My sister.

What feels like razorblades slice at my insides. The pain of Polaris still stuck in that horror show of a place leeches any sense of calm from me. I throw on a fake smile for Avery's sake. She doesn't need burdening with my problems when she has her own to deal with. "I'd love some coffee. Thank you. Can I get it in the biggest mug you have, please?"

The more I tool over the thought, I think I can see how this woman can still smile. The same way my sister has maintained a wall between her and all the nasty shit that has happened to her. If she didn't, there would be nothing left to salvage. A new respect for sweet Avery blooms as I watch her pour two fresh mugs of hot brew and pass them to us.

Ares takes his mug and raises it in salute. "Thank you, Avery. You've been a big help."

"Welcome, sir." She tongues the simple gold band of a lip piercing, the one small detail that tells me she has a little wild behind all that sweetness.

He turns the full weight of his attention on me and thoughts of sweet and innocent drop away. Shimmering silver mesmerizes me. "When you finish breakfast, come find me downstairs. I'll be waiting. Don't be long, *malyshka.*"

I wonder if everyone jumps when he gives an order. I shake my head. This Russian. One minute he'd look good on a morgue slab from my doing and the next I can't see him any other way than lording over me with those bedroom eyes. I hold zero fantasies that this man does anything he doesn't want to do, so the idea he wants me, a complete nobody, leaves me wondering what I have that interests him.

For a second I almost ask him, but I don't think I want to know the answer. Besides, would it matter? Not really. I'm here until my sister is back at my side or until I find another way to get her out of that hell hole. I'm not cut out for midnight shootouts, bike rides, wild riverside sex and dominating Russians. I can only kid myself for so long. I am not as strong as I look.

Chills I should not be feeling tingle their way down my spine and hit home when he leans in and presses a kiss to the shell of my ear.

His firm lips part and the cool gaze of his turns smoky. "What is churning behind those pretty eyes?" When I don't answer and decide it is a better idea to bite my lower lip instead, he brushes the back of his knuckles down the side of my face and considers me. "You need to work on your trust. If I ever take you anywhere it's never to lock you up again. That is a promise."

That is not where my thoughts are but now that he mentions it, the same question of what he wants with me comes back to perch on the tip of my tongue. But I swallow it down. I don't know how much of his truth I can handle in one evening. Bodies, cleaning crews. Mansions, expensive cars. The little bit I know of him tells me he'll answer with actions instead of words and right now I can't sit without feeling his last *action* on my ass and between my legs.

I watch his retreating back and wait until he's gone before I turn to Avery who has her coffee balanced at her lips and her eyes drinking in everything.

I clear my throat. "Sorry 'bout that."

"Watching him with you is fascinating. Men like him don't normally take a moment to reassure their women. They take what they want, leave the empty, used husk for someone else to clean up." Haunting words to match the distant look in her eyes. "I begged him to buy me. To save me. I didn't think he would but he did. I'll never have a harsh word for a man who was willing to buy my freedom and then give me a home. Treat me like another human being."

I understand her fierce loyalty now and know the admiration in her eyes for Ares is not attraction but undying loyalty.

I reach across and take her hand, giving it a light squeeze. Color floods her face. "I'm sorry for what you've gone through."

"Don't take this the wrong way." She worries her lips for a few seconds and then blurts something out that has me reevaluating every second of the last week of my life.

"If you hadn't been kidnapped and put up for auction I would still be their prisoner. Their whore put up as a piece of meat. I'm grateful you were there and even more grateful someone like Ares was there that night."

My whole world grinds to a halt. How do I respond to that? Yeah me too? Not really. Those words would be a lie. I swallow a thick ball of confusion, doubt, worry, and fear.

I nod slowly and squeeze her hand. A knowing look passes between us and I focus on more neutral territory. "Have you watched the news?"

She grabs a plate and pushes fresh eggs, bacon, and toast in front of me with a soft knowing smile. "No, why?"

I shake my head, not really wanting to go over the events. A headache settles right behind my eyes. Thinking about all the death and blood is bad enough; talking about it seems impossible.

We sit in silence for the time it takes me to drink two mugs of coffee. I focus on regaining my strength for whatever Ares has planned down in the basement.

I'm almost done when I see Avery prepare a second plate and pour another mug of coffee. From under the counter, she pulls a serving tray and loads it up, adding on a glass of orange juice and a few extra strips of bacon.

"For Ares?"

She nods and arranges the butter closer to the toast.

"Do you see him with any of the girls here?" I ask, holding my breath.

Wide eyes meet mine and her tongue swishes that piercing over the middle of her bottom lip from side to side. "You mean the club candy?"

I guess that's what you call them? "Yeah?" I know I have no right to be asking, but I have to know.

She stares at me for a second like I've lost my mind. Crazy thing is, I kinda feel I have.

She sweeps her eyes over the kitchen and then leans her elbows on the countertop. Those pretty eyes filled with curiosity. "I have a better question. Have you? Because I haven't. I mean, besides you." Her voice grows quiet.

I stow away my fake smile and pull on something a bit more genuine. I can see her and my sister becoming best friends. Something about Avery makes me feel relaxed and right now, that's a gift I hold close to the chest. Her eyes pin over the kitchen island and I follow her line of sight.

Ohhh...and suddenly I realize the blushing pink on her cheeks isn't for her puppy crush for the club's president but for another man entirely.

"Riot." I raise my mug of steamy coffee and he throws me a playful wink. He strolls through the wide arched entryway and then locks eyes with Avery. He looks wild and unchained. *Like he just went through a brawl that could have ended his life, Nova.*

I catch a hint of blood he missed on the underside of his chin in an obvious rush cleanup job. Seeing me watching he heads straight for the coffeepot, but not before I see him notice that lip piercing.

"Avery."

He uses the same tone on her that Ares uses on me. But I keep my lips sealed and stand back, coffee raised.

Instead of answering Avery dips her head and rearranges the tray of food like it all moved on its own in the last ten seconds. Well, isn't this interesting? The quiet, shy act is Riot's kryptonite. Only one other man on this planet can go from cool and calm to ravenous faster than Ares and he is not in the room. Avery better be careful. Her lion looks hungry.

Riot's shoulders rise and fall with a deep breath. Shadowed creases around his eyes and scruff covering his jaw tell me his night didn't go as smoothly as mine. Guilt fills me. Though he's cleaned up and changed his shirt, the scent of smoke and gunpowder cling to him.

I dig deep for some courage and step up to him. I give Avery a quick smile of reassurance and lower my voice. "Very few people have ever stood up for me. Protected me. Thank you."

I'm standing beside him and holding my mug out for a refill. He obliges.

Eyes the color of crushed citrine swing my way. "You're the prez's girl. What he protects, we protect. You take one; you get us all, sweetheart." He moves off and Avery's gaze follows his large hulking form until he's out of the kitchen.

"What was that about?" Avery scoots in, eyes on Riot's retreating back.

"I did something stupid last night and the crew stepped in and rescued my ass."

"I doubt you did anything stupid."

"I don't think Ares would agree. You know my sister is still there. I found the men who pointed the Volkovs at us. But I didn't know that until I stepped into the lion's den."

I didn't think Avery had an angry bone in her body but at the mention of the Russian brothers, her eyes turn a shade of murder that makes her look lethal.

I place a hand over hers where she grips the side of the counter. I guess I found a trigger. "If you need to talk, you know you can come to find me, right?" I offer. She turns pale and I can feel her fingers tremble beneath mine. "What happened to them? I mean the people who sold you."

She won't meet my eyes, but keeps them pinned to the last place Riot stood. I don't want to answer the question, but maybe knowing there is one less person out there hurting others will help her find some form of inner peace. "Ares took care of him. He won't be hurting anyone."

I see her shoulders visibly relax. I take the tray she prepared. "This is for Ares?"

"Yeah."

"Tell you what. I've got this. Why don't you follow Riot and see if he needs anything? He's had a rough night. We all have." I don't know how much club business Ares and his crew share with the others living in the compound so I limit the amount of information I offer up to the bare minimum.

235

Her shocked eyes tell me she'd not meant to reveal her attraction to one of Ares' crewmembers.

"Yeah, no thank you."

Playing matchmaker isn't something I normally do. Hell, making friends never hit my radar except with Ellie. She kind of stumbled into me one night while out making a late run for ice cream and rum. An odd combination I didn't think another soul liked but myself.

Turns out there were two of us. After moving to New York City I figured making a few friends would be nice. Look where that got her. But Avery and I share a horrible, unique circumstance and she looks like she could use a friend. I wrap an arm around her shoulder and rub the side of her arm.

"Take it from me; tomorrow is not a given. I think you know that. Riot seems nice and I think we could both use a little of that in our lives."

"There's no way he'll see me as anything other than used."

The sadness in her eyes kills me and I have another reason to want to see the Volkovs rotting in hell. I leave her with one parting food for thought. "How do you know unless you try?"

Out of the corner of my eye I notice a familiar leather jacket and jeans in the same shade of midnight black. The man wearing them strolls through the side kitchen door and shoots straight for the stairs Ares took a few minutes ago. I blink and the tray of food is an afterthought abandoned on the counter.

I don't remember moving. Just the feel of the soundless carpet underfoot and then I do something I've never done before. My arm goes around a thick throat and tightens until I hear a gasp.

I'm not this girl. The kind who goes around randomly attacking people, but I've had my eyes opened tonight and I've learned something—move first and take the upper hand. It's the only way to survive.

I'm swung left and then right. The room whirls and several sets of eyes are on me. Us. The man I'm choking turns a pretty shade of red and the surprise on everyone's face is priceless. Why the hell aren't any of them doing anything?

Hands grip my waist while another set pries my vise grip chokehold open. I'm plucked from the intruder's back and deposited on the floor.

"I thought I recognized you last night!"

Ares is a wall between us but I push him to the side. Or try to. A bulldozer would be easier to nudge a few yards than him. No matter. "What did you do with her? Where is her body? Tell me!" Ares' knife is in my back pocket and I surprise even myself with my quick reflexes. I point the tip at the man's chest. "You won't be taking me again."

I turn my wrath on Ares. "And you, you have five seconds to tell me why Volkov's man is standing in the middle of your man cave." I look around and figure it's the best way to describe the dark furniture, large-screen TV, and bar. The only thing that doesn't fit is the large conference table.

Tight lines etch the corners of Ares' mouth before he speaks. "Nova, meet Dragon. He's not Volkov's; he's mine. A Savage son."

Didn't see that coming. "Oh." Shit. "I see."

Dragon eyes the blade and flicks the end. "Word is you're pretty wicked with that thing."

"When I need to be."

He looks bemused. Sitting around the same age as Ares, I pin Dragon to be hitting close to forty. Late thirties at least. Like Ares, this man has no dusting of gray, but age shows itself in different ways. For Ares, it's in the way he carries himself. Confidence, experience, and power speak of his time on this earth.

For Dragon, it's in the way he stands. The angle of his gaze when he considers you. You know he's seen shit and done more. Darkness sits around him. One rivaled only by Ares'.

"Good, next time, strike first and *then* ask all your questions *if* the guy is still breathing."

I stand there for a moment reassessing my actions and the information I'd just been given. He has access to my sister. I don't know how, but I just know. "You guys like to give out a lot of fighting tips."

I turn to Ares this time, the knife back in my pocket. "You have an inside guy?"

A black eyebrow raises. He winds an arm around me and pulls me with him to the head of the table and onto his lap. "Have for several months now. Dragon is Savage blood. You can trust him. He's the one watching over your sister."

Bingo. I like being right.

Having my suspicion confirmed does nothing for my nerves. Of course, that could be because I forewent all the rules of being a lady and just tackled an unarmed man.

Even though they are freshly showered, all of them look like they could use food, a stiff drink, and about two days of sleep.

Rage. Riot. Devil. I look at each of them. They've been through hell.

"Why didn't you tell me this before? Before last night? I would have... Devil wouldn't have been hurt." His arm is in a sling and his bandage needs changing. Blood seeps through to stain his pullover.

He rubs a hand over his damp hair. "Don't worry about me. I'll live." Pain pulls his face into a grimace but he does a good job hiding it behind the rim of a coffee mug.

"See Doc after this."

Devil nods. "Already called him, Prez."

Ares moves the hair from my face. It hangs in abandoned tufts.

"You don't need to worry about us. And I doubt anything I ever tell you will sway your decision, but we've seen worse." Ares' expression tells me he believes his words.

Staring around the room I say, "You all sacrificed so much for me last night. And you almost died. Or at least could have been killed."

Devil scoffs. "Last night was a warm-up for what's coming. It had to happen. You take way too much on your shoulders. This is not on you."

"You just moved our timetable up is all," Riot adds on to Devil's words.

"Still thank you. I'll try not to do that again, but no promises." I figure I better keep it real with the plan percolating in the back of my head.

Ares addresses everyone. "Speaking of, we almost had our asses handed to us. We need more muscle. More men. We've been holding off patching in new blood. Tonight that changes."

"What about the law?"

"Forget the law. They can't do shit."

It's apparent I know nothing of how these men operate and I'm in way over my head. Besides I have something I need to do. I move to raise off Ares' lap but his arms buckle me in place. "You're the key player here. Without you, this won't work. You need to stay."

Ares looks to Rage who is changing his drink out for a large coffee. Black. "Call your brother. Did he get back from South America?"

Rage nods. "Last week."

"If he wants in, he has to pledge to the Sons and we'll patch him in."

Ares looks to Riot. "Your cousin is still interested?"

"Yes."

"Good. The same goes for him. He pledges with Rage's brother and they'll be part of the brotherhood for life. And that goes for anyone else who wants to be a Savage. We'll start patching them if they are willing to bleed for their brothers. But they'll need to understand one thing. My word is law. Nothing is done without my approval. We might not be with the law but we are not against it either."

"Understood, Prez."

It's scary but amazing to see how easily these men fall into line with their president. As if reading my mind, Ares turns to me.

"Like I said, the real power lies with you. These men are only as strong as their bank accounts. As soon as I receive notice of a large transfer I expect them to receive sometime today; we move. Lockdown their funds. They'll be scrambling thinking it's the Feds. That's when we move."

He's no longer talking to just me but everyone in the room. Now I understand the bigger picture and feel like an idiot for my actions.

"How will you know of their bank movements?"

"I have friends where I need them who feed me information."

Of course he does.

Riot turns to me. "You were down in the basement. You personally witnessed the number of guards they have. What are we up against? Did you hear them talking? Anything that might help."

Dragon scoffs, looking put out. And on a man of his size, it's almost commercial. "And what am I? Blind and deaf?"

Riot claps a hand over Dragon's shoulder. "I want to hear her take on it. Women are more perceptive and better at details."

That seems to shut Dragon up and all eyes turn on me. I take strength from the large arms around me and let the warmth of them ground me to the fact I am no longer in Volkov's basement holding cells being prepared for auction.

I close my eyes and conjure up my worst nightmare. "Those cells have two keys. The only way they are getting open and you are getting the girls out is with those keys. Total old school. No fancy biometric keypads. Guards work with similar guns to what Devil had last night. Everyone has them. From the ones guarding the girls to the ones standing just off the auction stage. They rotate them, too. I know because in the couple of hours I was there I saw three different guards rotate outside my door."

I pause, recalling what I heard while Dragon carried my friend's body off.

"I don't know how much you heard while the two idiots were talking. But they mentioned when you stepped out with…" My voice drops and I take a steadying breath.

"You don't have to do this, *malyshka*."

Ares moves to stand and do what I don't know? Carry me upstairs? Tuck me into bed like some shivering scared flower?

I place a hand on his freshly shaved cheek. "No. I do have to do this."

I turn to Dragon. "When you took Ellie away, they mentioned the Volkovs were selling a few other girls and me illegally." I hold a hand up. "Wait, that's not what I mean. The Volkovs, whoever is backing him, don't know they are selling some of the girls off and not giving them a cut. Beast

One and Beast Two, the guys who were in charge of making sure I was ready for the stage, have big mouths. If I recall they said: 'This is our city. Not theirs. Remember that.'

I hit pause and hold off sharing what came after that comment for when I have Ares alone again. Why they were so interested in Ares buying a girl left me with questions. Ones only he can answer so I don't see the point in asking them in front of the others.

"See, bet you didn't know that."

Dragon grunts but he doesn't argue Riot's point.

"How many women are left for the second auction?"

Dragon looks haunted at Rage's question when my eyes come to meet his. We both saw the horrors of the basement. Being one of those girls held behind those iron bars is a feeling I'll never shake. Escaping there was a miracle and a blessing. I realize that.

"There are far more now than there were a week ago, Prez." Everyone drops their weight in a chair looking as exhausted as I suddenly feel.

Except for Rage. He's pacing along the back wall, a cigarette hanging from his lips and a drink of something in his hand. Vodka it looks like because it sure the heck isn't water or the coffee he had earlier.

"There's five of us and a fucking army of them, *bratan*. We have to do better and we don't have long." He takes a long draw of his cigarette and releases the smoke slowly. I can visually see the tension in his body relax.

Ares grunts, nodding at Rage's words.

Dragon pulls something from the inside of his jacket and tosses a stack of something black and white down the length of the table. Not papers, but pictures I see.

"You said you wanted some faces and names. I got one of the two. They don't let me get too close to the suits coming and going. But I set up trail cams they haven't found yet. Got these of people visiting Volkovs' mansion."

Ares scoops them up, shuffling through them, but pauses on one. It's a blurry picture with a man partially facing away. I can't tell who it is, but it seems Ares can. The set of his mouth and the deepness of the crease along his forehead read like a signpost.

"Who is that?" I ask unevenly. His eyes turn glassy and death looks like it steals over his tight expression. Gaze unmoving, he says something in Russian before turning to Rage, ignoring my question completely.

Dragon finishes his coffee and moves like he's about to leave. "You need to know the brothers are getting restless. Be prepared to move fast when I call. The auction could be anytime. That stunt you pulled last night spooked them. About an hour after everything went down a man showed up telling them everything. Your girl's description was on his lips which put your name on theirs." Dragon scrapes a hand over his face. "They've moved the auction up to tonight."

"I'll confirm with the Genesis men."

Ares.

"No need, I was in the room when they made the calls."

Ares nods.

My heart is pounding. "And my sister?"

Dragon is on his feet at the end of the table. Hands with scarred knuckles grip the back of a chair. Years of fighting are evident. Each white and pink puckered scar tells me this man has never had it easy. Dark eyes pierce mine. "Your sister is alive. I can give you that much. They've had me out of the compound doing scout work so I don't know where they are holding her, just that she is still at their compound."

Beneath me Ares stiffens like he's afraid of what Dragon is going to say next. Something he already knows and I don't. I'm learning fast how to read the man which is a plus if it didn't scare me in every way possible.

"What aren't you telling me?"

Ares releases a sigh. "Tell her."

I brace myself and don't realize my nails are digging into Ares' forearm until he pries them off and wraps his hands around mine.

"She's been hurt in other ways, Nova. I'm sorry. They are putting her through submissive training. And not the kind you'll find at one of these fashion clubs where the sub gets safe words. This is hardcore abusive shit. Mainly verbal because they don't want to mark the merchandise physically. They are withholding food and other amenities if she fights."

"She is strong."

"Not as strong as you."

"I was always there to fight for her."

"When you see her again, she won't be the same person you remember."

I'm utterly, painfully speechless.

Blades of regret and panic pierce my heart. The girl's life has been kicked and stomped on since birth. First with shitty parents who went and died. If they weren't bad enough then we were passed to an uncle who saw us both as fodder for his midnight cravings and now. When the hell were we due for our break in life?

I shut my brain down before it leaves me a puddle of tears and regret.

Death, blood…this whole new world is nothing but betrayal and a fight for power—anyone who doesn't have it, wants it. And they'll use anyone to get it. One vicious cycle after another.

A world I want nothing to do with. I was purchased on the black market as a sex slave, for God's sake. I feel like my whole world has been flipped over and set on fire. And I can't do anything about it. I'm in a void and I feel like if I were to scream, the nothingness surrounding me would swallow it whole.

Dragon's phone buzzes with a message and seeing his face turn to stone in mere seconds has me on my feet.

"What is it?"

"I'm being called back. The brothers want to move the merchandise. Auction is canceled."

Clamps of dread restrict my breathing and I start to see stars behind my eyelids. I can't catch my breath.

"What?" This can't be happening. My sister will be sold off all because I couldn't sit still and wait for Ares. I had to move. I shake my head trying to dislodge the disgust and roaring anger. Going to Jacob's royally messed things up and now my sister will be shuffled into the underground trafficking rings. I'll never see her again.

Because Ares won't, I'm left with only one option. I know what I have to do. Only I don't know how.

Fifteen

Nova

Ohmygodwhatishappening screams through my head.

"Nova. Talk to me." Ares is out of the chair and standing beside me.

I don't realize I'm in the middle of a full-fledged panic attack until my head is shoved between my legs and the dots swirling behind my eyelids steal my vision.

A hand holds the back of my head between my knees and another is passing me a shot glass of vodka. Something cold presses across the back of my neck.

I close my eyes and focus on trying to get much-needed oxygen into my lungs.

Inhale. Wait. Exhale.

Inhale. Wait. Exhale.

"Get me the bottle." I hear Ares say.

Inhale.

His scent fills my senses. Lingering hints of the masculine scent of the soap he uses settles my nerves. How can a man I only just met do this to me? Have so much sway over my emotions? Nothing is clear as to why he cares for me. I have more questions than answers, that's for damn sure.

Exhale. His warm, gentle touch at the base of my back never leaves me. I use it to ground myself.

"My hair. Pull it back." I'm breathing heavily. Sweating. I can feel the raw clawing of the panic attack edging closer. "My hair. Please." I swat at my hair and struggle to pull it off my face. Off my shoulders. It's suffocating and I can't see. Walls of the dark basement edge closer, cutting off my air.

I struggle to get it off my face but Ares is there.

"Easy," he soothes. "Easy, Nova."

I am gasping with desperation. Nothing seems to be entering my lungs.

He takes my hair and pulls it back and I can finally breathe.

Finally.

The restricting bands looping around my chest ease and I draw a deep cooling breath. It rushes into my lungs and the burning subsides enough I don't feel like I'm about to die.

My eyes are closed and I don't try to sit up until my head stops spinning and the dots in front of my eyes fade from glowing orbs to dull pinpoints.

"I'll be outside if you need anything, Prez."

"*Spasibo brat.*"

A light touch settles on top of my head before it's gone and I'm left alone with Ares.

I sit up slowly. With my head still spinning I keep my eyes closed. "She's got to be so scared. She's never been alone in her life. I've always been right there from the day Mom and Dad brought her home."

"Tell me about her." He presses the glass to my lips and tips it so I can drink down the cool vodka. I welcome the chilled burn.

"What?" I cough.

I'm drawn into his lap. The basement is cleared out and it's just the two of us. I realize I must look like a mess. My hair is everywhere except where I want it to be—in my usually nice and neat ponytail away from my face. I brush it back and Ares wraps the lengths around his hand, holding it back for me. My clothes are filthy. Yet, he looks at me like I've just strutted my goods down a catwalk.

"Your sister. Talk to me, *malyshka*. Tell me about your sister."

My mouth agape, I stare at him. Both touched and skeptical. He's not exactly the gentlest lover and I've seen him put bullets in people. A gentle Ares is new to me. His tone takes on a calm nature. I can picture him luring his enemy in with it and then slaughtering them.

But I'm not the enemy here. At least I don't think I am. Am I being used? Or am I using him? I can't tell anymore.

"She's my exact opposite in every way. Black hair, tanned skin so pretty she always looks like she's just stepped off a beach. She gets that from our mother. She loves to dance, watch movies until the sun rises and despite this screwed-up world we live in she somehow sees the nice side of people. The only thing we share is the shade of our eyes and the love we have for each other. Because of being thrust into protection mode before I grew a pair of tits I've gotten so used to being the one making sure she had everything she needed."

"Parents?"

He pours another drink while I talk.

"Worthless. Mom died of a drug overdose in the backroom of a gambling house. That should tell you a lot about my upbringing."

There's a dark gleam in his eyes I am beginning to associate with death. He looks ready to commit murder on my behalf. I know nothing about him, yet I find myself spilling more information than I have to anyone else.

With that in mind, I lift my gaze to his. "My father followed her into an early grave a year later. Death by cop. He was moving narcotics for a group in California. He always told our mom he'd never see the inside of a cell. As a kid, I didn't understand that."

I look away. Every second I open my mouth the closer I get to a reality I do not want to talk about.

"It wasn't all bad," I continue, changing directions. "Mom and Dad always made sure we had food, a roof and I know they loved us in their own way. They never beat us. So that's something."

"You don't have to beat someone to abuse them."

That dark glint in his eye returns.

"Your scars," I say bluntly. Those marks crisscrossing his back is a story I want to hear.

He doesn't say anything. But he takes my hand in his and rubs the back of his thumb over the tips of my fingers.

Like I never spoke, he continues. "They never put your needs before their own." His jaw clenches, the jumping muscle twitching with what I assume is the same irritation sitting in my gut. "Had they, you would be with them right now. And not in my basement." A deadly silence descends over us and when his gaze pulls to mine I can't stop the chill running through me.

"They deserved to die for not protecting you."

I can't imagine what this man must have suffered through to make him think that way.

I don't touch that loaded statement and aim for more stable ground instead. "When they died Polaris and I went to live with our uncle in Montana. He had this beautiful three-story home on a beautiful ranch. Like this mansion, it had everything on the inside. Outside there were horses, cows, pups and my uncle's sweet wife was there too. I thought our luck turned around. Until a week after moving in he thought I would be payment for all his good deeds of taking in two burdensome orphans on the couch in the basement."

Ares releases a string of Russian. From the bite of his clipped tone, I may not understand the words but I feel them as if I do.

Strong fingers tighten around my wrist where he has his hand over mine.

I'm swiftly pulled onto his lap and his hands cup my face. I need sleep. I can feel its fingers dragging me down. But the simple feel of his heated touch on me has me wired.

"Go on."

"If he wasn't beating me, he was trying to take what he couldn't have. Fighting off a man three times my ten-year-old self isn't how I saw my life going."

Burning tears scorch my cheeks. Numbness steals over my body.

"When I would misbehave also known as fight him off from raping me, he would fist my hair, drag me through the house and lock me in the basement. She would do nothing but turn a blind eye. Twenty-three stairs lead into hell. I can't tell you how many times I counted them. A dirty, rat-infested place that only had one lightbulb and a chain in the back corner."

Goosebumps break out over my arms and my mind's eye fills with bad memories. The scent of musty dirt burns my nostrils. "He installed it just for me. The chain I mean. The only silver lining was whenever he threw me down there, he'd put my sister down there too."

"That's why you freak out when you're cuffed."

"And when forced into small places with locked doors. He refused to let me wear my hair any other way but down. He liked to pull it, control me."

"Yet you did not fear me when I did it."

My breath shudders from my lungs. "I know. I wish I understood why." But I leave it at that, the rest of my jumbled mess of feelings unpacked and stuffed into the dark corners of my mind.

"He's dead so there's that."

"Good. At this rate, I'd be killing off your entire family."

"Thank you." And this time I actually agree with him.

"You'll never have to face a horror like that again. You will never have to suffer at the hands of another man. I'm sorry, *malyshka*. Sorry I cannot kill a dead man for you. Sorry you ever have to be a part of this." He releases my hair and moves as if he wants to put distance between us.

I hate how easily he affects me. How my heart races the second he tries to put space between us. I hate needing him.

"No," I blurt. "No," I start again in a softer tone. "You don't scare me. I like it when you touch me." Fear of losing his touch or losing him sears through me hotter than lightning. "Please." I take his hand and twine our fingers together. I may not know the criminal I'm quickly falling for. But the man who plunked down money to save a sweet soul like Avery. That man I want to know. But I have a feeling the criminal life he lives is a package deal I'll have to accept as well.

I squash the panic that colors my cheeks. Embarrassing as it is.

"I like to hear you beg."

Surprise parts my mouth and his eyes fall to the tip of my tongue when I swipe it across my lips.

"Be careful, *malyshka*. Very careful. Unless fucking you right here and right now is what you want."

"You wouldn't." I'm torn between wanting to see how far he'll go right here, and right now. And hoping he's only teasing.

He drags the rough pad of his thumb over the path my tongue took; I watch mesmerized as he pops the button to my jeans and slides his hand inside.

I didn't think I could turn any redder, but he proves it's possible.

Flush with heat, I can only moan and accept the truth when he finds me wet. Thick fingers spread my tender folds and I gasp when he sinks two into my sheath. Heat flares and surprise drops my hands onto his shoulders. I watch the pulse point on the side of his neck throb in time with the one along his temple. Fear of being caught, fear of what he makes me feel. Fear of life after this is all over...all the above gels together to create mental quicksand for my emotions. I can step in and lose myself in this new world. Forget the fear. Or, I can skirt the edges, get just close enough I don't fall in yet enjoy the forbidden touches of this man. And keep my life when it comes time to leave New York behind me. And Ares only a memory.

I raise up and glide down Ares' fingers slowly. Hot, liquid silk spills to wet my folds and him.

"Good girl, *malyshka*. Good girl." His tone is pure alpha male—possessive, claiming. Unapologetic.

My pussy clenches.

So close, so fast.

The independent woman in me wants to slap those words off his lips, but the submissive side of me is the one who controls my hips. I buck and lean into his arms. He holds me close to him; our body heat all but melds together.

He gently pushes my legs wider over top of him and I ride him a little faster, seeking the pleasure and the praise. His eyes hold mine.

"Give me what I want. Let me have those juices. Give me what's mine," he orders.

For the life of me, I can't remember why I should be scared of the mafia man working my body with such expert precision.

Wickedness glides across his face in a smile. I can't look away.

My heart ignites into a flutter of anticipation. We're silent for a moment before he gruffs a question I suspected would come. "What changed? What made you Reina the hacker?"

He pulls me to straddle him and I gasp, feeling his arousal settle against my sex. Hot and hungry. Two layers of denim between us and I can feel the need seep through as if there is nothing between us.

"Ares?" He is what I don't need but crave. Wicked, wrong, and yet…

My core tightens with the ache to feel him stretching me with his thick girth.

"Shh, *malyshka*." For the barest span of a second when I look at him I perceive more than the criminal willing to kill for me. I see the alpha male ready to claim what he wants. And I'm the innocent woman caught in his sights.

He finds my throbbing clit and sets to teasing it furiously while his other hand tightens against my hip painfully. I love the burn, the emotions driving him to sink every last one of those fingers into my skin. It's what holds me to this moment and to him.

"Oh God, Ares!" I scream and find perfect bliss with one more thrust of his fingers. I cry out again and nearly splinter when shockwaves rake through me. He gives my clit another tender pat and pulls his hand free.

I look on as he lifts his fingers to his lips and cleans both of my juices. He growls his approval. I don't see it coming, but when his hand touches the back of my head and pulls me in I take the kiss. His tongue plunges inside and he takes what he wants, giving me the taste of my juices in return.

I savor the feeling of his tongue sweeping over mine. Our chests touch and with every inhalation, my beaded nipples scrape against the hardness of his pecs.

Mmm. Delicious.

Fingers clench the back of my head. He uses that handful of hair to control me. He breaks the kiss and pulls me back to trail hot nips and licks down the side of my neck. The fabric of his shirt bunches beneath my tight grip.

"Fucking delicious," he mutters over my skin and in the same breath says, *"Ty ne dolzhna byla byt takoy."* The brush of his lips, the hot path of his tongue over the places his teeth scrape send me reeling closer to another orgasm.

I don't know what he said but it sounds sensual.

"You were not supposed to be like this. So irresistible." His words are a murmured whisper I don't think I'm supposed to hear.

"Ares, please." I rake my fingers through his hair, tighten them around his thick locks. It's useless to try and control him. No one commands Ares. He does what he wants, how he wants.

I need to think straight. Telling him he shuts my brain down and my libido on isn't the smartest. Arming the criminal is always a bad idea.

His eyes burn with lust and wonder when he releases me and sits back. "Now continue. "

My eyes widen. "What? Now?" I shimmy my hips over his erection and remind him of the other half we need to attend to.

"*Da*, now."

"Um…" I try to stitch together my scattered thoughts and it takes me a minute. His hands busy themselves refastening my button.

"You're too tempting. The men will be back soon. You were telling me about your uncle. Continue."

I huff a humorless laugh, a shaky sound that reveals the state of my nerves. "When I turned seventeen my uncle tried to go after Polaris. I guess I was too big and strong. He liked them meek and defenseless. She was only eleven at the time. He fell asleep that night and I stood over him. A kitchen knife in my hand. I must have stayed there fifteen minutes willing myself to drive the knife through his cold, black shriveled up heart. Only a sniffling, crying Polaris grabbing my hand and pulling me out of the room stopped me. I didn't look back when I grabbed my sister and took off. That night I became the queen of my own life. Reina."

He's wrapped my arms around his neck and I drape my hands over his back.

The whole time I am speaking his mouth lingers over my pulse point. The one right below my ear and has me scraping my nails over his shoulders and back.

Beneath my fingers, I feel the signs of his own history. A past as scared and ugly as my own. Where mine are mental and emotional his are way worse.

"Tell me what these are."

He's silent long enough I feel he won't answer. "My father whipped me for protecting my mother from his wrath. His cane lashed into my back. I gladly took it."

We lock eyes and he doesn't move to stop me from fisting the ends of his shirt and pulling it over his head. Sitting shirtless in front of me I rub the palms of my hands over his flat abdomen, and heaven help me I can finally focus on appreciating his firm pecs without him tearing my attention away with an orgasm or kiss.

His skin is warm beneath my curious fingertips. His shoulders are made to spread a woman's thighs and I am tempted to lean forward, sink my teeth into all this delicious man meat.

But later.

Right now, I need to know the man Ares hides from everyone.

I peer over his shoulder. I've only gotten a glance of the scars when he briefly changed shirts in front of me. Up close I can see the ugly jagged edges where his skin tore and ripped under the punishing cane lashes.

"He did all this to you?" I fear his answer.

"Him. And my half-brothers. As the oldest, if I died, they inherited everything. They learned his cruelty from an early age."

"How old were you?"

"*Dvenadtsat.* Twelve. And spent the next five years plotting my escape from under his rule." Odd choice of words, but everyone is the king of their own domain, right. For a young boy and man, it must have felt like his world was ruled by a cruel dictator.

Any second he'll lockdown. I can already see the wall he keeps between him and his past erecting once again. Brick by brick he'll shut me off.

"Where is she now?" I ask quietly.

"Dead."

My stomach twists. His one word is void of warmth but cracked, shattered emotions knife through and break his voice.

"He killed her for loving me more than him."

I tighten my arms around him. "She was lucky to have such a wonderful son for the time you had each other. Did they catch him? Is he in prison?"

And just like that, the wall snaps in place. His expression zeroes to a blank mask with not even a fraction of emotions cracking through.

"Your sister." He shrugs on his shirt, covering those scars and effectively cutting the conversation.

"What about her?"

"You've been caring for her alone all this time?"

I nod. "Who else is there? Eight years. She's in college, a roof and food with decent clothing. I can't complain."

Wordlessly he lifts his head. I stare into his eyes. He's pissed. I can see it in the creases along his forehead and the flat line of his mouth. "And who is taking care of you?"

"I don't need anyone."

A peculiar look in his eyes shoves aside the anger I saw there a second ago. Now he looks amused by my way of thinking.

"Is that why you have that tattoo?" His thumb is back in my pants. Only instead of seeking to torture me into another orgasm so strong, I forget my own wellbeing he strokes the callused pad over my tattoo.

I place a hand over my lower abdomen. "Something like that."

"Tell me, did you set out to be a criminal?" The command for me to speak is subtle but I can feel his dominant nature. It's always there, just below the surface.

I lick my lips. "Did you?"

He doesn't answer, only sits there in that patient way waiting for me to answer him. Knowing I will answer him.

"I was legit at one time. When I look at a computer screen I see coding. I designed apps and software. Worked for a security firm for a while. Then a friend approached me. Told me the serious money is in hacking. Black hat shit that if I had enough balls could make me the most sought out with my set of skills and ability to hack anything with or without a backdoor. I wanted a stable life for Polaris and myself. Up until then I was moving around almost every year so my uncle couldn't find us."

Sorrowful eyes hold mine. "Good friend." He swirls the tip of his thumb over the back of my palm, eyes following the path of caresses. There's sarcasm to his tone.

I belly laugh. It is either that or fall into a fit of tears on this man's lap. Or is it *more* tears? I can't seem to get them to stop falling down my cheeks and at this point I don't know if they are from pain, sorrow, or real humor. "Try a real *dead f*riend," I correct him with a shiver of trepidation.

"He cleaned out a Colombian drug lord's accounts for a client. Three days later his body was found in a barrel in the Ozarks. They only identified him from dental work because he hadn't been there long enough to dissolve. And that is why I research all clients before taking them on."

"Smart. But no one will lay a hand on you. Not and live."

I pick at invisible lent on his collar. "How did you know I was having a panic attack, Ares? No one has ever helped me come down from an attack before."

"Do they get this bad often?"

"Just after my uncle's death. Like his ghost haunts me now or something. I don't know. I just wake up in cold sweats sometimes. Or if I'm particularly stressed."

He nods. "My mother suffered through them on quiet nights of all things. I learned how to help her cope. A vodka, a cool cloth, and talking."

I trace the ends of his sleeve where it is pulled up over muscular forearms. "She was lucky to have you."

He lifts a hand to my face and places a kiss on my forehead. "I was lucky to have her. And twice as lucky to have you."

His body keeps tensing up against mine, like strings of the past reach through to the present day and refuse to relinquish control over him. His arms tighten around me and we fully embrace each other.

He rests his forehead against mine and we stay like that just rocking and drinking in each other's comfort. The Russian and his captive bride. Or am I his fake bride? Bought bride? All three, I guess.

There's a darker story he's not telling. One sitting just below the surface and one that drives him like the hatred for my uncle motivates me. Only I don't think this man hated his mother. No. He's hiding something. I don't press him for more details, knowing we have bigger issues right now.

He stiffens when my hands come to his back but he doesn't move away. For now, I just let him feel me. Hopefully, he knows he's not alone. All I can do is hope he can take some strength from me too as I've done from him.

His phone pings and he pulls it out. The story about the Colombians and my friend is very true and why I don't like playing Houdini tricks with bad people's money.

The stone-cold look of his expression returns and I know it's time. Avery comes down the stairs and brings me my laptop but just as quickly slips back upstairs.

He moves me to take his place in the chair and walks over to a desk off to my right.

He returns with four different sheets of paper and places them on the table. I pick them up. Names I don't recognize are at the top next to ungodly amounts of money. The highest hitting eight digits.

"Who are these people?"

"Volkov accounts are all hidden behind shell corporations."

Guessing from what he had me do before he would consider uncuffing me I take a stab at what I'm being asked to do. "And you want me to empty them?"

"*Da, malyshka*. I want you to help me cut them at the knees. Make them bleed."

He stands beside me but instead of being a looming force I can't fight against, I feel the energy shift in the room and it sits solely on my shoulders. I have the power here, the control, and he wants me to know it.

His phone rings and he snaps it to his ear. "*Govori bystro.*" Speak fast. "Alek." The surprise in his tone pulls my eyes off the screen in front of me.

Rage and the men filter back in looking a little sheepish.

"All good?"

"Sorry I had a freak-out, guys." Nothing like being the nut case of the group.

"That's okay, baby girl. I do it like clockwork about every Saturday right after breakfast burritos."

Only Rage looks me in the eye and when he does I can tell he's not joking.

"To us freaks." I raise my half-filled glass. He walks over refills mine and then raises his. "Never raise a half-filled glass. Bad luck."

"Gotcha." We clink glasses and toss our drinks back. "I've never had a vodka breakfast."

"Glad to be your first, sweet thing." He winks at me and I hear a growl come from behind me. Obviously, Ares has one ear on our conversation and the other on his. He's speaking in low Russian and I get the sense it's a tense conversion. Then again Ares always sounds like he's either pissed, aroused or doesn't care. Or at least in my experience.

He hangs up and taps the phone on the table. "Send the jet to collect Ghost."

"Ghost?"

Shivering silver lands on me. "A distant cousin. Good with guns. I haven't seen him in years, but he's agreed to patch in." His focus moves to Rage who is sitting beside me. There's a silent conversation happening between them but deciphering it would take hours I don't have.

I pull up the dialogue boxes with trembling fingers. Warm hands settle over mine. I understand how this will help save my sister, but it's not fast enough. Ares isn't fast enough. I can't blame him either. He has to watch out for more than just one person. Everyone here depends on him. The crew. And he's right about the other women being at risk if he moves prematurely on the brothers.

Ares' fingers tip my chin toward him.

"You are protected here. No one and nothing will hurt you as long as you are here. Do you understand me?" There's a warning edge to his tone. Now that I have full control over all my senses, old habits want to kick back on. Trust issues sit at the top of my must-work-on list. Knee jerk reactions are a bitch like that.

I stomp on my fear. This is Ares' life, day in and day out. One he thrives in but my foundation of petty crimes means nothing when compared to his.

"I do this and I'm painting a bullseye on my ass."

My fingers fly over the keyboard as I solidify my own plan to save my sister. And myself.

Sixteen

Nova

I don't know when my luck is going to run out, but it hasn't yet. I send up a hallelujah and a few praise baby Jesuses as I sneak across the gravel parking space outside Ares' compound. Gravel crunches underfoot but there's no one around to hear me cross the large expanse. The gate is too far down the drive for anyone to see either.

It took me all of fifteen minutes to pull up a backdoor to the Volkovs' bank accounts and drain them dry. I didn't ask where the funds were being sent and Ares didn't offer. The less I know the better. It's bad enough I am the one behind the keyboard.

Ares requested I print out every transaction they'd had over the last two months. Forty pages' worth of data. There went another fifteen precious minutes I feared might have cost me. I can only imagine the wealth of information those sheets possess but he was only interested in one name.

Antonov.

I didn't imagine the stone-cold killer in him rising to the surface. All the quiescent power he reined in until then released in suffocating waves. I had to get out or risk being drawn into his orbit of destruction.

His focus is *not* on helping my sister. Mine is.

The second I hit enter on erasing the Volkovs' money, Ares moved into action. He called a meeting with Rage asking everyone to leave. That was my cue while Dragon was occupied. I didn't need to hear all the plans to know my sister is not their main focus. There will be collateral damage when they strike out against the Volkovs. Polaris will not be among those who pay for their sins.

Antsy, my fingers slip off the handle and I try again. This time I manage to open the back door of Dragon's van and slip inside just as he leaves the side kitchen entrance. I shove down panic at the idea of being in the back of a panel van again and focus on the end results. I latch the doors and tuck myself into a ball behind the driver's seat. The motor rumbles and thirty minutes later we're stopping outside a place with guards. I can hear them shouting for the gates to be opened.

Metal grinds against metal, telling me we've been granted access. Alarm bells go off inside my head but I ignore them. Dragon says something and then we are through. Dogs bark and I hear Dragon peel off in a rush of Russian to the guard.

He guns the motor and speeds up a long driveway. He shoves the van into park and the second the door slams behind him, I'm easing from the back. I spot a ball cap stuffed in the back of the driver's seat. I grab it and tuck my blonde hair under the dark blue material. Sunlight on my hair is like a freaking spotlight shining in the middle of a room. Not a good mix for clandestine operations.

I don't know if it is dumb luck or the Universe having my back, but I make my way to a side entrance undetected. It's a place locked down as tight as a prison. Iron bars cover all the windows and there are enough guards with leashed dogs walking the grounds it would be hard to stay unnoticed for long.

I try the handle and when it turns, I slip inside.

I wait for my eyes to adjust. Standing here makes me utterly vulnerable, but I'm so blind someone could be standing in front of me right now and I can't see them.

The last time I stood here was when Ares had purchased me. Avery had taken my hand and then we were shuffled off to an unknown future. At the time I thought I would die that night.

I take a deep breath and shake off the feelings of panic. With my eyes adjusted, I slowly begin to see the details of the inside. Dome lights illuminate a long hallway. Along the sides are several doors but only one red one. That has to be it.

I zero in on it and let my feet glide soundlessly over the plush carpet underfoot.

Hugging the walls of a softly lit hallway, it seems to take forever before I stop outside the red door. I listen. Nothing.

The handle gives when I twist. Their arrogance of never locking a door is their weakness and my benefit.

I step inside and the second my feet hit rough cement I travel back to my ten-year-old self.

"This is not like that," I whisper. "Polaris needs me." *Polaris needs me.* I repeat silently and take one step then another until I stand at the bottom of twenty-three stairs. A cold sweat trickles down my spine. My vision dims and the white dots dulling my vision threaten to overtake me.

I close my eyes.

Inhale. Exhale.

Pause.

Inhale. Exhale.

There's another hallway here stretching to my left and right. Instead of warm lighting like upstairs the feel of white overhead bulbs bright above me gives off institutional vibes—cold, sterile and void of life.

Whimpering catches my attention and I shove my past back in its vault and bolt to the left and back in the direction of my one-time prison.

I grip the bars clanked shut over darkened holes for doorways. "Polaris?" I gruffly whisper. No answer. I run to the next, and then the next. "Polaris," I try again. But none of the women inside have the same jet-black hair and blue eyes I'm looking for. It kills me, but I move on, vowing to return for every single person in these cells.

"Polaris?"

Instead of an answer, I'm looking for, I hear shuffling of feet over cement. Big feet. Only it's not coming from the cells in front of me, but from behind me. And suddenly I'm left with two choices: fight whomever I hear coming down the hall or hide.

Since I can't help anyone when I'm dead, option two seems the smartest choice. To my left and to my right there is absolutely nothing I can use to conceal my presence.

A cell stands open a couple of paces down a cold hallway. I jump inside and tuck around the ledge of a support beam. It's not much in the way of a hiding place but it's better than standing out in the middle of the passageway.

Two men I recognize shuffle past. Beast One and Beast Two. Bile rises to coat the back of my throat.

I wait until they are out of sight before I make my way back to the cells.

"Polaris." I keep my voice low.

"Nova?"

I spin around at the sound of a weak, broken voice.

"Oh God, thank you! Polaris. Polaris. You're alive." Overwhelming relief makes my knees weak and my hands tremble when I reach for her.

"Nova?"

I grip the bars to my sister's cell. It's bare of anything of comfort. Only the cold floor and a pot in the corner. No bed, no mattress. Just the bruising floor.

Immeasurable rage fills me. Thirst for violence never sat well with me before now, but I want blood for the sins committed against my sister.

Her chest is heaving, her eyes so big and the amount of fear coming off her makes tears water my lashes. Her innocence and youth. The glow on her cheeks and the smile on her face are gone.

Someone will pay for this. I wrap my fingers around the bars and curse not having a tenth of the strength Ares has and the fact I don't have a gun. Because right now I would use it and not stop until they either put one between my eyes or I did the same to them.

"We have to hurry." I cast about for cameras tucked into corners and sure enough the red blinking lights telling me someone is watching is there.

Cold fingers wrap around mine where I hold the unforgiving bar.

Scared tears hang from her lashes. "How? How do we get out of here, Nova?"

Her voice is small, weak.

I can't believe what I am seeing. Dragon had said the torture was psychological, not physical. But my eyes are not lying. Bruises cover the side of her face and her arms look more purple than her beautiful sun-kissed skin. She's wearing a flimsy sleeveless gown made of what looks like gauze instead of real cloth. It hangs off her thin frame in tatters.

"Why did they beat you?"

"They got tired of me fighting, I guess." She tries to smile but I can tell it hurts to move any part of her face.

"You must be cold." I take off Ares' shirt, dirty as it is, and pass it through the bars, leaving me in a thin camisole. "Put this on." She takes it. She lifts her arms and I spot more bruising along her ribs.

"I have a plan," I assure her. I take out Avery's phone. The one I pinched from the kitchen counter on the way out the door. I hit the power button and thank you baby Jesus; it has no lock code. The screen flashes to life and I flip through her contacts. Ares is the first on the list.

"The keys are in the room with the green door. That way." Polaris points to the left.

That changes things. I stuff the phone in my back pocket. "Are you sure?"

"A guy with black hair in a bun and dragon tattoos up his neck keeps them on a hook inside the door. Both sets are there."

So the bastard did know about the double keys. "Dragon."

She nods. "That's what they call him."

A vision of hope brims to life in my sister's eyes when I tell her, "Get ready. I'm getting you out of here and then we will disappear. I promise. I'll never let anyone else hurt you ever again."

Cold fingers brush over mine, but the young woman I helped raise doesn't have the same bright shine to her eyes. Icy blue is now a dull ghostly white.

Dragon warned she wouldn't be the fun-loving carefree girl she was before all this went down. But I hoped and prayed.

I can't think about that now. Moving quickly, I run the length of the hall and skid to a halt when it dead-ends at the green door. It's standing open and inside men are talking. I can't hear what they are saying but the hisses and growls tell me something is up. I guess that's why they haven't spotted me on the security feed yet. They're too busy arguing.

I stay plastered to the side of the hall and wait.

Inhale. Exhale.

My heart pounds so hard in my chest it's the only thing I can focus on. That and at any second some asshat security douche will detect my presence and I'll be locked inside a cell right alongside my sister and I don't think Ares will be able to save me so easily.

I swallow and pull up courage from the depths of my soul and tuck around the corner. The room is empty. I look up and find the hook where the keys should be just as empty.

"Damn it!" I curse under my breath.

A heavy hand comes down on my shoulder and my feet solidify to the floor. I might as well have super glue gunking me in place.

My knees lock, my heart stops. It's game over.

Somehow I find it in me to turn. Palm straight, thumb flexed, I rear back and aim for the throat.

But the man on the receiving end of my wrath is prepared this time. He blocks, throws my hand to the side, and pins me to the wall with a forearm to my chest.

I shove him away and he lets me go. I say lets because like Ares, this man doesn't take anyone's shit.

"Dragon..." I want to sigh in relief but it's short-lived when he doesn't say anything for a long dreadful minute. When he does speak my soul shivers from the power of fury seething from every pore on his body.

"What the ever-loving fuck are *you* doing here?"

Black eyes shooting daggers come to rest on me. He takes a phone from his front jean pocket and I grab it from his hand. "No, I know what you're going to do. Don't call Ares."

"That's what you are afraid of, woman? Him punishing you?" He pins me with incredulous eyes.

I turn a shade of red I've never been before. "I'm not leaving here without my sister."

"You are either thirty different shades of fucked in the head or brave. I can't decide which. Ares is the first fucking person I am calling as soon as I get your fucking sweet ass off this property. *If* you don't get us both killed first. My God. How did you—" His words die off as he connects the dots.

"Remind me to lock my doors from now on."

"There won't be a next time."

"Damn straight. None of us are going to survive your loyalty." He shakes his head. "I told Ares he needed to cuff you and keep you out of the way." His words are clipped, almost bitten off at the ends. Each one falls like tossed grenades at my feet.

My anger explodes. "Fuck. You," I snarl in his face, feeling braver than I should. "Nobody will cuff me ever again."

Dragon snatches me up and gets a good grip on my arm. I'm being hauled through a black door and down another hallway farther and farther away from Polaris.

"I told you I would take care of your sister. You need to trust when people say something they will follow through."

"I don't trust you. I don't trust anyone. No one has stepped up to save my sister or me. Ever. It's me and only me."

A pissed-off Dragon is in my face, lips peeled back growling. "When a Savage Son gives his word, it's considered written in blood."

I growl right back. "Like *I* said. I don't know you."

"But you know Ares. He's fought for you. And the brotherhood has bled and killed for you. What? That means shit to you?"

For a long second, I stare up at him in silence. He's not wrong. Not even a little.

"You're going to end up getting someone killed."

Using my anger as a driving force I land an elbow in his gut. He doesn't grunt or budge. He just keeps trucking for I don't know where.

I dig in my heels. "Get your fucking hands off me. I will not leave here without my sister."

He's not listening. Another ten feet and there's another door.

"Let me have the keys to her cell and I'll be out of here before anyone knows I've ever been here." I'm dragged into an unforgiving wall of muscle.

He hulks over me, his massive size dwarfing me in comparison. "Are you out of your goddamn mind, woman? You're lucky to be leaving here at all. *If* I can get you to the tree line before the dogs scent you. They like a good chase."

His leather jacket hangs open and he's too busy holding me to realize he's given me full access to his gun.

I grab it from the holster under his arm and he releases me just as quickly. The next three point two seconds of my life are nothing but a blur of black leather and male.

I'm against a wall. My legs spread wide over the thigh of a man my Russian said I could trust.

I'm beginning to think otherwise.

One hand holds the hand holding the gun to my side while the other rests over my chest just above my breast.

Breathing heavily, I hold his gaze. There's no way he's not feeling the pounding of my heart ripping a hole in my chest.

He leans in, the full weight of his body pressing me into the rough brick at my back. "No one touches my gun unless they want the full weight of what I have to offer coming at them."

Inhale. Exhale.

Lips peel back in a snarl. "Do. You. Understand. Me," he clips next to my ear.

Hard eyes blaze into mine. The scent of his cologne is light and soothing. Something the man is not.

In the past I would have cowered had someone shoved me into a wall and used their size to intimidate me. If anything, this whole experience has taught me size doesn't matter. It's the size of the fight in the person that gets measured.

I grab his nut sack and squeeze. "You better come at me with more than words if you want me to take you seriously. You think you're the first man to try and use their cock to control me?" I laugh in his face.

He inhales sharply through his nose but doesn't back down.

I squeeze a little more and that gets his attention. He peers down the bridge of his nose at me but his arms against my chest aren't as restraining. "Come at me again with all your testosterone and I'll make you a eunuch and use Ares' blade to do it." I mentally reach for my blade, but I don't feel it tucked into my back pocket. It must have slipped out in the van.

I shove at him and at first, he doesn't back away. I know he could crush me like a ladybug between his fingers but he stares down at me for a span of time I know we can't afford to waste. I can't be certain but I think there's respect in the way he considers me.

He eases off me and I slide down the wall until my feet touch the floor.

His lips nearly touch mine. "Grab my balls like that again, sweet bird, and Ares might have to fight me for you."

Did he consider that foreplay? My mouth hangs slightly agape. And I'm the crazy one?

"You can't stay here. The brothers are on their way down. The second I open this door you will haul ass to the tree line. Take these. I have my bike stashed at a barn half a mile up the road. Beat feet to ground and you can make it in ten minutes."

He shoves a set of keys into my hands and takes his gun back.

"There are three guards positioned on the roof. You better hope like hell they are on a coffee break."

"Dragon, no. Can't I—"

I don't have a chance to argue or plead or tell him I have not a freaking clue on how to ride a bike.

Sunlight pierces my eyes and I am shoved out the door.

"Run, damn it, and don't look back, sweet bird. The wolves will swallow you whole."

I get about ten paces before I dare a look behind me. The door is already closed. I dash back and try the handle but Dragon knows better and it's locked this time.

"Damn it!" I snarl, turn and book it to the massive tree line on the east side of the property. Twenty yards out my luck dies.

Dirt and pine needles fly as bullets pelt the ground at my feet. Snarling dogs close in.

"Stop!"

Not today, Satan! I pick up speed, but the tree line and its safety are too far away. I know I'll never make it. Wet grass underfoot causes me to slip. I slap at the ground and push up but I've lost my momentum.

I'll never make it. To my right, I spot another door. The cellar. I shift directions and aim for another side entrance. If I can get back inside, I'll find a place to hide. From there I can call the authorities. Ares.

Guns go off. Bits of dirt and grass fly.

I swing open the sides of the cellar door and run into a fist the size of a brick.

Seventeen

Nova

Beast One, the mammoth douche, looms over me, rocking from side to side like he wants to try out his Rocky Balboa moves on my face. He just needs me to peel myself off the ground first.

Hard pass!

The scent of copper hits me just before I taste the trickle of blood oozing from the corner of my mouth. A couple of inches left and my nose would be broken. The blow to my head rattles my vision and for a second I have a hard time focusing on anything but the grass I'm about to puke all over.

"I thought I smelled you."

He draws in a deep gust of air through his nostrils. "*Da*. Fallen angel with all that white hair. I'm going to teach you to be my submissive."

"You can't afford me," I spout.

Fat, stubby fingers wind around my arm in a bruising grip. I struggle, fight him off but he only tightens his hold.

I'm hauled over a shoulder and he carries me into the cellar. I kick and scream the whole time he moves us through one hall, up a flight of stairs, and then another.

Lovely hardwood does a bang-up job of cushioning my fall when I'm tossed off like a sack of meat. I tumble sideways, my hands out to brace for impact, but it doesn't help the pain pulsing out from my ribs on contact.

"Fucker," I grunt and take a size fourteen shit kicker to the other side of my ribs. Stars burst behind my eyelids. I wheeze. Fuck, that hurt like hell. I wrap my arms around my center and curl into a trembling ball.

Slowly I push to my knees and just sit there trying to put some air into my starving lungs. Shuffling of feet over the smooth flooring is the only precursor I get to the shock of pain I feel against my jaw. I go flying and skid over the polished flooring. The hard legs of a coffee table stop my progression across the room with a thud. This time it's my spine.

I stop breathing. I know I should be pulling in air but I can't draw breath through the soul-crushing agony eating my insides.

Fingers stab my hair and an unforgiving grip yanks me back to a kneeling position.

"I knew you would look pretty on your knees." Beast One's breath is putrid just like his cologne. He clumsily grabs for his zipper and I prepare for the fight of my life.

"Later, Volk."

Through narrow slits I spy a familiar set of black eyes watching from the opposite side of the room to match the familiar voice. "The Volkovs will want to speak with her."

Dragon has his arms crossed. Watching from the doorway. As in not lifting a finger to stop this asshole from using me as a punching bag. He looks completely relaxed leaning up against the frame like he does this sort of thing every day.

And he's right, I realize. Dragon can't forfeit his cover.

An ugly face fills my vision. "I remember you."

Another blow to the face and this time the sofa to the side of me cushions my fall. In my tumble, the phone in my back pocket falls. I scoot over it in an attempt to hide it.

I take the hit to the face like a warrior fucking bitch. I spit blood on the tips of Beast One's scuffed boots. His shit-eating grin makes me nauseous but I bury that under the false sense of bravado keeping me stable on my knees.

"Nice to see you remember me. I'll be the one to drive a knife through your heart. Remember *that*, asshole." My mouth is back to running and I spit another mouthful of blood out.

I hear multiple sets of feet pounding wood and Dragon moves aside as two men in suits that match the opulence of the place walk in. But no amount of money in the world would fix the scars scaling their necks and half their faces.

"Enough, Volk. Stop beating our guest."

One wears his hair down in an appearance to hide burn marks splashed up the side of his neck and jawline.

The other tries for a beard to hide the nasty-looking puckers but there are patches missing where the scars cover the side of his face.

Neither succeeded.

They cross the study and the one with the clean-shaven jaw kneels in front of me while his look brother hangs back, his head hunched over his phone screen.

There's a spill of Russian coming from his mouth and his expression screams panic.

Something tells me they've just discovered my early morning handiwork.

The one hovering over me turns and answers and his brother's thumbs are flying over the small device.

A finger lifts my chin. Hair falls around me. I'm breathing heavily but push through the blinding dots threatening to crush me under a wave of panic. Early afternoon positions the sun just right to send shafts of light to pierce my eyes. I take that pain and focus on it instead.

I remain unblinking.

"Does your master know you're missing?"

For once I keep my mouth sealed shut.

His Russian accent is not as thick as Ares', I notice oddly. I don't know why my brain wants to nitpick on such a meaningless detail. Probably because the man in front of me looks like he's hanging on the last hinge of sanity when his brother speaks next.

"It's not here." This time the second brother speaks in English. He sounds panicked.

His hair is ruffled and the smile on his face is as fake as Joker's. One good push and we'd all be in crazy town.

Disgust wells inside when he slides the back of his knuckles down the side of my face.

"My brother is saying our bank accounts have been drained. You just came from the bed of the only man who could do this." He's disturbingly calm and I wait for the mental break that will send him over the edge.

"Do you know where my missing money is?" he asks, wearing that same eerie smile.

"Like I would know," I lie to his face. I've had a lot of years of practice and it's once again coming in handy.

He pulls a handkerchief from his suit pocket and dabs at the blood on my lips. I look on, horrified when he brings it to his mouth and licks. "You'll make a sweet addition to my collection."

"Mr. Volkov." Beast two enters the room. I wondered where he was. "The women are loaded and will arrive at the port within the hour."

"That's fine. As of today, we take control."

"Ivan, every single account is dry. There's not a single cent left. It's the Antonovs. I know it. That rat bastard stole from us."

"Yes. But you're thinking of the wrong Antonov, Andrei."

Ivan's gaze never leaves mine as he speaks to his brother now pacing from one side of the room to the other.

Andrei mutters something and drags his hand over his face. It would be comical if I wasn't so damn scared they will

287

take their wrath out on me any second.

Out of the corner of my eye I see the one named Andrei jittery with his eyes darting to the doorway like he's expecting someone to walk through it at any second.

"Oizys says now, *bratan*."

"*Poshel na khuy*! Fuck you! And fuck him. I'm done with these Antonovs." Ivan is across the room in three strides. For a man of his size, his speed is pretty freaking impressive. He fists the front of his brother's suit and hauls him in until their noses are touching. His eyes are wild.

"I make the rules, brother. Me," he bellows until the floors beneath me feel like they are shaking. Spittle slips from his mouth in his rage.

"Say that to my face." The Volkovs' heads swivel toward the door. The flash of a muzzle and Andrei is in a heap on the floor.

I stare stunned. We all do. This is Oizys I presume. I huff connecting a few dots. Their parents had a twisted sense of humor naming their kids from Greek gods. Ares and now Oizys-a goddess, but I guess his dear mommy didn't care. Naming your kid after misery and suffering is messed up.

Time slows and second by second I see realization dawn. Ivan's face crumples with fury and fists start flying.

A man equal in Ivan's size steps through the door and grips him by the throat. Five fingers dig into flesh, squeezing until Ivan's face turns a flaming red. With the force of an ox, he lifts Ivan to the tips of his toes like he weighs no more than the suit he wears.

"Did you have something to say?"

Ivan struggles frantically but he might as well accept his fate. His gurgling makes my stomach clench.

"I didn't think so," the man I am still assuming is Oizys says with a cocked arrogant brow.

He shoves Ivan across the room and the man pinwheels into the wall. I can't take my eyes away as he slumps to his knees. I wanted them both dead. Wished to see the Volkovs buried in the earth. But the human part of me, the one who just wants peace for God's sake, weeps for the brother who crouches over the body of his lifeless twin.

I feel his pain, the tension of it gripping my chest tightly.

There's a new alpha in the room. Palpable as electricity during a thunderstorm. Power transfers. It no longer sits with the Volkovs. I peel my eyes off Ivan and let them fall on the new threat.

"Shit," Beast One says faintly and for once I actually agree with the douche bag. We are both in some real deep shit here.

Massive, dark-haired with a scowl just like Ares. His eyes are the color of forged steel and his shoulders have a similar shape—strong, pinned back as if held by sheer arrogance. There's a familiar aura of power about him but this man has a sinister edge to his energy.

"Ares?" I admit I can't see too much through my left eye. It's swollen and feels three times its normal size. But those eyes forged in steel have me taking a double look.

If the Volkov brothers looked loaded this man drips wealth and power. The newcomer approaches me. I try to stand but Beast One shoves me to my knees painfully.

"Animals on the floor."

I shake his hand off but it comes right back on to hold me in place. My ponytail slips, spilling hair to tumble over my shoulder. Ares' lookalike narrows in on it and fingers the fine strands between his forefinger and thumb. Shivers of fear trickle down my spine.

"Direct line to my brother, Ares?" He points the barrel of the gun in his right at the phone tucked beneath my leg. I guess it wasn't as hidden as I thought after all.

My brain trips over his words. What the heck did he just say?

My brows scrunch. I reject his words. "Who?" There's no way I heard him right. But my heart syncs with my eyes and says he's telling the truth. The freaking low-life, mafia, piece of lying crap. Ares, not his brother. My fingers turn to ice and there's no ignoring the *tink tink tink* sound of my shattered heart hitting the floor. Why did I think he would be different? I didn't want to know how he made his money. I didn't want to think he truly bought me to actually *buy* me.

This was all one screwed-up game for him. To what end? Have a little fun with other people's lives? Why did he have me drain the Volkovs' accounts? Is this some sibling rivalry?

Familiar eyes drill into me. Not familiar, I correct myself. Similar is all. This is not Ares. But the man I nearly gave my stupid heart to sure the hell has some explaining to do.

No, scratch that.

Oizys picks up the phone I'd hoped was concealed enough and holds the screen toward me. "We should call him. It's

290

been a couple of decades. Catch up on old times." His smile shifts and he bares his teeth. He appears to be every bit of a rabid animal.

I force my mouth to work. "No, thanks."

The smile turns humorless. "Nobody told the little bought fuck toy she's screwing bratva blood?" He considers me. "Everyone thinks I'm the bad apple. But I've never lied. I tell you I'm going to kill you, I do, *da*. But not Ares. He lies to your pretty little face. Who should you trust?"

Right now. I kind of nod and go along with his little monologue here. His hands are moving the whole time he's speaking. The gun in his hand waving around.

"Did you not know you were screwing the very family set to sell your sister?" He pauses and pierces my soul with his gaze. Shivers rake through from the scathing invasion.

"I love a good family row. Ares and me. We've had our differences for a while now. He blames our father for his whore mother's death."

Beast One shoves me forward and I land on my hands. "Good little bitch," Oizys murmurs in my ear. I can only imagine how I want to spit and claw at his face. My muscles tremble from the effort it takes to hold myself back.

He taps the end of my nose and I see red.

"You know you two are perfect for each other. Betraying your family is in your nature. I'm going to love taking you from him. You can be the bitch who sucks me clean after I fuck your sister."

He nods like he's convinced himself the crazy vulgar shit going on in his head is true.

"*Da*, the little black-haired raven. Your sister. I was going to sell her but after seeing her be such a good little submissive in training I can't deny how exquisite she will be." His growl of appreciation makes me sick to my stomach. "But her hymen and virgin blood will bring in some pretty money along with all the others. Something to think about on the long flight home."

My mind rushes over what he's saying. "Take me instead," I plead. "I'll do anything you want."

He scoffs, the sound disturbingly close to the one Ares' makes when he disagrees with me. Which is often.

Oizys' expression turns dark, amused. "Foolish girl, I already have you. And her."

The asshole snaps his fingers and my sister is brought in. Her head is tilted downward, her hair a shield over her face. "Speaking of."

She lands at my feet with a hard thud.

Pain laces through my chest at her frail body being manhandled. "Polaris." I try to help her up, but Beast One has his hands wound around my hair. He jerks and a sharp pain over my scalp brings me to a sudden, painful halt. I elbow him in the nuts and he falls to his knees beside me, cupping his dick.

"How does the floor feel?" I hit again only this time my elbow connects with his nose. I hear a crunch. Like paper in a fist. Blood runs down his face and it is a piece of art. I hit him again and love the satisfaction of seeing him hit the floor. The bigger they are, the harder they tumble in a pile of weeping shit.

Douche face snaps again and this time Dragon is the one holding me back from giving Beast One another reason to scream.

"Knock her the fuck out," Beast One roars, rolling on the floor. "I'm going to kill you in front of Ares, bitch!"

Over his writhing body, I see a quiet Ivan silently shuffling his brother's body out the door.

The sound of his name shoots pain through me. I bear the coldness of his betrayal. I'll use it as fuel. I should have listened to my gut. Something seemed off about him and I was right. He never wanted to talk about his past. Now I know why. Despite the outcome, I was right to come here. Right not to trust him.

But the troublesome voice in my head speaks up. What if I'm pregnant with the monster's child? I force away the thought and focus on what I can control now. Saving my sister and me.

Dragon flips Beast One off. "I don't take pleasure in beating women unless my dick is in them and it's their ass I'm spanking." His lips are in a fine white line. He's working hard to control his face but I can tell he had no idea about Ares either. At least I'm not alone in my feelings of betrayal. Ares will have more than his brother to deal with at some point.

"It's good to have boundaries." Oizys checks the cartridge of his Glock and locks it back into place with a snap which makes his offhand comment urge me to want to laugh in his face. I can't imagine this man knows the meaning of boundaries.

"Did you come in here thinking you would what? Save your sister?" His laugh grates over my raw nerves. The bite of the floorboards into my knees centers me.

His nostrils flare as he speaks. His teeth clenching and unclenching. Another trait he shares with his brother.

"Foolish girl. Did you ever stop and think why you were taken off the street? He'd been watching you for a few weeks. A little diversion left you alone long enough for me to grab you and your jewel of a little sister. You were my chink in his armor and you weakened him beautifully. I have waited a long time for this. I've been watching your lover, my brother, for months now. When he walked in here ready to buy you, be the hero…" His dark chuckle peels back the layers of his insanity and I have a front-row seat to the show.

He strokes a hand over my head like I'm some good pet which is just fine. As long as his attention is on me and not Polaris. "I knew it was only a matter of time before you showed back up here. I didn't have to lift a finger. When I kill you in front of him it will be like reliving old times."

His mother. Oh my God. What have I done?

He taps the barrel of his gun against my temple. "And here you are. Just as I planned, little birdie."

Glass rattles and a pillar of smoke outside the windows shoots skyward. The roar of motors and the sound of guns going off brings a smile to Oizys' face.

"And there my dear brother is. Right on cue."

EIGHTEEN

ARES

Anger brewing inside me has reached its limit. It's a festering blister inside me and today I will put an end to at least one of the plagues leached onto my ass.

My brother.

Dark sensations of murder and bloodshed prickle over my skin. Knowing Nova is inside, possibly receiving the same treatment forces me to rein myself in. Taking control over the darkness pouring through my soul is nearly impossible. Before Nova, I would have had no problem slaughtering without mercy or cause. Just clearing a path to reach my objective. I'm happy to know at least now I am doing it to save a pure soul like hers. Maybe it will be enough to get me into heaven with her.

I press close to the property wall and bury eight bullets into the guards keeping me from Nova. As far as I am concerned every single person involved in hurting Nova earned their body bags. What are a few more souls on my docket, anyway?

Bullets spray the wall above my head and I crouch, aim for the roof and sink one between the eyes of a sniper perched above. The Volkovs have a nice setup; I'll give them that. The last time I was here they had twice as many guards on the outside. They should have known better than to lower their defenses. I considered coming at them from behind, using the trees as cover, but I can't take the chance of booby traps or explosives.

Direct and straight for the throat is the only way I operate anyway. Let them see the hellraiser coming for them. My brother is expecting me. I don't see the need to hide the fact.

Nova has no idea what she has walked in the middle of. The second Dragon tossed those pictures in front of me, my suspicions were confirmed.

I look at Rage and he gives me a stiff nod. We both have our guns up and together we clear a path to the cellar. Walking through the front door isn't the smartest move. My brother will be expecting it because it's what he would do. His ego has him believing he won't be eating my lead by the end of the day.

He's wrong. Since the time I understood the definition of evil, I knew my brother to be a carbon copy of our ruthless old man. I don't feel an ounce of remorse for what I am about to do.

Smoke blocks us from view and I use it to my advantage. I signal for Rage to take the right and Riot the left. After discovering Nova missing I couldn't afford to wait for the backup we had coming in Reaper, the Genesis men, and the new patches…we'll just have to throw up a prayer the devil doesn't realize we're dead before we get a chance to hit the stairs to heaven if this goes south.

Our one saving grace is Ghost rolling up on his ride as we peeled out of the compound. A couple of quick words and my distant cousin fell in beside us and we roared down the highway with me in the lead.

"*Snayper*," he yells and we all flatten into the gravel. Bullets zing by and bury in the ground around us. Whoever is on the roof isn't aiming, just popping off in our general direction since the smoke is too thick to pin us down.

Ghost hustles across the lawn, kneels out in the open. He aims and the sniper pinning us topples head over ass three stories down. A work of beauty to watch.

"Done," he says matter-of-factly.

I haven't laid eyes on this man in almost fifteen years. He's a decade younger than me but he's filled his years with experiences we both understand and share. We both took lives for money. I left that behind me while he lived it until about six months ago when he gave me a call asking if I had room for one more.

I said yes in less than a second. He asked for some time to get his affairs in order. Cutting ties with the bratva is next to impossible, so I told him to take all the time he needed just to make sure he didn't get killed for his efforts in the process. I have to wonder what it cost him to be here killing in the name of the Sons of Savages and not back home under my father's crushing thumb.

A conversation I can't wait to have.

We move swiftly, hang low and let the rolling black cloud of burning oil mask us. Rage and I both hit the side of the fortress at the same time. Behind us the new Savage patches work to keep us from catching a bullet in the back of the head.

We slip inside. Ghost and Riot bring up the rear. Devil is close by.

"Clear, Prez," he shouts out and I give the signal to move.

We wind through the extensive hallways and make our way up the back staircases to the front of the mansion where I know Oizys is waiting for me. He'll want front-row seats to all the action and watch as the chaos descends around him. It's his playground so I know he won't be able to resist.

I signal for Rage and the other two to break off and secure the rest of the location. Rage fights my decision with a stone-cold look but ultimately peels off and heads to the top floor.

I continue toward the front of the house. I pass the library. No one is inside. An office. Also empty. The sound of a fight going on the grounds carries through the thick walls, muffled as if in the distance. I have to trust my men can handle themselves.

Out of the corner of my eye, I spot Ivan. He's standing in the center of a large ballroom, eyes cast downward. His back is hunched and if I didn't know any better I'd say the man looks defeated in the low light.

Half-drawn curtains shield him from most of the light. Only a sliver slants through the opening. It's enough. He's slightly turned from me but I can see well enough to notice blood smearing down the front of his suit and shirt.

I step closer. Hair hangs over bloodshot eyes. I don't have the time or luxury to draw this out. I need him out of my way. But first I need answers.

"Where is your brother?" I keep my voice low as if speaking to a spooked animal.

Devil comes up beside me. He keeps his eyes trained on Ivan while he speaks to me. "I can't find her. She's not in the basement at all. And all the women are gone."

I feared as much. They moved faster than I expected. "Where are the other girls?"

"Gone."

I step toward Ivan, gun drawn. "Where the fuck is she?" I snarl, losing my barely controlled temper.

Tilting his head, eyes filled with death swing around to me and I feel the chill of them from across the room.

"Dead." He gives a tight grin. There's something off about the man. Shadows cover half his body. There's a form at his feet and I can only guess it's from my brother's handiwork.

"He's dead," he says again in our native language. "Dead and all because of your brother."

The next five seconds slow. In the absence of light, I fail to see the gun Ivan has at his side. My finger is already on the trigger. I pull at the same time he does.

Dual muzzle flashes and the scent of blood hit my senses simultaneously.

Devil lunges, the bullet meant for me sinking into his back.

Ivan falls face-first over his brother's cold body.

"Fuck, God damn you," I roar, catching Devil before he can fall to the floor. I ease him down and settle his bleeding form over my lap.

"Why the fuck did you do that?" I want to pound my fist into him, beat the shit out of him for stealing my death from me.

Blood drips from the side of his mouth. He grins, red smeared over his teeth.

"It's not your time, man. Find her, Prez. Keep her safe and give her a parting kiss for me, yeah."

"Fuck you, Devil. Damn it!" I want to roar my wrath until the building around us lays in ruin.

"Don't forget about me."

My friend's chest shutters and death steals him away. "You died a death too early, my friend. It will not be in vain. I'll see you soon." I reach over and close his eyes one last time. The pain gripping my soul is nothing compared to the pain I will unleash on my brother.

I strip my cut and spread it over Devil's body, silently vowing justice. We all signed on knowing an early death was possible. But it doesn't make it right.

Rage bounds down the stairs, bullets raining down on him like angry hornets pelting the floorboards. "Incoming!"

Glass shatters and wood splinters.

We both roll, take shelter under the ledge of a protruding balcony and crack off shot after shot. Four men fall but it's not nearly enough to satisfy my thirst for blood.

I nod toward Devil and Rage catches my line of attention. "Watch over him. Don't let them touch him."

"Go find her." Riot joins us covered in blood. "Not mine," he reassures me. "We got this."

I check my ammo, put in a fresh clip, and turn to the only section of the house we haven't checked.

I see him standing over a shivering Nova. My mind clicks back over the memories of my mother on her knees in front of my father. She pleaded for him to leave me alone. To focus his wrath on her. Pain stings across my back as if fresh cracks of his cane belt across my flesh.

My hands flinch, my step falters.

This is not the same, I remind myself.

Oizys has a gun to her head while another man holds her by the hair. He'll die for that.

I regain my focus, step into the room.

"*Bratan*. I thought by now you would be dead," I say in a hollow tone as I walk into the front parlor.

My brother turns, his million-dollar smile a slash over his mouth.

Blood covers the front of Nova's tank top. She's breathing heavier than normal. Bruises the size of my fist cover the right side of her face and she's clutching at her ribs. My brother just solidified his death warrant.

Who I assume is her sister is on the floor beside her.

I don't risk leaving my focus on either of them for long. I can't afford to give my brother more ammunition against me than he already has.

"*Moy brat!*" He throws his arms wide; his gun seems almost a part of his hands. He's stripped of his suit jacket leaving his other gun easy to pull from its shoulder holster.

"Do you remember what I told you the last time I saw you?" I ask. "Tell me, do you remember?"

"Like I remember the contorted face of your mother as our father ended her. That you would kill me the same way. Well, I'm here for you to try."

The last time I drove my fist into his face was the day he laughed as my mother slowly had the life stolen from her. Today will be the last on this earth.

There's no posturing or preliminaries. I drop my gun and cross the expanse in only a few strides. The feel of his face taking my fist is the first relief I've felt in over two decades. My soul feeds on the surge of satisfaction. He stumbles into the back of a chair. I grip handfuls of his shirt and pull him down while driving my knee into his diaphragm.

My focus narrows and the fighting inside the compound dies away.

Testosterone fuels the fight twenty years in the making. Fists fly. Snarls flare to life and curl through the room. Savage and bloodthirsty, we fight. Both of us know this is to the death.

"It's been a while since we've had such a nice game." Oizys swipes at a trickle of blood at the corner of his mouth. "Bring it, brother! When I have you bleeding on the floor in front of me I will keep you alive long enough to watch me end your precious whore." Oizys snarls and delivers a steel fist to my ribs. I relish the feeling of pain. Absorb it and use the rolling burn as the driving strength behind my next blow to my brother's jaw. The force throws him against the wall.

Evil gleams in those black eyes. He tries to raise his weapon but I knock it from his hand and it clatters to the floor. Oizys' eyes widen from the affront. His nostrils flare as chaotic rage courses through him. His pupils dilate, turning his dark eyes as black as his putrid soul. Rage distracts him and I deliver another fist of iron to his ribs.

"You even look at her and there will be nothing left of you for our father to identify."

Another blow to the ribs and my brother reels backward. I advance, taking the fight to him.

Agony blooms over his face. He inhales ragged breaths and a tight wheezing sound escapes his lips. Sickness from old memories threatens to grip my stomach but I rein back control over my body. As a boy, when we fought I never had the advantage. Here we are on a level plane.

My father always saw to it that my younger brother had what he needed to win against me. There is a level of cruelness about Oizys I didn't possess back then.

But that is not an issue now.

I follow the blow with one to the face. Rear back and do it again and again until the hell spawn falls to his knees and my knuckles are covered in his blood.

"Ares, no. You need to stop," Nova cries out. From fear for my soul? I scoff. There's nothing that can save me now.

I hear her but the raging beast in me is snarling and thirsty. I have to feed the beast. My brother cannot live to hurt another soul.

I stab my fingers into his hair and yank his face up to mine. Breathing heavily I can feel the piercing pain of at least a couple of cracked ribs.

"Beg me to live!" I roar. "Beg me and I might send you back to our father in a body bag instead of as a bag of ashes so he can see what I've done to you."

"And I'm the monster. Be careful, *moy brat*; you are dangerously close to becoming me." Harsh and labored breaths shake his chest. Peals of laughter escape my brother's bloody mouth. I shake his head and drive my fist into his mouth until the sound stops.

"Ares." Sweet and tender. Everything I am not. The light stretches across the expanse but nothing can reach me this deep in the darkness.

Hope has the man inside me reaching for the anchor of my white-haired angel's voice but my demons are stronger and won't stop until the filth at my feet draws its last breath and I hand his soul over for judgment.

"Father is dead, brother. I killed him." His black eyes shine with bitter amusement despite the obvious pain I see there too.

Fires of hell erupt within me. "No!" I bellow. I wanted the pleasure of ridding the earth of his disease.

"He was taking too long to die. The fucker wanted to keep his power. I wanted it. I took it. Just like I'm going to take your whore and her sister."

There's a commotion beside me and I see Rage and Riot burst through the arched entryway, bringing the Genesis men with them. Terror-filled blue eyes land on mine. There isn't a second's warning before chaos ensues.

The asshole holding a gun to Nova's head swings his arm around as if he stands a chance against the five of them. Nova does the only thing that can stop my heart midbeat.

She lunges, tackling the unsuspecting beast of a man.

My brother uses my distraction to surge to his feet. Pain distorts his face but he seems driven to return the beating I gave him.

I smile, relishing the idea of taking him to his knees again.

The crack of a gun goes off. Glass shatters and rains over me. Nicks and slashes of cool edges slice into my face and neck.

"Stooooop! Stop now or I swear to God as my witness I will kill you both."

The barrel of my Glock points at my heart.

Regret tightens in my chest the longer I look into her eyes. Why did I let it go this far? I should have stopped my brother a long time ago.

"You two can beat each other into a bloody pulp for all I care. But I will not be part of your savagery." The gun swings to my brother who smiles back at Nova. "Polaris. Let's go."

The quietness in her voice is in distinct contrast to the hatred in her tone.

I risk a bullet but take another step in her direction. Another bullet zings by my head.

"Do. Not. Move. Last warning."

I freeze and slowly raise my hands in a gesture for her to know no one will hurt her. Especially me.

"Nova," I say in a warning voice.

"You're going to be a beauty when I get you on your knees and choking on my cock."

I turn on my heel and shut my brother up with a left hook. He stumbles back, glass crunching underfoot. He falls to a knee, hunching over.

"You want me to shut up; you'll have to kill me first."

I hear the strong inhalation of air and feel his body tense as if preparing himself. But being more focused on Nova I am not fast enough.

I don't feel the shard of glass slice over my throat until the blast of a bullet sinking into my brother's chest drops him to the floor at Polaris' feet. His arrogance drove him to think he could take us both out before being stopped.

The smoking barrel turns toward me and a wild-eyed Nova looks ready to take me out, too.

"Don't move or you're next. I swear to God I will end you." Her eyes drop to my lifeless brother then swings to me. Her chest heaves but she doesn't drop the muzzle of the gun. Not my woman.

"Nova."

Warm blood trickles down my throat. Someone upstairs is smiling down on me right now or likes seeing me in torment. A couple of centimeters over and my brother's attempt at killing me would have worked.

"Nova," I say again in a softer tone. She's spooked. Any wrong move right now and I'll be joining my brother at the hand of the woman I love.

Revelations are a bitch of a thing. They normally don't come unless you're about to meet your end and by that time it's too late.

"You lied to me." Her voice trembles worse than her hands. I'm almost proud of her for how steady she's holding that gun on me.

"You are just as bad as they are. I guess you were trying to tell me. When you said you wanted out from under your father's rule. I didn't put two and two together."

"Your father—"

"Is," I swallow and correct myself. "Was the head of the Antonov family. Bratva. Cruel. Savage. Bloodthirsty and more powerful than most. Yet thirsty for more."

She cocks her head; those pretty eyes of hers swim with unshed tears. "And here you are. Doing his dirty work for him? Is that why you waited? So they could take the merchandise before you struck? How do I know you are not trying to take them out so you can move in?"

"I've worked for the last ten years to be strong enough to fight him. I just needed proof my family was behind the trafficking."

"Lies."

The tightness in her voice and the betrayal in her eyes has me wanting to drag her into my arms and beg for forgiveness. My protective instinct to see her back to the light and shield her from the darkness of my life. My past.

Rage and Riot hang back. The Genesis men are another issue. A level of surprise is on all their faces and I know I'll have to deal with the fallout at some point.

I see Harlon looking at Polaris who is breathing heavily. Frightened eyes dart to the door and back to her sister. Cillian eases up behind her but he's not fast enough.

Polaris comes between us and faces her sister. "Nova, Nova listen. Don't do this. You're better than them. Let's just leave."

"I can't. I just killed a man."

"Because he was going to kill me."

The pain in Polaris' voice is palpable. An energy all its own.

"Thank you. Thank you for saving me." Polaris wraps her arms around her sister and Nova finally drops the gun to her side.

"But I didn't." Those tears in her eyes shred my insides. The need to take her in my arms consumes me.

"You did, Nova." Harlon comes to stand beside Polaris. He draws her shivering body into his and wraps his suit jacket around her delicate shoulders.

"I heard the Volkovs talking. They all wanted Ares dead. He was the only thing standing in their way from getting what they wanted. They were going to kill him and his brother and take the business away from the Antonovs."

I see Nova's resolve toward ending me falter.

I look to Harlon. There's no way I will let another take a bullet for me. Losing Devil hasn't hit me full force yet. I know it will. Until then I can at least protect my love's sister from my sins the way I could not save him.

I nod my chin to Harlon, Santi, and Cassian. They read my silent signal and pull Polaris to safety. Not that I think Nova would dare hurt her sister, but I won't risk accidents happening.

"They've taken them to Canada and from there they are sending them overseas. The two they had watching over us liked to talk." Her eyes drift to the beast of a man not too far from my brother. The terror in her gaze is as strong as the hatred in the pit of my stomach for my family's greed.

I look to Rage and he pulls a still shocked Riot along. I don't need to verbalize what they need to do.

Harlon bends and lifts Polaris in his arms and leaves just as silently as they came.

It's just Nova and me now. Smeared with my brother's blood and my soul sated from his death I stand in the center of another hell.

"Nova."

"Don't Nova me, Ares. You lied to me. I trusted you."

"No. You didn't. You put yourself in danger because you didn't trust me to save your sister."

"And I was right." Tears fall furiously down her face.

Seeing her torment from my actions nearly kills me. I shrug out shirt and let it fall in the glass at my feet.

"Can you love me? A killer?" I fall to my knees, hanging my head. "The shame I feel for asking you to love a man like me is overwhelming. Yet here I am. I plead. Don't walk. If you do, you might as well put a bullet in me."

She stares at me in stunned silence.

"You lied to me," she seethes. "Lied. How can I ever trust you?"

"I protected you with that lie. Or at least I thought I was. I lied to everyone. I was ashamed of where I came from."

"I loved you. Can you believe that? Loved a man who bought me and then used me."

"I never made it a secret as to why I bought you."

Her gun hand twitches. I can feel her slipping away from me.

"My hands ache to hold you. My arms crave to carry your burdens. Can you love me still?" I fall forward to my hands. "Beat me. Seek your revenge for my lies but please, Nova Masters, please do not take your trust away. Everything I have is yours. My wealth, my life. It's yours. My heart. My soul. My blood. My love, as little as it's worth, it's all yours if you can only love me as I love you. *Ya obozhaju tebya.*"

"Keep your money, Ares. I never wanted it to begin with. Never wanted any of this."

I hold the remnants of my shattered soul together with nothing more than the fires of pain fusing the pieces together as her footsteps drift away.

NINETEEN
NOVA

I have a decision to make. I haven't seen Ares in a month. I'd been so willing to leave him sitting in my past when I had my sister to save. Now that she's okay, relatively speaking, I can't help but think about what I want.

And the news of Devil's death sits heavier than lead in my stomach. As irritating as he was, the man saved my life. I dash a tear away. How can these people deal with death and loss almost daily? It's probably why they party so hard. They never know when it will be their last.

I stab at the ice floating in glass of water. It's about all I can handle lately. The ice bobs under the surface and finally settles in the waves. Just like my heart. Only I haven't resurfaced from the pain of walking out on Ares kneeling on the floor bleeding asking me for forgiveness.

It burns not to run to him. To fall among the shattered glass cutting into his knees and pick up the pieces of our love. But he hurt me. How do I forget that?

The voice that keeps speaking up despite my efforts in drowning it out with as much alcohol as I can drink grows louder by the day.

I hurt him, too. I know that. I am responsible for his brother's death. How do I face him after doing something so horrendous? I can't close my eyes without seeing his body on the floor, his blood spilling out to stain everything it touched.

Acid swirls and boils in my stomach.

He opened up to me and shared his past. I did the same. I failed to trust him even though he said he would help. I didn't give him that chance. I see that now. But I couldn't risk that he would fail me. Like every other person in my life.

Blurred city lights feed through the blackened windows. Summer days in Chicago are beautiful, but the nights are spectacular. All the glittering lights and busy streets nestled within the backdrop of dusk. I imagine all the big cities look this way, but the view from the fifth floor of Genesis is breathtaking. If not a little nostalgic.

I can feel my sister's nervousness before I see her reflection in the glass. She walks in behind me and her shimmering reflection mirrors what I sense. The day I walked out on Ares, the men of Genesis offered Polaris and me a place to regroup. I couldn't get out of New York fast enough. A couple of days later they offered us both permanent residence in the penthouse over top of their club in return for helping them dig through their files looking for inconsistencies. The irony is they are as dirty as Ares and the Savages. But here at least I was given a choice.

I've learned a lot about myself in the time away from Ares. A lot. More than I ever thought possible for me.

"Ok, I'm ready. How do I look?"

I shelter my rambling thoughts and turn on the dazzling smile my sister is expecting. She joins me where I am sitting in the sunken living room overlooking the city below. A large white couch lines the entire space with various throw pillows in burgundy for a splash of color.

I swallow back the pain and regret. Seeing red sends a wash of panic over me for the atrocities I've committed. Deep down, maybe I am no better than Ares. I've killed. A hard truth I will have to live with.

My sister twirls in front of me. "You're stunning," I say and I mean every word.

Pretty red-tinged lips quirk into a smirk of disbelief. "It's a business suit."

I raise my glass. "And it fits you perfectly."

Polaris still hasn't regained the weight she lost under the cruel hand of her torturers.

She joins me on the couch, pulling a pillow over her lap. "You're going to love it here. I was checking out the various rooms and levels earlier—"

Polaris laughs softly. Pre-kidnapping it would have been a boisterous, infectious laugh that would light a room up. Now it's a faint sound I strain to hear.

"You can't just go into the rooms, Nova."

I shrug and sip on my champagne. "Why not? I knocked. I wanted to see the new digs my sister will be working six days a week. Did you see what they have in the golden room?"

She raises her brows in a way that says *duh, of course.* "It's called the golden room for a reason."

I smile.

"You're sad. I can feel it."

Hiding it seems futile. Since childhood, Polaris has always been able to see deeper than surface level. "I miss him and his overbearing, controlling, infuriating ways." I refuse to cry and smudge my makeup. A rare occurrence but I wanted to be dolled up nicely for some selfies for Polaris' first night as Genesis' head executive assistant.

Polaris takes my hand and twines our fingers together. She moves over and we sit with our heads together just watching the night. "Do you think I made a mistake?" I ask.

"I think you needed space. With your work here done and Santi, Cillian, and Harlon holding the dirt you dug up from the people stealing from them and using this place to run women through. You're free." Polaris shifts on the couch and we look at each other. "You need to do what makes you happy."

I huff out a heavy sigh. "You're right. Maybe I'll go down to South America. Put my Spanish skills to good use down there for a while." I push off the couch and Polaris pulls me into a big hug.

"You're safe here, Polaris. Use your time here to heal, okay. Finish your degree in business and just focus on yourself, okay. For the first time in our lives, you have a clear path to success ahead of you. Take it."

"Ladies."

We turn in unison to see Harlon, Cassian, and Santi standing in the middle of the penthouse. They're dressed to stop hearts and all wear smiles to match the fancy suits. If dressed to kill were a thing these three have it down to an art.

"Gentlemen." I release my sister and she crosses to them. Harlon holds an elbow out and I watch my sister lace her hand through the crook of his arm.

"Ready, Ms. Masters?"

"I think so." An untrained ear wouldn't pick up on the shiver in her soft voice. But I do. I also notice the heated, possessive glances coming off Santi and Cassian for my sister. For the last four weeks I've stared at their matching wedding bands, but I've yet to see a wife for any of them. There's a deeper story there. One I'm sure will come to light soon enough.

I'm about to say something along the lines of don't hurt her, typical big sister stuff when Polaris turns back to me. "Hey, Nova?"

"Yeah?"

"Don't be gone long, okay?"

I wrangle my emotions into something that resembles cool and calm, but my insides are weeping at all I've lost.

I force a smile on and turn up the juice making it shine like a million bucks.

"Oh, before you go would you do me a favor and check the white room? Third floor. It's the one—"

I'm already nodding. "Got it. It's the honeymoon suite. I get it. Yeah, what do you need?"

This place runs like a hotel, but it's really a lavish nightclub with the option to rent a room for those who want privacy. All have themes and colors assigned to them. Private shows, lounges, women's section, guys' section. If you can dream of it, this place has it. And it's been used by the local mafia as a neutral ground that extends ten miles beyond the doors of this place. An asset the Genesis men have built up over the years and earn big time on. It's like paid security and protection. Except something terrible has gone on behind their backs. This is their territory and the local mafia families have used it as a hunting ground for trafficking women through.

They'll have a fight on their hands to take back power. I can only hope my sister doesn't get swept up in it as I did with Ares.

"I left something there. You'll see it. Would you mind?"

"Sure."

My sister heads off to her future as I take a quick detour to level three before I get to mine.

I hit the number three on the elevator and the doors slink closed. The Genesis men paid me handsomely for all the dirt I unearthed on their enemies. Maybe I'll go to Europe for a while. Learn French. Get to see all the ancient ruins before heading to South America. I can't say any of it puts a bounce in my step. It's all actually depressing as fuck.

The doors swoosh open and I head to the white room, turn the handle and nearly fall flat on my face.

A million candles are lit, covering every available spot except a single path. I follow it with my eyes and it leads me to a man dressed in all black.

"Ares?"

"Nova Masters." At first, he looks like a mirage with how the shimmering flames dance over his impressive size. Hair spills over his forehead like he's run his fingers through it a half-dozen times in the last hour.

I force my chin high and my back straight. "What are you doing here?"

He's wearing dress slacks that fit him perfectly. His shirt, also black, is neatly tucked into the band of his pants. The sleeves are neatly rolled over beautiful forearms. His jacket is nowhere to be seen. He's the picture of money. Darkness and power.

He shifts a little and the shadows move over him. They conceal the upper part of his face from me but I can clearly see his Adam's apple bob and his jaw pulse with tension from him grinding his back molars.

He's nervous. Maybe even scared.

"Winning your heart back. I know you don't want to see me, but I can't go another day without you in my life." Conviction weighs his words down.

"Polaris."

He nods, confirming my suspicions of who set this little reunion up.

"She's conniving when she wants to be."

His hands slide into his pockets. "She loves you. She meant no harm."

"I know."

The whole time he's talking Ares comes closer until he's standing right in front of me. I can feel the warmth of his body heat and I want to fall into his arms and forget about everything. Forget the lies; forget my past. And forget it's because of me his brother is dead.

Ares reaches around me and closes the door, twisting the lock into place. I'm locked in with the enemy. Russian Bratva. Savage. Ruthless. Murderer.

I can't toss my stones too hard. I'm no better than them. I've killed. I'm a hacker for God's sake. I've done shady shit for money.

"I need to go." There's not a lot of conviction behind my words.

And he knows it.

A sputter of protest falls from my lips when he picks me up and holds me to him. He takes my mouth in a hard kiss and I feel the very second I lose the battle. *What battle* that voice pipes up again and this time I agree.

The hard planes of his muscles force my body to mold to him.

"Ares, we can't do this."

"You can leave at any time. But I will only chase you down and pull you back to me." His lips peel back in a challenging grin. "But before you go, listen to me first. My name is Ares Maxim Antonov. I was born into crime and raised at the knee of a murdering thug thirsty for blood and power. But my mother made sure I didn't turn out like him and paid the ultimate price for that."

"Ares—"

"Let me finish. I was raised to be a murderer who could never love. I've done both now after you. I've fallen for you despite the odds. I love you, Nova Masters."

I press my palms against his shoulders and push, but he doesn't release me. "How? How can you love me when I killed your brother? How can you look me in the eyes and say you love me?"

"Because by doing so you saved me from the darkness. You pulled me from the pits of hell and gave me a chance to walk in your shadow. You carry the light. You are my light."

I truly have no words. "Ares."

"Say you love me."

"I do."

"Then let's take that, use it. We will need to be strong and the only way I can do that is with you at my side. My brothers will want revenge for Oizys' death. I need your strength to fight back the darkness and not get pulled into that blind rage again."

"What if I walk?"

"You won't get far."

Glaring at him I want to cross my arms over my chest, turn on my heel and march out the door. It would take me ten seconds to get to the elevator. I doubt I would make it a foot over the threshold with how his eyes narrow into slits reading me so easily. But still. Damn it. "That is the cockiest, most controlling, possessive thing I've ever heard a man say."

"And it's true. Try to run and there is no place on this planet you can hide from me. I have connections everywhere. And my cuffs still work."

He peers down at me with those dark eyes and a chill runs through me. I believe him. The time he gave us apart was him being respectful of my decision. But he has limits and I guess this is him showing me I have a choice to make and to do it quickly.

His hand slips beneath the knot of hair at the base of my neck. The darkness of his threat fades and what is left behind makes me breathless. He grips the ends of my slip dress. The only warning of what is about to happen is the flash of heat in his eyes.

One tug and my dress is over my head and on the floor. He reaches around and my bra is next that leaves my panties and heels.

He swoops me up with an arm under the back of my knees and the other at my back. Before I can protest or consider if I want to protest, I'm on my back and he's kneeling over top of me.

He grips the sides of my panties. A frilly pink thing that matches the color of my dress. Something my sister picked out for me when I rather opt for jeans and boots. Admittedly, that would have made this moment particularly hard. Thinking about it more, she dressed me knowing this would be happening. I make a very quick mental note to thank her for watching out for me.

Above me, Ares thumbs the soft material. "These are pretty but in the way." He yanks on either side and the lace rips, falling to the sides. He moves it away and kneels in front of me. His mouth devours my pussy and he groans the second his tongue slips between my folds.

I groan knowing he found the pool of hot liquid he causes at the slightest touch waiting for him. "Sweetness and all mine."

My legs are hiked up and he sweeps his tongue over my dripping hole. He swirls the pad of his thumb over the nub and I'm instantly bowing off the bed.

"Ares!" I scream. My body has been starved for his touch and now that it has it the climax that shoots through me is fucking gloriously instant. Heat hotter than the sun rages through me. I don't get to see when he strips but when the bed dips and he moves between my thighs I press to my elbow.

His heavy cock drips with pre-cum. Fat and swollen the head begs for me to lick it.

Ares points the tip at my pussy and swirls all those juices dripping from the crown through mine.

"Fuck, you drive me insane and ground me all at the same time." He says a rush of Russian that makes me cream harder. I don't know what he says and it's not the time to ask but I will make it a point to learn his language as he's learned mine.

"Ares." I press my heels into his ass and raise my hips to meet his throbbing cock. "Fuck me, Ares. Ruin me for all other men."

"*Vse moye.* All mine," he roars and sinks until his heavy balls slap against my ass. My walls clamp around him, hold him inside me.

"I missed you. I nearly went insane from not having you near me."

He kisses a path down my torso and takes a hard peak between his hot lips. I cry out and hold his head to my breast, wanting more of the deliciousness.

I shamelessly pitch my pelvis forward and take more of him deeper. He growls, letting me know he feels the way my body sucks him in.

I moan into his mouth when he breaks away to steal my lips with his. There's a ravenous hurriedness to the way he pries my mouth open with his tongue. I give in to him and savor the feel of his tongue sweeping over mine. I rock my hips, fucking him as much as he fucks me, both of us breathless and hungry for the other.

I run my hands up his back and this time feeling those scars don't make me feel heartbroken for the boy who received them, but proud of the man who wears them with pride. He saved others from pain, though it nearly killed him. And he was willing to do the same for me.

"I love you. Ares, I love you more than I've ever loved someone. Being away from you tore my heart out. I just didn't know how I could face you after what I did."

Finger collar my throat and his fingers grip me possessively. I gasp and moan, loving the feeling of each finger branding my skin. My pulse thrums against his touch. "Never fear me. Never hide from me again. Promise me."

"Promise."

My back bows off the mattress and he picks me up, leaning back on his heels. He settles me over his lap and I begin to move over his cock. Taking him deeper and deeper with each unhurried stroke.

His arms bear my weight and I lean into them trusting him to keep me safe. Trusting him with my body, heart and soul.

Wet, hungry lips wrap around one nipple and suckle before moving to the next.

My head falls back and I am swept away by all that is the man I love. His scent, his touch, his body.

"You belong to me not because I bought you, but because you freely give me your heart."

"Yes," I confirm, raising my head to lock gazes with him. "Yes." He spreads out on the bed and draws me on top. I ride him, our movements in sync. I cling to him and meet every upward thrust he gives with one of my own. Together we stoke the fires inside us. He grips my hips, burrowing so deeply inside me I'm left gasping his name.

"That's it, *malyshka.* Give me all of you. I want everything with you. I want your screams, your juices, your body, and what's here. He pulls me to a sitting position and places a kiss over my heart.

I cup his face. "It's yours. I fear it was since the first time you put me in cuffs."

Flames from the candles dance in his dark eyes. Heat sweeps over me and I continue to ride him.

327

"Fuck me, *malyshka*. Take my cock and milk me. I'm going to feed your pussy all of my milk; I want to see you round with my baby. I want to care for you, love you, and never let another soul come between us again.

I still. "Ares," I start, unsure how to continue with what I have to say.

"He sweeps my hair from my shoulder. Up until that second, I never realized it escaped the knot I had it in.

"What is it? What's wrong?"

I take his hand from my hip and settle it over my stomach. "I know, *malyshka*. Your life. Your death. Your way. I can only hope I fit within those words. Let me show you how I will love you. Save me from my darkness and I promise to save you from yours."

"You already have."

His dark brows pinch together. "What do you mean?"

"I'm pregnant."

Goosebumps spring to life over my arms when saying those two words out loud for the first time. I didn't even tell my sister.

"Pregnant? Pregnant," he repeats reverently. His expression is that of wonder and awe. So unlike the scowling man I first met.

"When?" He traces his fingers lightly over my back, tracing each bone with a possessive touch I feel to my very core.

"Your bike. Down by the river. You took me with no protection."

"I remember. It was the best night of my life. I thought you were dead until I found you standing in the middle of that asshole's bar fighting like you were a warrior princess. I fell in love with you that night."

"I did the same. You rescued me and I didn't even know it."

He rolls us over and he pins me to the mattress with his massive weight. I take it and wrap my arms around him, wanting him closer still. He pistons deep inside me and I rock my hips to meet his thrusts. Together we seek our releases.

There's nothing slow about it either. The second he took me I knew my orgasm would be explosive. My body craved his as much as my heart did to hear his voice. We're breathless and holding each other so tightly that when I scream my release his roar mixes with mine. Our chests vibrate and I can feel my life force twine with his. Wise people from the far corners of the world say soulmates are real. That those who find them are lucky to have such a force of energy binding them to those who would give their life for yours.

I believe them now.

Growing up such a thing sounded foolish. How could I ever trust someone as savage as my god of war? But in reality, there's no one I trust more. No one I will ever love more. He's perfect for me. My savage justice. My warrior. The man who went to war to save me.

"I love you, Ares."

I feel his mouth curl into a grin where he's kissing the dip in my neck. "Let me show you how much I love you, my white-haired angel." He moves his hips and his spent cock is rock hard once again and nowhere near done with me.

Good. Because these candles have hours left to live and I am just getting started.

Thank you for reading Savage Justice! The Bratva Savages continues with Savage Thief, Dragon's heart-wrenching second chance romance. Read on for the first chapter of his book or go ahead and grab it in ebook or Kindle Unlimited by tapping here or visiting my website at www.penelopewylde.com.

SAVAGE THIEF - CHAPTER ONE

ASENA

Daddy told me to stay away from monsters. He is forever saying all men are capable of evil and lurk in the shadows ready to destroy the little princesses of powerful kings. That one must be wary at all times or end up victims of their dark deeds.

I never believed him.

My controlling, overprotective daddy likes to believe all princesses are made of light and rainbows, unable to sin.

I scoff. I don't want his protection and I'm no damsel in distress in need of saving. This is no fairy tale of sweetness and pretty glitter, either. What I want is dark, gritty. Decadent and raw. Filthy, in a word.

Don't get me wrong I love a good fairy tale and sweeping feel-good heroics like every other princess. But sometimes— okay, all the time—I see myself with the villain.

So I ask you this, what if the princess of this story likes the darkness and wants the monster to catch her? Does that make you hate her or love her?

And in case I'm not being obvious enough, I'm the princess in question. The queen-in-training to the Titan empire. Mafia blood courses through my veins, my status invisible to all those outside the family. Only the criminals of my daddy's world can see through the veil of innocence to recognize the blue in my veins and the jewels on my head.

But I don't want the title nor the crown.

I want *him*.

I'm helpless to protect myself against the dark desires coursing through me. Should I fear them, revel in them? Banish all the wicked thoughts of possession and lust from my body and mind?

If you have a remedy I don't know about, please do share. I've tried everything in the books to forget the man I shouldn't want. It only makes me want him more. Like some reverse spell, Hoodoo or Voodoo shit, I swear with my hand on a stack of bibles.

Since that's the closest thing I have to answers, I'm left with only one option. I'll have to go searching for them and that means I'll need to do the unthinkable—I'll let the monster I seek get his wicked hands on me. Only then will I have the answers to all my questions.

Who knows. Maybe once I purge his wickedness from my system, I can get my life back. Lord, let it be so because I'm tired of the internal torture ruining me.

I carry these thoughts with me across the vast manicured lawn of my daddy's estate, thankful for the moonless night.

My heart races and my pulse thunders just beneath the surface of my heated skin. Lush grass slips between my toes as I make my way deeper into the shadows in search of the very monster I've been warned against.

Patience has never been a strong suit of mine. A Titan trait, or so I'm told. Truth is, I've held out for two long years. It's not easy burying the truth inside, but I managed. Isn't that long enough? If not, then how long am I supposed to wait before these raw emotions consume me alive from within?

More questions I don't have the answers to.

Wet leaves lick across my bare thighs where my night shorts ride high. I should be embarrassed by my desires. Or maybe at the very least ashamed, but the ache inside me only calms when *he* is near.

John Hark.

A Titan enforcer. A modern-day outlaw.

Killer.

Monster.

And the man I love.

I flick each of these swirling thoughts away like bothersome afterthoughts.

Shivers climb the length of my spine and a rush of adrenaline refuels my hammering heart trying to beat a hole through my chest.

It's almost pitch-black so I cling to the sides of massive shrubs until the edge sweeps away to reveal a narrow, softly lit path I used to play on as a child. Cool stones press into the bottoms of my feet as I hurry. At the end of the walkway is where my monster awaits.

I knew I was in trouble the second the man walked into our lives like a hurricane hell-bent on creating chaos. He came to us on a night much like this one which I should have taken as a sign of something dark and foreboding coming my way, but hindsight and all that.

It was his arresting black eyes that I noticed first as Daddy introduced me to the new Titan enforcer—a fancy way of saying trigger-puller, trust me.

The way the dark stranger's hand slid over mine, each finger encasing my smaller hand until the warmth of his palm caressed over mine. Powerful. In control. Almost like he wanted me to feel the strength of his warm, arousing touch. But it was the way he looked at me that stole all my senses. I swear, some unseen force fused me to the man the second our gazes connected. I felt heart-struck from that night on.

His dark eyes stared into mine as I gave over my name and the world beneath my feet shifted unnaturally. As though a power forged and melded our lifelines together. Crazy, right? Yeah, I don't know. It sounds messed up to even think about, but that doesn't make it any less true.

He only reaffirmed the connection after repeating my name in his rough, firm baritone. And right there in the middle of my daddy's office, I fell in love.

Again, I tell you. Heart-struck.

Fucking crazy.

Mysteries and secrets hid behind those thick lashes and apparently, I didn't care then and I still don't.

Two years of living in silence are enough. The need to know everything about him consumes me. And despite knowing I'm doing the forbidden, here I stand on his doorstep, barefoot, barely dressed, and willing to give up everything for a taste of what I shouldn't want to a man the world fears.

Looking over my shoulder one last time, I silently push his door open enough to slip inside. Just as quietly I return the door to its closed position and don't let out my held breath until I hear the snick of the metal behind me. I find the lock and crank it clockwise. Only then do I truly take in my surroundings.

Almost immediately I regret my actions.

I freeze mid-step. Hark's deep voice winds along the cool current of conditioned air and reaches into me lighting the hottest of fires. I place my foot down and let curiosity carry me deeper into his guest bungalow.

Dimmed lights throw the entire open-style space into various shades of black and gray. Sofas, chairs, bookcases. They are all darkened forms only discernible from their distinct shapes. It doesn't matter. I know them by heart. Just like I know which direction I hear the masculine grunts and growls coming from.

I take another step deeper into the bungalow and the thudding of my heart makes me strain to hear over the rush of blood in my ears.

Oh, God. There it is again. A sound of pure ecstasy. Deep, primal.

Is he here with someone else? Green fingers of jealousy claw deep grooves over my soul.

Please, Lord. Don't let it be true.

"I'll kill them."

I pause. Take a deep breath. No, I won't. But sometimes I wish I had my father's ruthlessness.

I bite at my lower lip and quickly weigh my options. Turn and run like a wilting flower or push on? Fight for what I want or let it slip away?

A masculine curse curls through the bungalow sending chills over my cool skin.

I shut my eyes and swallow thickly. Okay, then. The second option it is.

I edge down the hall, past a small kitchenette, and deeper into a room with a large bed in the center. My heart drags behind me on the floor. Fiery tears rim the edges of my lashes.

From toes to fingertips, tingles of adrenaline prickle over my entire body. With the place thrown in shadows, it's easy to spot the bright light flooding the far side of Hark's master bedroom where the bathroom door stands slightly ajar. Steam rolls out and I'm drawn to it. I have to see who he is with. See who stole my place before I quietly take my leave.

Thankfully the door inches open silently. I tentatively step from the darkness, my foot moving from the warmth of the carpet to the shocking coolness of marble.

Steam clouds the sides of the glass and through the mist, I realize I am dead wrong. Hark isn't here with anyone at all. His back is toward me. He grunts again, this time harsher, deeper like he's in pain. Goosebumps rise over my arms and pucker my nipples painfully.

I move closer, so close if I reach out, I can slide the glass door open and step into the shower with him.

But not yet.

I freeze, mesmerized by the rippling muscle. His harsh groans are louder than the fall of water over his large body.

Speaking of, I nearly groan at the gorgeous sight of the man under the shower spray. Millions of drops gel together to sluice over deeply tanned, glistening skin and I swallow back a whimper, craving to lick those sprinkles of moisture off his delicious body.

His massive back features a glorious tattoo spreading out over all that well-defined muscle in intricate black ink. Large scaly wings unfurl down the backs of his arms and his trim waist. Across the expanse of his wide shoulders and flared laterals is the body of a black dragon with golden eyes.

Its head is posed downward, smoke and embers curling around the edges of his snout as if biding its time to unleash a wrath unlike any other. I can imagine when Hark lowers his arms the beast appears even more breathtaking in its complete form

I dip my attention off the skin art and lower over a firm biteable ass and legs just as well-formed as the rest of him.

And then Hark turns and my whole night shifts from possibly losing my virginity to most definitely giving this beast my body.

I gasp softly, fear of being discovered adding to the concoction of mixed emotions swirling inside me.

I wait for him to notice me standing at the edge of the stall, but his eyes are thankfully closed. He drops his head back, the water drowning out any possibility of him hearing my heavy panting, too.

I track the falling water and realize the grunt and groans are not from a man in pain, but of one deep in the grip of pleasure. And I mean grip. Thick fingers wrap around a thicker cock and he's working his long, fully aroused length with hard, fast jerks. He pumps his hips, thrusting into his hand and the ache in my core turns to an uncontrollable pulsing throb.

He steps from the water, throwing his other hand up to brace against the glass wall. With the water now hitting his back I appreciate the pinched expression on his rugged face. His eyes are still locked and his lips peel back with a low, animalistic growl. He strokes his beautiful cock, the head swollen and angry-looking.

Shivers of excitement wrack through me and in that second the amount of heat pooling between my thighs drenches the thin material of my night shorts.

Much like a dragon's rumble, this man's pleasure reverberates through the bathroom and feeds into me. Every grunt and rumble strokes over my throbbing clit as if the man himself finally has his hands on my body.

I reach up and press my palms over my silk-covered nipples to try and ease their ache. But it's no use. My body doesn't want my touch anymore. It wants his.

And then he speaks.

"Fuck, God, make it stop already!" He strokes, hard, fast but the explosion of his release doesn't come. I can help him, that's why I came here. But should I? Self-doubt has me second-guessing my actions. It is possible he's fantasizing about someone else? Maybe the thought of them has him seeking his pleasure in the privacy of his bathroom?

I chance a look up and at that exact second coal-colored eyes slam open and pin me in place. Something akin to a thousand watts of electricity sizzles through my veins, destroying me from the inside out. In the same second, it renews the all-consuming lust coiling inside me. Damn this man. What has he done to me? My breath hitches and lodges in my chest, burning. Only this time it grows with a life of its own and spreads throughout me until I don't know if I'll ever truly be free from the dark cravings whispering in my ear to take what I want.

Heart-struck. It's not something easily explained. It just is. A place between love and pain. You know what you want, know it's dangerous. But it's entirely off-limits.

A flash of anger flickers across his face. Rapid beats of his heart are evident in the erratic thump of the artery in his neck. It's the only clue as to how affected he is by seeing me. Those piercing dark eyes glitter with danger just before his mouth moves with a tone to match the ire.

"What the fuck are you doing in my bungalow, Asena?" He's not shy about the fact he's jerking off, either. His hand continues to move over the slicked steel length of his cock as he considers me. The world along the fringes of my sight blurs. Oh God, I've never seen someone so beautiful. So powerful.

My thighs squeeze tight against the throbbing need pulsing there. Showtime. Can't run and hide like a little girl now.

I swallow back the last remnants of doubt and raise my chin defiantly. My gaze shifts from the hand stroking his cock to hold his gaze. My invisible crown firmly in place.

"You didn't come to the house to share in the celebrations. I thought I would come and see if you were alright."

Hard pecs shift with the bark of laughter he releases. "And am I, Asena? All right that is?"

Leaving the shower running, he steps from the water and doesn't stop his progression until he's out of the stall and standing a breath away from me. Water runs everywhere but he doesn't seem to care or take notice.

My name on his lips is a rarity. In fact, I don't remember the last time he used my given name. It is always *princess* said with a smirk on his lips and a teasing tone to his voice.

The sight of his aroused, naked body anchors me to the spot. I stare shamelessly. Water drips over the most perfect masculine body. Cut lines, deep grooves. I forget to breathe for several seconds as he stands there, gripping his beautiful cock in one hand, the other I'm hoping ready to catch me when I jump his bones.

Seems like I'm not the only shameless one.

Despite the warmth from the steamy shower, the cool air from the overhead vents mixed with my arousal has my nipples pressing tight against the confines of my silk camisole.

His eyes drop and the second the heat of his gaze caresses over the peaks, another wave of warmth pools between my legs.

I reach out and trail a finger over the fine lines of scales curving around his massive bicep.

Harsh lines cut between dark brows. If I were smart, I would heed the warning in his tone and the piercing burn of his unchanging eyes. But my brain isn't what drives me tonight.

It's the uncontrollable lust coursing through my veins. The weight of need floods my senses preventing me from sleeping. From feeling hunger. The only craving I feel is for this man and the dark pleasure I know he will give me.

"No, Hark." I drag a single nail down his chest and scrape it over a nipple to the sound of a deep growl. "You don't look okay to me," I say tentatively. Feeling brave, I continue. "You *look* like you're in terrible pain." Eyes lifted to his, I lean in and curl the tip of my tongue over the hard disk of his masculine nipple, sucking off a droplet of water.

A dark smile curls the edges of his lips. A forewarning of his next move. He stops stroking himself and is on me before I know what is truly going on. We are across the bathroom, moving faster than I think safely possible. But he doesn't lose his footing as he clamps a hand under my thighs and lifts. We slam into the nearest wall, the heat of my sex pressing against his lower midriff.

343

Water drenches the front of my camisole and a harsh flare of fear spikes through me when he notices my piercings.

His hips jerk seemingly involuntarily. His jaw clenches and a soft cry peels from my lips when he buries a hand in my hair. If Hark's chilled look could end a life, mine would be vanquished by now. The beast's chest rises and falls with pent-up...rage? Desire? They almost look the same to me. I don't know. His narrowed gaze is hard to get a handle on, but his thick erection is most definitely sending me mixed signals.

I lift my ass and reach between us, taking him in hand and that's when I freeze.

"Hark," I say breathlessly. Surprise widens my eyes and his lips part with a groan as cool metal brushes against my fingertips and I realize I missed a detail. A very important one we have in common.

Oh, fuck. I need to see him again. He grunts when I tighten my fingers around him and brush my thumb over the tip before tracing the bar of metal piercing his length.

There are times in life when you literally have to take it by the balls and give it a little squeeze.

Holding his gaze I stroke him from root to tip once more before I move my hand down further and take his velvety sac in my hand and tighten my hold. He doesn't flinch as I expect. He only leans into me a little more, his gaze lasered in on mine like he's calculating how deep his grave will need to be if he takes me up on my none-too-subtle offer.

I flick my finger over the piercing in his foreskin and the delicious intake of breath I hear beside my ear makes me flush with heat. My breasts swell and the tight peaks brush against his hard chest.

He raises an eyebrow. "You think you can play with the help, little princess? See if one of daddy's men will pleasure that tight pussy before you run back to him and say you were raped? Are you looking for some kind of entertainment?"

Shock hinges my mouth wide. My eyes dance between his but I can't gauge if he's trying to scare me or if I've scared him.

"Is this some kind of joke, Princess?" His voice is dangerously low and I have to strain to hear him over the blood rushing through my ears and the spray of water at our backs. "Tell me! Did dear daddy send his virgin daughter to my quarters to get a rise out of me? See how loyal I am?"

He moves away from me abruptly, cool air swooshing in to replace the fire between us.

What? Shock and then anger roils through me. Using my gaze as a weapon, I laser him with my ire. "Fuck. You. John Hark."

His rumbling chuckle raises my hackles further. "Or, is that what you're here for?" He quips in a humorless tone. "One last present for the sweet little princess on her eighteenth birthday. A good fucking. So which is it? Option, one, two, or three?"

I recoil as if slapped. "Do you have to be so crude?"

He moves away abruptly and I lose my balance on the wet floor. I stumble forward and straight into his arms. His hands are back in my hair instantly. With a harsh tug, he turns my lips up to his.

"You're not playing with fire here, you've moved into the flames and they are going to burn you alive. Something you're nowhere near ready for. Go find a boy toy to fuck around with before I personally show you the door."

"I know what I'm doing and your harsh words don't scare me." Am I being stupid or reckless? Maybe both. But I silently dare him to make his move.

Panting wildly I can do nothing when he crashes his lips into mine. Nothing but take the brutal, punishing kiss as he holds me securely to him. Miles of hard muscle press against my smaller frame. Hard pecs, solid abs. We touch from nipples to hips. Second by second, the adrenaline is replaced with unhealthy amounts of lust.

He rips away from me and storms to the other side of the bathroom. The muscles of his body bunch and coil as he prowls back and forth. Damp hair falls over dark eyes and like this, untamed and wild, he looks like a masterpiece. Beautiful. Lethal. Barely contained.

Between his legs his heavy cock sways, the head glistening with his seed. I poke the tip of my tongue out and wet my lips, hungry for a taste of darkness.

I can feel him raging against wanting me and what he knows will likely end with him at the opposite end of a loaded gun if anyone discovers me with him.

Taking the boss' daughter is a death penalty but will he walk the fine line of danger with me?

I grip the soft ends of my camisole and lift my arms, tossing the material at my feet. Next, my dainty shorts join my top. I didn't bother wearing undergarments. He comes to a full stop and his hand falls back to the base of his erection. Pain contorts his handsome face.

"You don't know what you want, Asena. You've barely lived."

As if I need another reason to keep staring at his angry cock, he wraps his long fingers around the swollen steel length and draws down with a tight grip. When he moves upward a long rope of pre-cum spills from the tip to wet his fingers. I'm mesmerized. Not only by the splash of his seed but by the glint of light off the piercing. Will it hurt when he forces the head inside me? Will I crave the pain and scream for more? My heart speeds up.

I knew this wouldn't be easy.

"What the fuck are you doing? Go back to your party and your friends." Carnal cravings consume his eyes. He can hide it behind harsh words all he wants. It only makes me want him more. I might be a virgin, but that doesn't mean I don't know what sex is. And what lust looks like. I know firsthand what it feels like and how all-consuming it can be.

He scrubs a hand down his face and only now do I realize the stubble darkening the edges of his chiseled jawline. Normally clean-shaven, the wrecked look makes him all the more alluring and forbidden.

"Screw my party, Hark. Everyone is asleep anyway. And don't you dare throw our age difference at me. I've watched you know," I start, suddenly unable to hold his eyes with mine. "Um, you with other women." My admission sends a nasty flood of shame to color my cheeks.

He chuckles; the sound is wicked to the core.

I drop to my knees, spread my thighs wide, and let my arms drape to my sides.

He only stands in the middle of his large bathroom unmoving. As if he knew all along I stole glances of him with lovers.

"They fall to their knees and wait for you to tell them what you need. I can do that. I can be what you need."

His expression turns savage. "You can never be what I need. Never, do you hear me!" He roars. "Go the fuck home, Asena. Now!"

"No!" I slash my hand through the air. "I'm not leaving. Teach me. Show me. Use my body for whatever you need."

He says nothing. Stubborn man.

"Hark," I say with a husky whisper.

"Asena. You're going to get me killed." My name comes out as if it cuts him with a thousand shards of glass—rough, painful. "Fucking woman," he grits, his teeth gnashing them together. For the first time, I see the hardcore monster break character and show me the tender underbelly.

"Leave," he chokes out. "Leave before I fuck the darkness into you and there's no turning back from it. From me. I have blood on my hands and you have a crown on your head. There is no you and me."

There's an edge of regret with undercurrents of something I can't quite place. It sends chills through me and my instincts scream for me to run. Except I don't fear the man as I should. He's nearly twice my age and three times my size. In truth, the only thing I fear is him pushing me away.

"If your father or the Druid finds you here, what do you think will happen?"

The Druid. Sean Doyle. My throat squeezes at the mention of my daddy's right-hand man and most loyal assassin. The man who prays over his victims in Gaelic before snuffing out their lives. He fancies himself a saver of souls.

I just think he's batshit insane.

An unbidden chill scales my spine.

"Don't worry. Everyone thinks I'm asleep in my room with all my girlfriends."

Black eyes narrow on me. The trail is a hot path from the slope of my neck to caress over my nipples. Wicked fantasies gleam in the dark expanse of his gaze.

"Asena, you fucking witch."

And just like that, for the first time in my life, I feel like I'm making the right choice. That this man, as deadly and dark as unrepented sin, is the man I'm willing to give my heart and life to have.

I spread my thigh a little wider and his chest rises with a long deep breath. Holding his gaze I move my hands to the V of my thighs and spread my folds so he can see what he does to me.

"Let me please you, Hark. I can be what you need."

"What is it you think I like, Asena?"

Lifting my lashes, I stare up at him and speak the truth. "Your women submissive. Willing to do anything you command. I've…" I gulp back the embarrassment and push ahead. Nothing can be built on lies, right? So out with it already. Sandpaper scratches against my suddenly parched mouth and throat.

"You what sweet innocent little virgin Asena?"

Did he know? I swipe the tip of my tongue over my bottom lip. "I've watched you fuck others and I want to know the feel of you taking me as you took them. I want you to be my first. My last."

Continue reading Savage Thief in ebook and Kindle Unlimited by tapping here or visiting my website at www. penelopewylde.com.

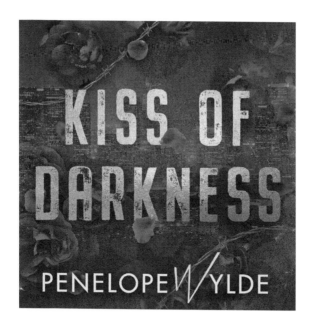

KISS OF DARKNESS DUET

Tarnished Kisses - Book 1
Shattered Kisses - Book 2

Witness the men of Genesis—Harlon, Santi and Cassius—fight to keep their crowns while the darkness within claws them deeper into the shadows.

Undertakers. Villains. Monsters.

Days and nights run red with blood until there's nothing left but death at their feet.

Until her.

The three ruthless mafia kings take the broken and cruelly treated Polaris under their wings, unsuspecting of the new war rising—one led by villains that will end in ashes. There can only be one outcome. Her love will either save them from their torment or they will destroy her with their darkness.

I have a brand new breeder series launching February 2024!

Six mafia kingpins are shackled to their thrones.
Loveless. Heirless.
Until they decide to break their chains
and steal love anywhere they can find it.

**Pre-order the entire series of standalone novellas
by tapping below:
Owning Amethyst, Ruining Lili,**

Possessing Bella, Stealing Grace,

Mafia Daddies of Chicago is a mafia, age-gap romance novella series of stand-alones. Each delicious 'n spicy title is stuffed with dirty, messy love you can read in one sitting. There's a touch of danger and the HEA is a must. But getting there is where the forbidden fun happens. Expect ruthless OTT alphas and heart-wrecking instalove!

Newsletter + Free Books

Want more hot alpha heroes? Join my mailing list, get two FREE books and never miss a juicy, WYLDE romance release!

Penelope's Newsletter

Catch all the current releases available only on Amazon where you can read for free with a Kindle Unlimited subscription.

Penelope on Amazon

ALSO BY PENELOPE WYLDE

I have organized my book list by dark romances and light romances. Check below to discover your preferences.

DARK ROMANCES

Each book on this section comes with a trigger warning. I cover dark themes, write violence on the page and each story features high heat romance.

BRATVA SAVAGES:

Savage Justice

Savage Thief

Savage Chaos

Savage Sin

Savage Hunter

KISS OF DARKNESS

Tarnished Kisses

Shattered Kisses

DARK MAFIA CROWNS
-THE MORETTI KINGS-

Stolen Pleasures

Unraveled Pleasures

MAFIA DADDIES

Owning Amethyst

Ruining Lili

Possessing Bella

Stealing Grace

DARK MAFIA VILLAINS TRILOGY

Her Dark Mafia Kings

Her Dark Mafia Beasts

Her Dark Mafia Sinners

CLUB SIN:

Room One

Room Eight

Room Two

Room Seventeen

Room Seven

Room Six

Room One Hundred and Six

Room One Hundred and Five

SAVAGE LOVE:

Mercy for Three

Honor for Three

Justice for Three

SAVAGE MAFIA

Stolen by the Mafia

Bred by the Bratva

Bred by the Villain

DARK REVERSE HAREM ROMANCE DUET:

Dark Mafia Kings

Dark Mafia Queen

HER FILTHY HAREM:

Her Filthy Professors

Her Filthy Mafia Men

Her Filthy Bratva Bodyguards

LIGHT ROMANCES:

Each book on this list is a safe read. What does that mean? No trigger warning is required. Darker themes you find in my dark romances are not found in these light books. That said, the **HIGH** heat level is the same across all my books.

FORBIDDEN PROFESSORS:

The Professors' Sweet Treat

The Professor's Bought Bride

The Professor's Sweet Virgin

FAKE BRIDE DUET

Wrong Bride

Right Groom

CHERRY POPPERS.

Cherry Sweet

Cherry Bossed

Cherrilicious Ink

Wild Cherry

HARD MEN IN UNIFORM:

Claimed by Her Soldier

Belonging to Her Soldier

SAVAGE MOUNTAIN MEN:

Her Savage Mountain Man

Claimed by Her Mountain Man

Sharing Their Mountain Bride

His Snowbound Mountain Virgin

About the Author

Penelope Wylde loves playing on the dark side of romance, making her characters work for their happily-ever-after. Join her for a twisted ride through the gritty shadows before reaching the light. That is, if you dare to be WYLDE.

She writes overly possessive heroes and anti-heroes who are pure sinners at heart who bring enough heat to the pages to melt your hearts…and your panties. Billionaires, mafia, reverse harem, and bikers…the more forbidden the romance the more she loves to peel back the layers and discover what makes her characters tick.

She makes a wicked margarita mix, owns two hundred shades of red nail polish and is always found reading one forbidden romance or another when she's not writing.

www.PenelopeWylde.com

Made in the USA
Monee, IL
03 September 2024

65113880R00208